TRIBUTE

Ellen Renner

Tribute

HOT
KEY
BOOKS

First published in Great Britain in 2014 by Hot Key Books
Northburgh House, 10 Northburgh Street, London EC1V 0AT

A CIP catalogue record for this book is available from the British Library.

ISBN: 978-1-4714-0031-5

1

This book is typeset in 10.5 Berling LT Std using Atomik ePublisher

Printed and bound by Clays Ltd, St Ives Plc

Hot Key Books supports the Forest Stewardship Council (FSC),
the leading international forest certification organisation, and is
committed to printing only on Greenpeace-approved FSC-certified paper.

www.hotkeybooks.com

Hot Key Books is part of the Bonnier Publishing Group
www.bonnierpublishing.com

This book is dedicated to Malala Yousafzai, one of our world's Knowledge Seekers.

Swift.

I named her for the bird. When she first came I saw something brown and drab: a small animal that spent hours huddled in the corners of my father's house, weeping. She hid her face behind a curtain of sooty hair. I didn't want my father's gift: it was boring, plain, disappointing. I didn't want my Tribute child until the day I saw her run.

She ran through the stone corridors of the palazzo as though she was flying. She sped out of the shadows, past long rectangles of windows, sunlight flashing on thin legs. Her hair spread behind her like the wings of a swift scything the sky.

When I commanded her to come to me she knelt on the floor, hanging her head. I crouched down. I put my five-year-old face nose to nose with hers. At last she looked at me with liquid amber eyes. And in the darkness of her irises I saw golden sparks flickering. Sparks of yearning – of hope at war with fear. At that moment I knew we were the same. That we both wanted the impossible: to fly. To hope when hope is madness.

I took her by the hand, which is forbidden. I named her for the bird I loved most, and we ran through the marble halls together.

1

I taste the bitter wind, feel it lifting me. My wings carve the air. The courtyard spins below: flashes of grey limestone, olive-green vegetation, up-tilted faces.

Mind magic. Our tutor has supplied a hawk – a female merlin – and I'm struggling to cope with the animal's primitive brain. It's almost worth the effort. Circling on a thermal, above the twisting world, I glimpse a sort of happiness. So why do I hate these lessons? None of the other student adepts worry that it's somehow wrong to enter another creature's mind. Why do I always have to be the odd one out?

Because I will not be my father's child.

A girl stands to one side, away from the others. Her hair is a red-gold mass. Her lips are slightly parted, as if she is about to speak; her eyes greenish-grey and frowning. Despite the merlin's warm feathers, I shiver. It's uncanny to look down out of the sky and see yourself through another creature's eyes.

I turn away and twist sideways to soar, circling up inside the prisoning walls of the courtyard. Higher, higher, until the tiled roof of the Academy falls away, until I am far above the city, with its circlet of olive groves and earth-red fields. I hear the wind in the trees and dry winter grasses, the whisper of running water; smell the warm blood of sparrows and rabbits hiding in the undergrowth.

The pain of longing fills me. It is as though there is a hand clenched around my heart. Escape! Fly over the net of fields to the distant blue haze of mountains. But I can't live in the hawk. To leave my human body for too long is death. And I cannot die yet. I have a debt to pay.

A flash of white. A dove flutters twenty feet below and a red haze of images floods the merlin's memory: blood, warm and bitter; ripping into soft plumage; gulping rich gobbets of flesh. We fold our wings against our sides and dive. All is silent but for the whistle of the wind in our nostrils and the thud of blood in our ears. Fierce joy. Heartbeats. Slender neck stretched in terror. White wings frantic.

I try . . . I do try. Two times now I have failed to kill. My heart thrills to the merlin's desire, but I can feel the dove's fear as strongly as my hawk's hunger. We jackknife in the air, twisting sideways, wings tucked, talons out and spread. A glimpse of my face, far below. Pale, as though about to faint. I tear the hawk away in a rage of failure. We swerve, missing the dove by a feather's breadth.

The merlin screams in frustration and the binding is broken. I fall with a sickening swiftness.

For the next few seconds I'm too busy fighting giddiness to pay attention to my tutor or the words he's shouting. I concentrate on securing the merlin's tether – the thin strand of conscious thought that keeps the bird twisting lazily on the thermals, unable to soar free and escape. My lesson has been disastrous enough without losing one of the Academy's hawks.

'If you haven't the stomach for the kill, withdraw and leave the bird to get on with it! You prevented, Lady. Don't try to deny it.'

I blink the last of the dizziness away and turn to face him. Aluid's bulging eyes threaten to pop from their sockets.

'A mage must be able to use the eyes and ears of any animal they turn to their purpose.' My tutor's voice grows pompous. Aluid smooths the front of his saffron-coloured robes and thrusts out his chest. I recognise the signs: it will be a long lecture. He should thank me for giving him so much enjoyment.

'To fly great distances ourselves is tiring. A hawk or eagle can do it for us. But not if we interfere with their natural habits. This is the third time you've stopped your hawk from killing. It is not lack of skill . . . so what, Lady? Squeamishness?'

I shake my head. How can I explain what I don't understand myself? The other students have gathered near, a semicircle of curiosity and mild malice. Watching their tutor bait the stuck-up daughter of the Archmage is one of my classmates' favourite entertainments.

I gaze over their heads to where the merlin circles, a graceful shadow in the sky. I hear the dove on the ground nearby, scratching for shelter.

'Again.'

I stare at Aluid. He can't mean it. Contorting your mind to fit the strange shapes and pathways of an animal's brain is among the most tiring of magics. After three sessions my head aches and my body feels sucked dry, as though I've just climbed to the top of the Tornados mountains beneath the sun of a midsummer's day. 'N-no!' I stutter.

'You refuse?' Aluid straightens. Red pushes up under his sallow skin.

'With respect, Tutor –'

I feel him take the hawk. Aluid wrests the creature's mind from me and sends us all plummeting towards the dove.

It would have been insulting had I been ten and untalented, but to invade a creature under the control of a sixteen-year-old student adept is unforgivable. Disbelieving laughter fills my ears as the others realise what has happened. My tutor doesn't notice that I haven't left the bird. I fight to pull my consciousness away – ill with nausea at an intolerable intimacy of mind and mind.

I fall. We fall. White wings flutter as the dove takes to the air. Too late. Slow, plump, warm food. Rich blood. Tender flesh.

Aluid's concentration shifts. I feel him merge deeply with the hawk in anticipation of the kill, and at last I have room to wriggle free and slip back into my body.

Images fill my mind: memories of violation, of the secret I've held in my heart for so many years. Helpless anger, hatred, bitter loss – the companions of my childhood flood through me and I lose, for a crucial second, my only weapon: self-control. I glare at my tutor through half-focused eyes that see another time, another tormentor. I reach up a stiffened arm and strike them both across the face.

The hawk squawks. Awareness slides back into Aluid's eyes. The merlin, freed, gives a joyous scream, wheels into the sky and is gone. The dove flutters to the ground.

My tutor puts a hand to the reddening mark on his cheek. His nostrils flare; his lips are white lines of fury. I stare at him in horror as the old nightmare fades. It's only because I am Benedict's daughter that I'm not lying in the dust, writhing in pain. Laughter dissolves into shocked silence. The circle of students presses closer. I feel their staring eyes, hear their breathing quicken in anticipation.

How can I have been so stupid? My tutor may have humiliated me, but most do that. Aluid has the power to hurt me far more than I have hurt him. But will he use it? It seems he will. My stomach twists tighter at each word hissing through his clenched teeth.

'That bird was worth a hundred and fifty secs.' My tutor draws in a honking sniff of outrage. 'You can ask your father to advance you the money. After you tell him you have violated the third precept. I will accompany you to the palazzo.' He smiles a tight, anticipatory smile. 'Now.'

My father, Benedict, Archmage of Asphodel, possesses a library which is one of the most beautiful rooms I have ever seen. Carved redwood bookcases stand between the long windows, each shelf laden with volumes bound in leather and tooled in gold and copper. If you are allowed to take down a book and lift its heavy cover, you find illuminations decorated with ground lapis lazuli and gold leaf. Scribes long dead transcribed the words, copying each letter in elegant tracery. Scribes who could not read what they wrote. It is a room that fills me with horror.

Aluid holds the heavy wooden door wide for me, bowing

with a courtier's grace, an insolent smirk on his face. I long to slap him again, but as soon as I step into Benedict's library I'm trembling too much to give my tutor another thought.

My eyes seek it out immediately: the paperweight. I hardly notice Aluid leave to fetch my father. My feet take me forward until I'm pressed against the cedar-wood desk. The paperweight is a heavy glass disc the size of an outspread hand. The rounded top is inlaid with silver in an intricate design of twisting curves – Benedict's mage mark. It shines in the slanting afternoon light, exquisite, costly, the symbol of my father's power. But its perfection is marred: at one edge of the disc a red stain wells up through the silver tracery like a bleeding wound. The mark of blood.

One long-ago spring night when I am nine, I wake to find myself alone.

'Swift?' I call. When she doesn't answer, fear of the dark grabs my throat and I struggle for breath. Where is she? It's her duty to be with me. To keep the darkness away. Suddenly, my panic is replaced by a greater fear, for I know where she is.

'Time take you, Swift!' I scrabble under the bed for my slippers, bump my head and mutter all the swear words I know. She's taught me most of them.

As I sneak along the palazzo corridors towards my father's library, my mood is as dark as the night. But now that I am properly awake, I'm more afraid than angry. Swift is the only person I have ever loved; the only person who loves me. I would die for her . . . for a

Tribute child. It's stupid and shameful, but it's true.

'Please,' I pray to Time. 'Protect her, even if she is only a Tribute child. Don't let my father have set wards on the library.'

Time is good. Blessed be Time. Heart thudding, I push open the library door a narrow crack and squeeze through. She's there, sitting at my father's desk, a candle beside her, a book splayed open. She is reading. Blasphemy! But I am the one who taught her . . .

Relief makes me giddy. I rush at her. 'Fool!' I hiss. 'Do you want to die?' And I hug her to me with all the fierceness of love.

Swift pushes me away. Points to the book on the desk. 'I'm glad you came. I need to show you this.'

It's a dusty old history book. Benedict's library is full of volumes on mage-craft, but Swift avoids these. Instead, she searches out stories of the past. 'Idiot!' I hiss. 'You know what will happen if you're found here. Why do you risk your life to read about dead people?'

'I want to know the truth.' She stares at me, her face intent, her eyes glowing. It scares me, that hunger. 'This was written by a Maker. It tells all about their rebellion. The Makers didn't defeat the mages because evil spirits helped them. That's all lies. Ordinary kine, people like my mother and father, Tribute slaves like me, rose up and rebelled. Magic was wiped out on the other side of the Wall. If it happened there, it can happen here.'

Heresy! 'That book is from the forbidden shelves,

isn't it?' I stare at her, appalled. We've got to put it back. Now! I slam the book shut. As I do, my hand brushes against the paperweight that sits on my father's desk.

'Look!' I grab Swift's arm. A light glows in the centre of the glass disc. The swirls of silver on its surface seem to move, like a snake slowly unwinding its coils. There is a strange buzzing in my ears.

'Don't touch it!'

She's only a Tribute child: she can't help being frightened by magic. I ignore her and place my palm on the paperweight. It's warm. And through the glass I feel, like the beating of a heart, a pulse of fear and pain. And now I'm frightened too. I snatch my hand away, grab the book and turn around, pulling Swift after me.

But it's too late. My father stands in the doorway.

Benedict walks forward. Takes the book from my numbed hands. Swift presses close to me.

'This is not on the permitted reading list.' Benedict examines the cover. His eyes lift to me, move to Swift, cowering behind. 'If it was indeed you who read it.'

'Of course it was.'

'I wasn't aware you were such an eager student of history. Or of anything very much. Am I to believe that a new-found thirst for knowledge has dragged you from your bed in the middle of the night?' His smile is sour. 'And why is she here?'

'I'm afraid of the dark.' And that is true – not that he would know.

'Weakness.' He sighs. 'And you are a bad liar.' His eyes turn to Swift. I hear her catch her breath. I reach backwards and take her hand.

'You . . .' he says slowly, '. . . have been a mistake. A misjudgement.' His face grows stony. 'I have been self-indulgent . . . But no matter. I will mend my error.'

We know. Both of us. We know.

'Leave her alone!' I shout. 'If you touch her, I swear, I'll kill you.' I mean it. I have never meant anything so much.

He looks at me with distaste. 'Control yourself, Zara! You carry your mother's taint of emotionalism. Go back to bed. I will decide your punishment tomorrow.'

Reprieve. I'm too shocked with relief to think. I scurry towards the door, pulling Swift behind me.

'The Tribute child stays.'

His voice freezes us to statues. He hasn't needed to use magic. I turn to face him. 'No.'

'You taught her to read. You know the penalty. She will pay it.'

'She can't read!' It's a hopeless lie. I know he won't believe me – that I will be punished for my rebellion. I stand at bay, hating him, fearing him. But never dreaming of what will happen next.

Benedict is motionless, his eyes locked on mine. He breathes rapidly, his lips pulled back from clenched teeth. And I am suddenly deathly afraid. My father's emotions are never easy to read but now I sense . . . I know . . . that some border in his mind has been crossed. And that there is no going back.

One moment I am whole, separate, my thoughts my own. The next, Benedict invades my mind. He is inside my head; scattering my thoughts, dominating my will, controlling my body. I no longer possess my innermost self. The bit of me that should always be mine alone is now his. I try to fight – to push him out – but it's like trying to hold off an avalanche. The taste of him is vile, the humiliation so gut-twisting I long to vomit, but I can't breathe or move, even though nausea is choking me. My father examines my memories methodically, coldly, then withdraws his consciousness. I fall to the floor, retching. I'm shaking with horror. A mage may mind-control an animal, or even kine – non-magic commoners – but no mage ever invades the mind of another. It is an unspeakable crime. Benedict has broken the first precept.

Movement. I lift my head to see Swift running at my father. Something flashes silver-grey in her hand and disbelief gives way to pure terror as I realise she has a blade – there is no hope for her now. Benedict must see it at the same time, for his face twists with shock.

She is granted that much victory. And then she is flying through the air. Her body slams into a bookcase with a sickening thud. Half a dozen books slide from the upper shelves and fall on her.

I stagger to my feet and stumble to my father's desk. He ignores me: I can do nothing to hurt him. He strolls across the room towards Swift. I grab the paperweight with both hands. I will smash him. Hatred rises in my throat like tar. The weight of the glass disc surprises me. I struggle to lift it overhead. That sound again . . . a buzzing.

'Put it down.'

Swift lies motionless on the floor behind Benedict. He seems to have forgotten her. His eyes – glittering with something my child's imagination mistakes for fear – follow the movement of the paperweight as I heft it higher. I have his attention now.

I'm growling like a street dog. I feel my mouth stretch into a snarl and I throw the thing at him, using my mind as well as my arms. 'I'll kill you!' I scream.

I am nine. I have barely learnt to melt stone. Did I really think I could hurt the Archmage? But I do hurt him. As I feel him take the paperweight from me, I splinter off a fragment of glass and send it flying through the air. I aim for his eye, but I miss. It buries itself in the flesh over his cheekbone. Blood spurts from the hole in his face like water from a fountain, but Benedict doesn't make a sound. He catches the glass disc with his mind; returns it to the desk; extracts the splinter from his face and melds it back into the paperweight, a bloody smear on the glass. And he hurts me.

Oh, he hurts me. Every muscle in my body spasms into cramp. The agony is unbearable. I roll on the floor, screaming. Begging to die. I think he will kill me. I see a look in his eyes . . . but then his lip curls. The pain retreats but darkness gathers and wades towards me. I fight him. I scream for Swift, try to crawl across the floor to where she lies like a dead thing. I glimpse her face. Her eyes are open. I see her blink. Then darkness, cold and wet and unrelenting, grabs my throat and I fall.

I am unconscious for days. They tell me that when I finally wake, I cannot speak. Much of that year remains dark and lost. I don't try to remember.

I never see Swift again.

2

In the years separating that life from this, I have visited Benedict's library many times – night-time expeditions when my only company is Swift's ghost, guiding me to those books she needs me to read. But twice a year I'm forced to endure being in my father's presence in this place. At those times I stand in front of his desk, my tutors' reports spread over its polished surface. While he lists my failings as daughter and mage, I look at the paperweight. And remember.

Mages do not make things. That is work for non-magic kine, for the guilds. Except for the mages of Tierce, the city of glass. The adepts of Tierce vie with one another to create the most beautiful objects, melting sand, silica and pigment with their minds and forming the glass into intricate shapes.

My father's paperweight is one of the masterpieces of Tierce. I still wonder what truly happened seven years ago – how much I actually remember and how much I imagined. Did the glass really respond to my touch? Was there a buzzing, or was it the blood surging in my head – my own fear and rage – I heard? That night is so dark in my memory I can't be sure.

Now I lean over the desk, watching the swirls of metal

frozen in the glass. I can hear myself breathing – too fast – as I reach out a finger and touch the paperweight. It feels cold and dead. Are the silver threads moving? I bend closer . . . then jerk backwards as the door clicks open and my father enters the room.

It takes all my will and years of practice to stand calmly and meet his eyes. They are a clear yellowish-brown. Lizard's eyes. On his right cheekbone is a shiny round scar. His hair and neatly curling beard are still dark above the white lace collar he wears over his black robes. But although he has hardly changed, at sixteen I have grown nearly as tall as he. I keep my face empty, my eyes blank. He has never once mentioned what he did to me that night. We both know I will never tell anyone. My mother was declared mad. I carry her taint.

Aluid is nowhere to be seen and I allow myself a small sigh of relief. At least I won't have to watch his eyes bulge with outrage as he lists my crimes.

'The third precept, Zara?' My father walks to his desk and sits down. I am not invited to sit. 'That is distasteful. It smacks of hysteria – lack of self-control.'

'Aluid invaded a hawk I was flying.'

My father lifts his head a fraction of an inch; his eyes narrow as if deciding whether to believe me or not. 'He conveniently forgot to mention that fact. Well . . . I can hardly blame you for anger. But.' His eyes flash. 'Your reaction was that of a kine! Presumption by someone such as Aluid, or any mage, is to be met with the mind and the mind alone. I do not ever want to hear of you using your fists as a weapon. You are to remember who and what you are. Is that clear?'

'Yes, Father.'

'And what provocation did you give your tutor?'

Telling him the truth will infuriate him further but if I don't tell him, he'll hear it from Aluid. I take a deep breath. 'I prevented the hawk's kill.'

I can't read the expression in his eyes, but the air between us turns sour. The silence grows longer and still he looks at me. Then: 'You become more like your mother every year. You are the image of her, and you seem to have inherited her mental frailties as well.

'Yet you are my blood as much as hers!' The words hiss through clenched teeth. I flinch but my father has already regained control. He studies the paperweight. One manicured, blunt-ended finger traces the silver lines of his mage mark winding over the curved glass. His eyes lift to me and the cold determination in them is terrifying. I catch my breath.

'You are my only child, Zara. My blood runs in your veins and I will not have it wasted. Your gifts are undeniable. I am the greatest adept of the age and your mother was extremely talented. But you lack mental discipline. Find it, Daughter.' He stares at me, his brown eyes unblinking. 'Or I will instil it in you.'

My knees grow soft with fear.

My father's voice continues: 'I want no more botched lessons or half-hearted attempts. No more subversiveness or you will reap the consequences. Do you understand?'

I beat back a wave of faintness and nod.

'Good. Now . . .'

For once, Time is on my side. Before Benedict can announce

23

my punishment, someone knocks on the door, then pushes it open. My father's chief aide, a grey-haired mage named Challen, enters. Her sharp eyes dismiss me. 'Pardon, Archmage. Pyramus wants to see you. Urgently.'

My father lifts his head like a hound scenting prey. *Danger!* I freeze and do my best to become invisible – I need to know what this is about. Pyramus will be bringing news of some new plot. *But which one?* Benedict remembers my presence. He turns to me with a frown of irritation, gesturing for me to leave. 'Return to your studies, Zara. Apologise to your tutor and do not give me cause to see you again this twelveweek.'

I bend my head submissively and hurry from the room. Pyramus stands outside the door looking, as he always does, like a shopkeeper dressed up in mage robes. No one would guess that this small, plump man is one of the most dangerous adepts in Asphodel. He nods respectfully to me as I pass. What does he know? I break into a scrambling run as soon as I am out of sight. I tear along the corridors, praying that I'm wrong, but I fear that I – and the one person in the world I might call a friend – may be in deadly danger.

The Academy crowns the tallest hill in Asphodel, a limestone fortress of magic, its red-tiled roof faded to pink by centuries of southern sun. Four wings enclose a courtyard. Each side of the square represents one of the elements – air, water, fire, earth. A magician's tools. We play with the stuff of life itself.

I make myself slow to a walk as I reach the top of the hill and mount the wide marble stairs leading to the portico. The guards either side of the entrance barely glance at me. Some one hundred and fifty student adepts attend the Academy, our long white robes constantly aflutter in the hill winds that slip through every crack in the old stone walls. We few are the most gifted young mages in the city, destined for positions of leadership and power. Anonymity is impossible. And with my height and red hair, I'm all too obviously Benedict's daughter. Which is something of a handicap for a spy.

My heart pounds impatiently as I stride through the peristyle. Lessons have begun and the courtyard is empty of students. Winter's silence is broken only by the splashing of the central fountain, the rustling of ancient rosemary bushes. This place contains all the indifference of Time.

A sudden sense of futility spurs me into a run. I dart to the stairs that scaffold the courtyard and sprint up the wooden treads. The top floor of the Academy is no longer used. The clay tiles paving the corridors are cracked and grimy. The frescos on the walls are faded, the painted figures ghostlike. For years there haven't been enough students to fill these old classrooms. No one comes here except rats and mice, and the cats that hunt them. And Gerontius.

At the far end of the eastern corridor is a door no different from any of the others. Except it is warded. As I lift my hand to knock, the latch clicks up and the door creaks open on rusted hinges.

'Come in, Zara. I had a premonition you would visit today.'

'Liar!'

I know this room so well I hardly see it. But it's suddenly important that these things exist: the faded tapestries covering the walls, the walnut desk, the battered leather armchair. Centre of all, Gerontius himself, sitting at his desk, a book open before him. Large and hairy – white beard framing a face red-veined from love of wine – and dressed in robes that went out of style three decades ago.

Frightened as I am, a smile creeps over my face. 'You are the biggest liar I've ever met. Your wards told you I was here. You've never had a premonition in your life.'

'I wouldn't wager on that.' Shrewd eyes stare at me through puffy lids. 'But it doesn't take magic to know you're not here for a glass of wine and a chat. Sit down and tell me why you've come.'

I pull a chair to face him and perch on its edge, fists clenched against panic. He's so solid, so real, this old man. Surely he's been here forever, one of Time's own children. He was my mother's favourite tutor. Long ago he gave me a message from the dead that changed my life. I owe him everything: who I am, my very survival. And, looking at his wrinkled, fat old face, I realise I love him. Tears burn my eyes and I blink them away. There's no time for love – only fear.

'Pyramus,' I say. 'He knows something – he's meeting with my father now. Has he been sniffing around?'

The old man puffs out his cheeks; expels a long, low breath. For a moment he says nothing, then slowly nods. 'Of course. When does he not?'

'There's something, isn't there?' I see it in his eyes. 'Tell me!'

'The less you know –'

'Stop protecting me! I'm not my mother. I'm Benedict's spawn.' I glare at him. 'Never forget that. I don't. Besides, I'm not a child.'

'No.' He frowns at me like a sullen bullfrog. His hands are shaking. He's frightened. Oh gods! I feel ice grip my bowels. It's as bad as I feared.

He nods slowly, his eyes on my face. 'You're right. And you'll find out soon enough. One of the Knowledge Seekers disappeared two days ago. His guild and family don't know where he is. He could have had enough and run for it. He might be dead in a ditch. Or he may have turned informer. Thing is, he was my contact. There was nothing to do but lie low and wait. But this news rather suggests I'm compromised. That's it then . . . it's time I went, Zara. Your father will be after the names in my head and we can't have that. Think what would happen to the poor man if he found out about you, for instance.' He snorts.

Gerontius is putting up a good front, but I don't believe it one bit. 'Where will you go? They'll be watching. You won't be allowed out of the city.'

'I'm not without resources, child.' But his voice shakes. His eyes are watery. Gods. I can taste his fear. It fills the room like night mist. Panic floods my body, churning my stomach.

'What resources? Gerontius! . . . *Time's grace!* What are we going to do?'

The old man looks at me. Then, slowly and carefully, he closes the book he has been reading and pushes himself upright. He lumbers around the desk and takes me by the shoulders. I cringe slightly at the unaccustomed intimacy of touch.

'There isn't time for explanations.' His eyes look past me into his own thoughts. 'I made my plans long ago. Thank you for telling me. Now . . .' His fingers tighten on my arms. 'Get

27

the hell out of here and stay clear of me, no matter what happens. Swear it by Time's grace, girl!'

I stare at him. He shakes me. 'Swear!'

'I'm not going anywhere until you tell me what you're going to do. I can't just leave you!'

'You always were a worrier.' He smiles. 'Now. Remember your mother and what she died for. Remember Swift. And, if you can bear such an unsavoury old man, remember me.'

And then I know: he doesn't plan to leave this room alive.

'Gerontius! *No!* I won't let you!'

He sweeps me into a bear hug, gently kisses the top of my head and releases me. And before I can say anything – do anything to stop him – the old adept gathers his magic and shoves me out the door on a gust of wind. I fly across the corridor, slam into the opposite wall and tumble to the floor, bruised and dazed. The door crashes shut behind me and, as I stumble to my feet, I watch the wood change to stone before my eyes. And then I'm pounding on a wall where there's no longer a door – or any sign that a room exists behind the thick stone. Gerontius has walled himself inside his own tomb.

And I have been Death's messenger.

3

I left him. Left him to die and ran away. I don't think I had any choice. As quickly as I crumbled the stone, he would have replaced it. Fighting me would have wasted the little time he had – time to die. But in the place and manner of his choosing. And with his mind still his own. Better that Gerontius should kill himself than Benedict take him. The Archmage would have done to him what he did to me all those years ago: break open his mind and read what was inside. The first precept does not apply to heretics and traitors.

I'm the only one left now. Gerontius killed himself to save me. It doesn't make me any fonder of myself.

I sit in my room. I've closed the shutters to my windows. I don't want to watch the sun setting on this hateful day. The fading light filters through the slats, striping everything with thin bars of white. Pointing out, ever so ironically, that I'm a prisoner. I feel numb. And so, so alone.

I reach down inside my tunic, pull out a slender leather tube, prise off the lid and slide out a roll of paper. There's barely enough light to read by, but I know the words by heart. I just want to see the sprawling shape of the letters. To touch the

the blots and scratchings-out. To hold the only thing I have left of her.

Gerontius gave them both back to me – Swift and my mother. He took them from the dark and made them live again.

I didn't know my mother's story until the winter I turned ten. I had been living a half-life for nearly a year. Then one frozen afternoon the strange old tutor – the one the other neophytes mocked for wearing moth-eaten robes and living in an abandoned room on the top floor of the Academy – asked me to stay behind after the lesson. I had been the only student to fail to rust a piece of iron.

I hunched on a bench, shivering gently and staring at the terracotta tile between my feet, tracing its faded red pattern with the toe of my boot and waiting for the humiliation to start. I waited. And when nothing happened, I looked up.

Gerontius was leaning with his back against his desk, arms crossed, watching me. After we looked at each other a bit longer, he spoke: 'There's more of your mother in you than your father. But how much, I wonder?'

My mouth fell open. No one spoke of my mother. Ever.

'Shut your mouth.' The old man raised an eyebrow. 'You look gormless. No child of Eleanor – or Benedict, for that matter – could be as daft as you look.'

I shut my mouth and sat up. Part of me came alive for the first time in a year. Now that I was paying attention, I sensed what should have been obvious to me all along: Gerontius was nervous. And he didn't like my father. When he said Benedict's name I could feel his dislike ringing loud as the city bells.

'You're cleverer than any of this lot, yet you don't even try to learn. Why?'

I felt my mouth grow thin and stubborn. It was only another lecture. All the tutors nagged and pestered and punished. None of them could make me work. I would rather die than grow up to be an adept like Benedict. I cursed the fact that I'd been born mage-kind, which I knew was madness or heresy or both. I did just enough at the Academy to keep my father from . . . No. I wouldn't think about that. I shuddered and looked back at the tile.

'Something happened to you last year. I know what it was.'

I didn't dare look up. My heart began to thud. What was coming? What did this old man know about me?

'You named her Swift. It suited her at least, but you never bothered to ask her real name, did you?'

My head jerked up. I leapt to my feet and edged backwards. But before I could get to the door it slammed shut behind me.

'No running away, Zara. Your mother wasn't a coward.'

It took a moment before I could find the breath to get the words out: 'How do you know?'

A sad smile crept over his face, faded. I felt loneliness, faint as the scent of last summer's rosemary, waft through the room. 'Because I loved her like a daughter,' he said. 'I'm betting you take after her. I could be wrong but I don't think so. I've read the letter, you see. Maybe I shouldn't have read it, but I'm gambling on you and the odds are stacked against me. As they were against her.'

Letter? The other students were right: the old man was mad. But mad or not, he had loved my mother – there was no mistaking his emotion. Even so, I would be a fool to trust him;

31

to ask the questions teeming in my head. But the temptation was too much.

'Who are you talking about? My mother, or Swift?'

'Both of them.' He smiled again at the confusion in my face. 'Your mother was the best student I ever taught. Including Benedict, rot his soul. I never understood why she slept with him. But Nature makes fools of us all when we're young. It's been a long time since I've had to worry about that, thank the gods.'

Gerontius rubbed his nose. 'Eleanor was a heretic, Zara. Your mother believed kine are human, just like us. Shocking, isn't it?'

He watched me, his broad, red-veined face with its tiny, shrewd eyes as bland as if he was discussing how to pull water from air and use it to dissolve iron. I was terrified. Was this a trap? Was it my father, being clever and evil? Or was this man a miracle?

The old man's eyes narrowed. I was too stunned to control my face. If this was one of Benedict's tests, my tutor had already seen enough to condemn me.

'Shocking,' Gerontius repeated. 'Except you believe it too. We call them "kine". Cattle. But you know better. Unless I'm mistaken, you're an empath – like Eleanor. You have my sympathy. It's a sore and challenging affliction, being forced to share other people's pain, anger, joy and love. But at least you can't pretend they aren't human. I'm staking my life that I'm right. You loved Swift. And you hate your father for killing her. Well, you can hate him for killing your mother too. They won't have told you that.'

The blast of emotion that blazed from the old man branded

32

his words as truth. This was real. My life was changing. Again. And I didn't know what was more shocking: the fact that I was no longer totally alone – that I had finally met someone who hated Benedict as much as I did – or that my father had murdered my mother. She was only the shadow of a memory – she died when I was little more than a baby – but knowing Benedict had taken her away from me, as he had Swift, carved a new channel of pain in my soul.

I was shocked, yes, but not surprised. It all made sense now: all the things my father had hinted and said over the years. Why he looked at me with muddy eyes and I tasted bitterness, loss, and the will to control me as he had failed to control her.

'I'm sorry,' Gerontius said at last. He groaned, shoved himself upright, and strode towards me with a heavy tread. 'But I've got something that might help you sort out who you want to be. She writes a good letter, does little Swift. Handwriting's a bit dodgy, but you'd expect that.'

He *was* a miracle, this man. I felt tears stream down my face. She wasn't completely gone. There was something left.

'She came to me,' he continued. He picked up a paper from his desk. 'She found out about me; don't know how. I think she somehow sniffed out the Knowledge Seekers and got in touch with them. Astonishing really. She'd only just turned eight. She was clever. Very, very clever. *What a bloody waste!'*

He glared at me as though I had killed her. I flinched at the blast of anger and frustration.

'I'm a teacher, Zara. I hate the waste of potential. It's why I became a heretic, like your mother. There haven't been many of us over the years. Most end up dead . . . or mad. But I have to hope that someday we can change things. If we don't, in the end we'll go the way of the Makers. Sometimes I wonder if it wouldn't be for the best.'

It was the most shocking thing he had yet said.

Then he smiled and held out an age-speckled hand, offering the paper. 'Take this away with you,' the old man said. 'Read it. She asked me to keep it safe in case something happened to her. To give it to you when the time was right. She believed in you. Don't let her down.'

I took the letter. The paper it was written on had once been the blank end-page of a book. The torn edge was smooth and straight. I saw Swift's fingers folding and refolding the crease, painstakingly separating the page. It would have wounded her – damaging a book.

I glanced up into Gerontius's face, at the unbearable understanding his eyes.

Then I turned and ran, terrified he might change his mind . . . that it might, after all, have been a trick, a mistake. Later, alone in my room, I held the letter with trembling fingers and read these words for the first time:

> *Dear Zara,*
>
> *I need to write to you the things I cannot say.*
>
> *I'm sorry, but I have to leave soon. I am going to run away to the other side of the Wall – to the Maker cities. The Makers will let me read. They will help me learn all the things I need to know. I will be free.*
>
> *There are books about the Makers in your father's library, although the mages who wrote them tell many*

*lies. Finding out the truth is hard. There are people
in Asphodel who can help you. They are called the
Knowledge Seekers. Ask Gerontius about them.*

*Don't trust your father. He is one of the liars. I have
to tell you he killed your mother. I'm sorry for you, for I
know what it is to lose your mother.*

*When I am gone, find out about the Makers. Find
out about your mother. It is all there in your father's
library. He cannot bear to give up anything, and so he
keeps all the things has done there, no matter how evil.*

*Promise to come and find me as soon as you can. I
love you always. You are like a sister to me – the other
half of myself. I am not leaving because I don't love
you. I leave because if I stay here, I will never live. And
I must live.*

Forgive me, and remember.

Your sister,

Ita

At the bottom of the page, she had drawn a picture of a swift
in flight. It's a strong image, drawn with the directness of a
child. Now, sitting in the barred darkness of my room, I reach
out a finger and touch one of its unfurled wings.

4

Gerontius's disappearance is fast becoming a legend in the Academy. The students talk of nothing else, making wild guesses as to what happened to the tutor who seemed as much a part of the building as the stones themselves. His room has vanished as though it was never there. My father's people must have taken the wall down and found the old man's body. Did they take him away or simply wall him up again? I'll never know and it doesn't matter. Gerontius is dead. One by one, Benedict has stolen away the people I love. I swear by all the gods I'll make him pay for each of them. In blood.

The street winding uphill to the Academy is sprinkled with students, the ones who are habitually late, like me. I shrink away from them. I feel as translucent and fragile as old glass. Snatches of gossip drift to me on the cold wind: *Gerontius found a doorway through Time. Gerontius found a way to defeat Death and his secret is hidden somewhere in the Academy for anyone clever enough to find it.*

So predictable! The old man would laugh if he could hear them. I reach the steps and dart up, trying to block out the voices bubbling over with conspiratorial excitement, wanting to be away from them and their stupid fantasies.

As I mount the last step, I glimpse my father's Guardian standing in the portico. He's a tall man with a broad face, blunt nose and dark hair pulled into a heavy plait. His brown eyes hold the blank look of all Guardians. His name is Otter and he spooks me. Guardians always do. Because of the emptiness in their eyes and how it comes to be there. Otter's eyes latch onto me and fear knots in my stomach. What business does Benedict's Guardian have at the Academy? Is he keeping an eye on me? Did my father find something incriminating in Gerontius's belongings after all?

I've been balancing on the edge of control for days. Now something inside me snaps. I stride across the portico, my eyes locked on Otter's face. He watches me approach with the stillness of a Guardian – a stillness that comes from supreme physical confidence – and as I draw near I'm uncomfortably aware of the size and strength of the man, of his muscular arms emerging from the sleeveless tunic, of the bronze Guardian bands encircling each wrist and the shiny white scar on his right shoulder where he was branded with my father's mage mark.

I come to a halt in front of him. He looks me in the eye, which is unnerving. Most kine won't look directly at you. Guardians are not normal kine, though. They are not even normal Tributes. Their minds have been invaded so much they lack free will. Brain-cleansing, it's called. A version of what my father will do to me if ever he finds out I'm a heretic like my mother. A chill crawls down my spine.

'Why are you here?' I demand. 'Are you following me? Did my father tell you to spy on me?'

37

'Everything I do, Lady, is on Lord Benedict's orders.' His voice is low and pleasant, and totally without emotion.

Leave it! Leave him and pretend he doesn't exist. I ignore the sensible voice nagging in my head. I don't want to be sensible. 'Why did my father tell you to follow me?'

'Perhaps His Lordship is worried for your safety.'

This is useless. Worse: talking to this man is dangerous. I feel the gaze of the straggling students who pause to watch, curiosity outweighing the fear of a demerit for tardiness. And then, something odd happens – the Guardian speaks unbidden: 'Her Ladyship would be wise to return to the palazzo immediately after lessons today. These are perilous times in Asphodel and it pays to be careful where one goes and what one says. To anyone. Including me.'

He bows and withdraws without quite turning his back. But I have been dismissed. Or have I been warned? What in the name of the seven gods is going on?

When I get back to the palazzo that afternoon, the atmosphere is fizzing. My skin prickles as I walk through the courtyard. The cold sun of late winter is low in the sky. My shadow snakes ahead of me over the limestone pavement. Mages, courtiers, guards – everyone I pass is tense with anticipation. Something is happening. But what? And then, as if in answer to my question, the evening breeze gusts through the courtyard, bringing a sudden chill and the distant clatter of horses' hooves. Riders, approaching from the north.

I stop mid-stride and turn my head to listen. Messengers and emissaries from the other city-states come and go from the palazzo like nesting swallows, but this ringing of iron on stone is made by more than one or two horses. The feeling of excitement in the courtyard flares. A pair of mages I recognise as low-level administrative officers burst into a sprint and disappear into the palazzo. Guards run to the main gate and begin to unbar the massive wooden carriage doors.

I draw back into the half-dark of the peristyle. The tension in the air has infected me and my breath comes shallow and fast. The cavalcade marches closer, moving with the quickening steps of tired animals sensing rest.

North. Nothing lies north of Asphodel but the ancient ruins and scattered farms of the plains . . . until the Wall. A party of horsemen travelling from the Wall makes no sense. Tribute soldiers march on foot. Military messenger-mages journey alone and at a rapid trot. So who are my father's visitors?

Otter appears, jogging down the palazzo's wide steps, striding across the courtyard towards the gate, a brace of guards at either shoulder. I withdraw further into the shade of the peristyle. There's a secret here; one which might prove useful to the Knowledge Seekers.

The massive carriage doors creak wide, hinges squealing in protest. The guards just have time to secure them in place before the horses clatter in, hooves ringing, bridles jangling. For a moment, the movement and sound, the sudden stink of well-travelled humans and animals, stuns me into stupidity. My confusion thickens as I see who the riders are: a handful are military mages – low-level magic users who have chosen the army as an alternative route to some degree of status. The remaining riders are Tribute guards. And there is one other:

slender, dust-spattered; and exotic as a rare bird in close-fitting woollen trousers, a shirt that might once have been white, and a jerkin of scarlet leather fastened with silver buckles. His hands are tied to the pommel of his saddle.

As I take in his cropped blond hair, the gold hoops in his ears, the boots he wears in the northern style, reaching halfway up the thigh – as I see the sword scabbard flapping empty and useless at his hip – shock runs a chill finger up my spine. The books in my father's library have taught me well. I know what manner of being I am gawping at, open-mouthed. A Maker! My father has captured a Maker and brought him to Asphodel!

This has never happened before. Mages don't collect Makers – they kill them. And while I have long dreamed of meeting one, in my fantasies this happens in a distant future. A future when I have settled my debts with my father. A future when I will be free to make Swift's journey for her – to visit the land where she would have become who she was meant to be. I never imagined that I would see my first Maker here, in the courtyard of my father's palazzo.

As I peer through the milling animals, my heart catches in my throat. The Maker can't be more than sixteen or seventeen. He sits easily on his horse, head thrown back in defiance. His cropped hair should be the flaxen yellow of the North but it's dun-coloured with dust and sweat. Restless eyes scowl, brightly blue, from an angular face smeared with dirt. The left side of his mouth is cut and swollen, and a bruise blooms between purple and yellow on his cheek. The boy glares at the buildings lining the courtyard, unable to conceal a mixture of wonder and fear.

I stare at him, and the breath leaves my body. There is nothing beautiful about this boy, with his dirt-bristled hair, glittering eyes and bruised face, but I feel his soul, fierce and free. He reminds me of the merlin.

I watch, unable to drag my eyes away, as Otter unties the boy and reaches up to help him from his horse. The Maker ignores the proffered hand, swings a leg over his mount's neck and leaps to the ground. He staggers as he lands and his face flushes red. The boy stares straight ahead as Otter takes his arm and propels him towards the palazzo.

My last glimpse is of a dirty blond head and scarlet jerkin bobbing amid leather-clad guards as they march him up the steps. I carry on gazing at the courtyard, at the stable hands leading away the horses, seeing none of it, my heart twisting strangely inside my chest.

All my excitement at having news for the Knowledge Seekers has died. I can't think about anything other than the boy. Whatever my father has planned for the Maker, it will be unpleasant and probably fatal. I want to save him. Stupid. I can't save myself.

5

The last of the horses is led away and I am alone. The sun drops behind the mountains; light and warmth vanish in an eyeblink. The north wind prowls the courtyard, bringing faint sounds of the city. I stand, motionless as one of the mossy old statues in the wall-niches, watching the palazzo windows blink into life. My eyes are trained on a particular one. When candlelight flickers behind its glass, I take a deep slow breath and wonder if I am brave enough to chance it.

A spy should always think through problems carefully and logically. I should stop myself right now. Instead, I lunge across the courtyard and sprint up the main stairs and inside. The door guard allows herself a brief look of surprise. But it's well known that Benedict's daughter is odd. Several of my classmates have told me that the betting shops have put the odds at my being declared mad, like my mother, at eight to one. They are probably right. I've been spying on my father for seven years, but never before have I attempted to eavesdrop on him. I may be too impulsive to make a good spy, but I'm not stupid. Usually.

Right now Otter is taking the Maker to Benedict and I need

to hear what happens. I want to know why my father has brought this boy here. And what he intends to do with him.

I'm out of breath – and absolutely terrified – so I can't be totally mad. I race for the back stairs and slip up them so quickly that I arrive at the second floor in time to hear the Maker and his guards stamping down the corridor towards my father's library. I sprint up another flight of stairs and push through the door to the third floor, where I stand for a few precious seconds, panting and waiting for sanity to return.

It doesn't. I'm going to do this thing. The inside of my mouth goes thick and dry. This floor is given over to staff offices but the administrative mages should all have left for the day. The steward's office is directly over my father's library. It's locked, of course, but it takes very little concentration to insert a careful thought into the keyhole and convince the lock to open.

I slip inside, grateful for the chilly moonlight. There's no fireplace in this room – that would be an extravagance for clerical staff – but the library's chimney takes up nearly the whole of one wall.

I choose a large stone bedded into the chimney breast with a generous layer of mortar. Taking great care to build my concentration gradually so there is no sudden surge of magic to attract my father's attention, I soften the mortar with moisture from the air and ease the chunk of limestone out.

Trickles of sweat are running down my back when the stone finally comes to rest on the floor. I step onto it, push my head through the hole, and something soft, horribly sticky and full of soot wraps itself over my face. I gasp in a mouthful of clogging muck and begin to choke.

Stupid! I forgot there would be cobwebs. Centuries-worth of them. I jerk away and crack the back of my head on the opening. Then I'm leaning against the chimney breast, clawing at my face. Smothering . . . choking . . . all my best nightmares. I dig and spit the gunk out of my mouth. *Pestilence, pestilence, pestilence!* I curse silently, wishing I knew better swear words. It takes several deep breaths before I calm down enough to try again.

This time I use the sleeve of my robe to wipe the opening clear before easing my head inside. A column of smoky air drifts up the centre of the cavernous chimney. Heat laps against my face. Occasional sparks fly up, rising like tiny shooting stars searching for a way back into the sky. With them comes the sound of voices. Fire carries my father's words to me.

'. . . refusal will not serve you or your people. Your leaders gave you to me to hold as hostage against the peace, and I expect you to mend our clocks and train the apprentice I will provide. I have been promised that, despite your age, you are the best clocksmith in your city. I won't accept failure. If you persist in being stubborn you will be punished. You have one day and night to rest from the journey and adjust to your situation. Then I will expect you to mend our shrine clocks. You have the chance to make history, Maker! To bring a halt to centuries of war. Think on that in your cell. Otter, take him out of my sight. I lose patience!'

There's a scuffling sound, the closing of a door. Smoke rises, bringing silence. My father will be at his desk, thinking, planning, listening. I don't dare risk repairing the chimney. I ease down onto my bottom and rest my back against the slightly warm stone.

Peace. If I hadn't heard it myself, I wouldn't believe it. My father has bartered a truce with the Makers! And to guarantee the peace, they've given a clocksmith as hostage – a boy who will repair our shrine clocks. Clocks that have been dying since the Clockmakers' Guild rebelled nearly half a century ago, mistakenly believing they were too valuable to mage-kind to be killed.

If the Maker does repair the shrine clocks, Benedict's hold on the loyalty of every mage in the city will be strengthened. But . . . a truce? *Peace?* I don't believe it. Benedict doesn't want peace. My father's greatest ambition is to wipe Maker-kind from the earth and exterminate the race who, five generations ago, killed every mage on their side of the Wall in the Kine Rebellion. To stop the infection spreading to our side of the Wall. I know I'm right. The curling smoke carried my father's dark emotions along with his words.

It's well past midnight when at last the flames in the chimney die down and I hear Benedict's footsteps pacing away towards his bedchamber. I replace the stone and re-harden the mortar, clumsy with exhaustion and distracted by the question ringing over and over in my head: what does my father *really* want with this Maker, with this boy whose fearful, angry face I can't forget?

I sleep badly and wake late. Cold water rinses away some of the tiredness. Ignoring the grumbling emptiness in my belly, I throw on my robes. No time for breakfast. I stumble across courtyard, blinking in the morning sunlight. Did last night happen? Did I dream the Maker boy with his sharp blue eyes and scarlet jerkin?

The lump on the back of my head aches in reply. Not a dream. But I don't have time to worry about Benedict's plans for the Maker now. I'm late for the Academy. First lesson is with Aluid. That's another demerit at the very least. I force myself into a trot. But before I've gone three strides I notice a Tribute, a small girl in a faded black tunic, pattering across the pavement. She runs up to me and makes her obeisance.

'Please, Lady,' she pants, stumbling over the words in her nervousness. She can't be more than seven. Her hair is short and blonde, not long and dark, but still I feel my heart flinch. I draw myself up tall. I must look even more forbidding to the child, but I can't do anything about it. It hurts to look at her.

'What is it?' I ask, smothering my impatience to be gone and trying to make my voice, at least, gentle.

'Please, Lady, his Lordship the Archmage Benedict requires to see you.'

Panic. 'Now? But I have lessons . . .' My voice trails away. At least Aluid won't be able to punish me for tardiness. But I would much much rather face him. Does Benedict know I was eavesdropping? Has he been waiting since last evening, allowing me to grow confident until he pounces? Is it even worse? Did Gerontius leave something incriminating behind after all?

I'm a spy. Fear is part of the air I breathe, but now I'm scared breathless.

'Where is His Lordship?'

'In his library, Lady.' She bends knee again and is off like a rabbit.

46

I stand staring at nothing for a full minute, until my mind unkinks and offers forth a thought: *If Benedict knew about your heresy, he would send adepts and guards, not a Tribute.*

By the time I've climbed the stairs and paced down the corridor to the library, I'm breathing normally and my hands are steady. The guard opens the door as I approach and I enter the room without breaking stride. My father is alone, seated at his desk, looking through a sheaf of papers. He waves a hand at me, ordering me to wait. I stand as far away as I dare, my eyes – as always – searching out the paperweight.

'Zara?'

I force my gaze up. Benedict is watching me. It takes all my control to keep my face blank.

'Yes, Father?'

'Gerontius.' His eyes never leave me.

I manage to stop my expression changing. Not the Maker then. Is that good or bad? My face feels like a leather mask. 'Yes?' I ask.

'He was one of your tutors?'

'He taught most of us. I expect he taught you when you were my age.' *Careful!*

Benedict ignores this with his typical single-mindedness. 'What are the students saying about his disappearance?'

'Just what you would expect.' I hear the contempt in my voice. Another mistake, but I can't seem to stop making them. My loss is still too raw. Anger beats back fear, making me reckless. 'The gossip is that the old man found the path to eternal life.'

'And you don't believe that Gerontius found the path?'

47

He's paying attention now. 'Or is it the existence of the path itself you doubt?' I'm skirting on the edge of heresy and we both know it. Sanity prevails and I choose my words carefully.

'Gerontius was old and odd. Everyone knew he was eccentric. No – I don't believe he found anything other than Death.' I load my voice with so much scorn my father must surely notice my overacting. But he relaxes, leans back.

'And that's all? Nothing more? No rumours of unusual . . . philosophies?'

I shake my head, frowning as though puzzled.

'Did he have any special acolytes? Any students he seemed to favour?'

So this is it. My father sometimes questions me about my fellow students. He knows that the inevitable challenge, when it comes, will come from youth. A shiver runs through me, and a crazy desire to laugh. My father holds me in contempt – still thinks of me as the nine-year-old child who didn't have the strength to resist him. I wish I could see Benedict's face as I tell him *I* am Gerontius's acolyte – that someday I'll destroy him and avenge those he's taken from me.

'No, Father,' I reply calmly. 'Everyone made fun of Gerontius. It was disrespectful but hardly surprising. The old man was a bit of a joke. He should have retired years ago.'

Forgive me, old friend!

My father rises from his desk and walks to the shrine cupboard. He opens the door of pierced rosewood and studies the clock inside. It has been broken ever since I can remember. Every night I give thanks to Time that the shrine in my bedchamber still works. A shrine with a dead clock is uncanny.

'This will soon be mended.'

'I don't understand.' I've had years of practice at being a good liar.

'I have brought a Maker to the city.'

'A Maker!' Surprise is easy to pretend. Last night I saw the boy with my own eyes. This morning his presence in the palazzo seems as fantastic as if my father has announced that he has purchased a dragon and is keeping it in the courtyard to catch cockroaches.

'He will repair all the shrines in the palazzo.'

'But . . . a *Maker*? Did you capture him? What about –'

'While he's here you are forbidden to be in his company or talk with him.'

'Oh . . .' I feel my mouth fall open in dismay. Benedict never answers my questions. I'm lucky not to be reprimanded for insolent curiosity. I snap my mouth shut and shrug as though my father's command is of little interest to me. Again, I sense a dark current in Benedict's emotions. He hasn't told me the real reason the boy is here.

'Yes, Father. As you say.'

'That's all.' He bends over his work and I am dismissed.

I escape, but instead of continuing on to the Academy, I return to my room. I will have to risk playing truant for the rest of the morning. I need to get to the market and find the thief. I have news for Twiss. News for the Knowledge Seekers.

6

I race to my chamber and find my dark headscarf. It was easier to spy for the Knowledge Seekers when I was smaller, but there's nothing I can do about my height. Among the books in my father's library are stories about long-ago mages foolish enough to attempt shape shifting. It's possible for a skilled adept to change the structure of a living creature, but the results are usually fatal. Such magic is used in battle . . . or by executioners.

I pull on the plain brown robes I wear when I don't want to be noticed, stuff the scarf into a pocket for later. It's been too long since I've overheard anything useful. My father seems to trust me less with each year. As I slip through the corridors leading to the courtyard, I pray I don't run into Otter. And hope none of the administrative mages I pass wonders why I'm dressed like this, why I'm not at the Academy.

Once free of the palazzo, I stride through the city streets, reining in my impatience. As the hubbub of the market reaches my ears, I pause in a doorway to twist my hair up and cover it with the scarf. Of course, the mage marks on my cheeks and forehead proclaim what and who I am – but only a courtier would recognise Benedict's mark. And my mother has long been erased from official records. Most will take me for one of the rootless mages who roam the city-states in search of novelty.

The Maker's face still tugs at my imagination and my blood is singing. I feel reckless – invincible – which is both dangerous and stupid. When I first began spying for the Knowledge Seekers I was constantly terrified. But I've come to crave the excitement and risk. And the secret knowledge that I'm at war with my father.

I hurry through the marketplace as quickly as I dare. All around me stallholders call their wares: *Cabbage and potatoes! Fat cabbages for sale! Fine leeks! The last winter apples – buy before they go!* It's been a hard winter and even in Asphodel many kine have the bony faces and hollow eyes of the half-starved. Heads turn away and eyes drop as I pass. Swift told me that kine think it bad luck to look a mage in the eye.

I leave the noise of the food stalls behind and turn down a side street that leads to the silversmiths' quarter. The houses are small. Plaster crumbles from stuccoed walls. Where it remains it's faded pink, blue or ochre. Lemon trees raise rounded heads behind garden walls. Stone fountains spurt chill water and the clear sunshine of early spring falls slanting into the street. It shines on the wooden signboard of Tabitha the Silversmith.

I glance around to make sure I'm not observed, push open the low gate in the wall and enter a small courtyard. A robin scolds from the acid-yellow blossom of a late-blooming witch hazel. The house has an oak door, silver with age. It swings open at my touch and I step into a room full of sunlight and the sound of bells. Tabitha bends over a small pot, tapping it with a hammer. The hammer is a blur; the pinging noise like a flock of metal starlings in full voice, and the silversmith's face is rapt. As always, when I come here, I'm entranced.

I move forward into her line of vision and the noise stops at once. Tabitha lifts clear grey eyes, which widen as she recognises me. She stands and bows.

'Bruin, the blacksmith.' Her eyes are firmly focused on the floor as she says this. She will not look at me again. For six years now, Tabitha has been my first contact, the first link in the chain of communication with the Knowledge Seekers. Her fear of me fills the room like a sulphurous stink.

'Thank you,' I say, and leave.

Sometimes I am sent from shop to shop, from stall to stall. A young thief, Twiss, serves as the Knowledge Seekers' go-between. She may be based at the forge today, but there's no guarantee I'll find her there. Twiss could be flitting through the streets, carrying secrets from one rebel to another. Worse, it's nearly midday: counter time.

Twice a day the counters visit every smith in the city to weigh the iron and make sure none has been stolen to make a weapon, and Twiss will make sure she's nowhere to be found. If I've missed her I'll have to wait until tomorrow to pass on my news – I can't risk another trip to the market today.

But I'm lucky. The moment I peer into the smoke-filled smithy, I see her. She's working the forge, pumping the bellows with all the force her thin arms can muster. I pause in the door and watch. The thief is a dark-skinned girl with close-cropped black hair and the pointed face of a cat. She must be eleven or twelve, but looks no more than eight. She's dressed for her trade: barefoot and bare-limbed despite the cold, her tattered trousers and sleeveless tunic close-fitting and the colour of shadows.

The thief's happiness glows hot as the coals she heats. It's always the same when she's at the forge. Bruin is one of the leaders of the Knowledge Seekers; a grim-faced man with fire and iron in his soul. Not someone I would have expected a small child to attach herself to. Yet over the years I've watched an unexpected friendship grow between them. Twiss's eyes never leave the smith.

Bruin towers over her, all bristly black beard and leather apron. His powerful arms are bare and he's pounding a lump of iron on his anvil with a huge mallet. Sparks fly at every stroke. The room stinks of smoke, hot metal and sweat.

'That'll do, Twiss. The counters'll be here soon. You'd best be off.' Bruin plunges the piece of wrought iron into a basin of water. Steam hisses up, and he wipes his face and smiles at the girl. 'You're shaping up a fair smith. I'll be having a word with your old lady about 'prentice papers.'

'The Mistress'd sooner see you 'prenticed for a thief but you're too blame big!' Twiss lets go of the bellows and grins happily at the blacksmith. There's the feeling of a familiar joke repeated and enjoyed. Then the thief spots me and the smile dies.

Twiss is one of the brave ones: she always looks me in the eye. Bruin is another. I suspect he may be heretical. I've never met another kine who treats me as though I'm nothing special, as though the blood running in my veins is no different from his. Now he glares at me, as if daring me to bring him bad news.

53

'Is it the foundry?' he asks. 'Have they got wind of it?'

A shiver runs down my back. I hardly dare think of the foundry. A secret foundry means death – horrific death – to any kine. The Knowledge Seekers have illegally mined iron ore and built a moveable blast furnace. For nearly a year now they have been making a stockpile of swords, knives and spear points. The work is painfully slow, but some day there will be enough to arm every kine in the city. The war will be horrific. My research has told me something of what happened in the Maker world.

I shake my head, shoving all thoughts of the foundry and what it will mean from my mind. 'No. I've heard nothing about that. But there is news: Benedict has captured a Maker. The Archmage claims he's made peace!'

'Peace?' Bruin's face grows dark. He turns his head and spits. 'Someone's been feeding you lies, girl!'

'But it's true! Benedict has bartered a truce with the Makers. The hostage is a clocksmith. He was handed over by his own people.'

I hear a hiss of indrawn breath from Twiss.

'The Archmage wanted a clocksmith to repair our shrine clocks,' I explain. 'And I think he offered them the truce as bait. But I don't think for a moment he intends to keep his word. Not once the clocks are repaired. The Maker boy is refusing to work, b-but he'll have to.' I swallow and force my thoughts back to the job in hand. 'And . . . I think there's something else going on. Benedict is planning something. I don't like it.'

Twiss's eyes narrow. She's been listening intently, memorising my words. She'll be off any second, carrying my news like a messenger bird. Bruin takes the lump of iron from the water and thrusts it back into the fire, working the bellows with his spare hand. I would think that he hasn't heard me except that his forehead is furrowed in thought.

'Wait on, child,' he orders Twiss as she moves for the door. 'You were right to tell us.' Bruin's eyes shift to me. 'But your job's only half done. Now go find out what the bastard really wants with this Maker.' Those words, spoken elsewhere, would earn him a slow and painful death. The smith returns to his work, hammering the glowing iron, a scowl of concentration on his face.

I watch Bruin a second longer before I go. I'm a mage. All my training tells me that I should punish him for his insolence, yet I find myself strangely pleased that he's spoken to me as though I too were a common thief.

7

I'm too excited to sleep – or even to eat – although rest and food are what I most need to get through the night ahead. Finally, my shrine clock chimes three of the morning and, as I creep along the corridors of the palazzo, avoiding the night-guard stations, I try to imagine what it would be like to be a member of the Thieves' Guild.

It's good that there's a moon – I don't want to risk mage light. I shiver and wish the palazzo floors were wood rather than marble. Except that they would creak and I'm making too much noise already. I can't seem to stop my robes brushing the walls, my bare feet scuffing.

Twiss's tribe would never have me. The idea of a mage apprenticed to that outlawed guild makes me smile as I pad – almost silently – along the ground floor. Thieves steal from kine and mage alike. Benedict has tried for years to exterminate them. It's his one failure as Archmage.

I open a shuttered window, ease over the sill and drop onto the stone pavement of the courtyard. My heart taps quick as Tabitha's hammer as I dart across the open space. I hide in the moonshade cast by rose bushes; circumnavigate slender columns of topiary pointing to the stars. I don't *think* I believe the stories about the statues – that they were prisoners turned to marble or bronze in the age of great magic – but I avoid their shadows.

I crouch at the base of the ancient bay tree and stare at the prison entrance. Who is on duty tonight? Everything depends on that. Flying is powerful magic. If the duty mage is an adept they will feel the elements shifting, if they're awake and not drunk. And then they might wonder who was doing strong magic this time of night and come to investigate.

Still . . . my eyes lift to the prison roof . . . there's no other way in. I'm going to do it. My blood burns in anticipation. *Disobedience!* I let myself revel in the feeling for a moment then push it away.

And I'm airborne! Adept's magic, and a skill I mastered early. Ordinary mages can barely hover above the ground for a few seconds – I fly. Concentrate, thicken the air beneath and push. It's more like walking on columns of feathers than flying. Balance is everything . . . and focus. It uses up energy at a ferocious rate, and I'm physically drained when I drop onto the prison roof. But I'm shaking more from nerves. I crouch low and wait. The moon shines down; the tall cypress trees circling the palazzo bar the roof with shadows. Silence.

I swallow to ease the dryness in my throat and move as quietly as I can to the edge of the roof, clinging to the gently sloping pantiles. There is a small window on this side of the prison. The window is always open; its wooden shutters rotted long ago. A forgotten window. Doves fly in and out during the day and bats at dusk.

I step off the roof onto a column of thickened air and lower myself to the window. A smell of dust, of decayed feathers and the dried faeces of small animals catches at the back of my throat. I reach out, grasp the sill, and pull myself inside. It's an old storeroom of some sort. In the faint moonlight, I see a filthy wooden floor, the boards half rotten. Something scurries along one wall and my stomach lurches. I hate rats.

The door is opposite. I'm sure now that the duty mage isn't an adept. Or is drunk. So I float above the floor. It's not just the filth – I don't trust those boards to carry my weight. The door is locked; the lock rusted solid. I rust it further. Push. And curse. I'd forgotten the hinges would squeak. The mage might not be an adept, but she or he will have ears. As will the prison guards.

I'm tired now – I should have eaten. I stand in a dark corridor beside the half-opened door, heart pounding, and wait. Nothing. Time's own luck is with me tonight. I must be more careful or I'll lose what might be my only chance to talk to the Maker. As I think of him, his face appears in my mind, and I decide to take one more risk. The prison is a labyrinth of cells but I need to find him quickly.

I settle onto my heels, my back against the wall, and send out a thin thread of consciousness. Most of my mind is still in my body. I'm far too frightened to risk more. I focus on the image of the boy and send the thread snaking through the prison. I sniff him down, like a bloodhound.

One floor down. In a locked room and not one of the cells in the dungeon. Benedict obviously wants him alive and healthy. The boy lies on a bed in a corner of the room, beneath a barred

58

window. But he does not sleep. I search and find the nearest guard. She paces the corridors one after another, her route a set pattern. I memorise it and return to my body.

In less than five minutes I'm outside the Maker's door; the guard should be out of sight and hearing for another five. It's long enough to touch the lock with my mind, push the metal fingers holding it shut into alignment. There's a soft click and the lock is open. I twist the heavy doorknob and slide into the room.

That was easy! I grin to myself. Perhaps the Thieves' Guild will have me after all . . . and then someone lunges at me and there's an arm around my throat. I struggle to speak but he's choking me. Instinct takes over; I thicken the air between us and shove the boy away. He staggers back and I send a ball of mage light spinning between us. I'm breathing hard and not just from effort. Ever since the night in the library, I cannot bear being touched. I stare at the Maker, daring him to try again.

The reflection of my mage light dances in his irises, turning them a bright kingfisher blue. Something catches in my throat at the sight of him, at his nearness. He's standing in a half-crouch, arms loose at his sides. A fighter's stance. The Maker glares at me, only the rapid pulse flickering in his neck betraying his fear. Perhaps it's the danger, but suddenly I can barely breathe. He looks from the mage light to my face and I see shock. But that is quickly replaced with a more familiar expression: loathing.

'What do you want, *mage*?' He hisses the word like a curse.

'To help you.'

And now, face to face with the Maker, I know I've been a fool. Why should he trust me or answer my questions? Worse,

I can't trust him. I can't tell him I'm a spy in my father's palazzo; that I'm Benedict's daughter but am working with the Knowledge Seekers. Even if he wanted to keep my secret, no mind is safe from the Archmage.

'Help me? Why would you? You're a mage!' The look of loathing on his face intensifies.

'So?' I snap. 'Does that mean I can't try to help you?'

'Yeah.' He nods sarcastically, but he's breathing more quickly now and I feel his fear expand. 'That's exactly what it means. Why are you really here? Did the Archmage send you?' He looks me up and down in a way that makes me want to slap him. 'Are you supposed to seduce me into being a good boy? Well, tell your master he'll have to try harder. Besides, I don't sleep with demons, I kill them!'

Blue eyes blaze above sharp cheekbones. He's made an attempt to wash, but his face is still bruised and his hair stiff with road dust. He watches me like a bird of prey, body tensed for battle. I can feel his his anger, his desire to escape. But not blood lust. Fear and hatred, yes. But this boy has never killed anyone. I'm certain of it and it gives me the courage to continue.

'I've been really stupid,' I say and feel a surge of triumph as he blinks in surprise. 'I should have realised you'd be scared of me. But you don't have to be. My mother died because she wanted to help the kine.'

'Kine? Your mother died because she liked *cows*? Great!' He snorts a bitter laugh and shakes his head. 'Just to make things totally wonderful, now I'm being stalked by a mad demon.'

'Mages are not demons! We're as human as you. And I'm not mad. Well . . . maybe I am . . . oh, *pestilence*!' How many

60

ways can I mess this up? And what I have to say next isn't going to help.

'"Kine" is the mage word for non-magic users.'

He blazes into anger at once. 'You call us *cattle*? That's disgust—'

'Yes, it is. Now shut up and let me finish!'

He glares at me, battle-light in his eyes. I stare right back. The Maker crosses his arms and waits, his whole body shouting sarcastic comments.

'Thank you!' I take a deep breath. Unlike this boy, I've had years to learn to control my temper. 'My mother was an adept. A mage of great talent who undertook years of schooling to join the ruling elite. She had everything – power, status. But she gave it all up because she knew it was wrong to enslave non-magic users. She died for her beliefs. Mages like us are considered heretics. We're locked up or killed. But we exist. A few of us.'

I pause, but he merely watches me. Giving nothing.

I try again. 'The Archmage claims he's made a truce with the Makers, but I don't believe he wants peace. I think he wants to wipe your people from the earth. I'm here to talk to you, nothing else.'

I haven't forgotten his taunt about seduction. It's a perfectly logical conclusion for him to have made, but I don't like him any the better for it. I push my irritation aside. 'If we work together perhaps we can figure out why the Archmage has really brought you here.'

His face tells me I'm not getting through. Stubborn, arrogant boy! Why did I ever want to help him?

'You can believe me or not!' I snap. 'That's your decision. I've risked my life to come here tonight! What have you got to lose? I'm not asking you to tell me anything the Archmage doesn't already know.'

His sharp blue eyes narrow, considering. He's not like me: he doesn't rush at things.

'You claim you're risking so much,' he says at last. 'Well, why do it then? To help your enemy? I don't believe that. What's in it for you?'

'I told you. My mother –'

'Died. Yeah. You said.' The loathing in his eyes has faded to dislike. But his mistrust stains the air between us.

There's something else as well, something he's fighting to keep under control. Anger, of course. He's been delivered into slavery by his own people. But there's a deeper, sadder emotion. The Maker has lost everything and everyone he loved. I try not to feel his pain but it's no use. Some people I can barely read. Others seem directly connected – I can't stop myself feeling their emotions. Swift was like that, and the thief, Twiss. And so is this boy.

'I've lost people too. Everyone. That's why . . .' I've run out of words. I can't reach him. I've failed.

My vision blurs. My nose starts to run and I swipe at it, furious with myself. Who am I fooling? I can't save this boy. For years I've been playing pretend, like a child refusing to grow up, imagining that somehow I will be the one to change things.

I don't want to be a mage! I don't want the power to kill with my mind. I don't want any more Tribute children, any more suffering. I don't want Swift to have died for nothing . . .

but she did. Benedict murdered her. He killed my mother. He will probably kill me someday. Wanting something won't make it happen, no matter how hard you pretend. The Knowledge Seekers will never defeat the mages. I'm a fool.

'I'm sorry.' There really isn't anything else to say. It's all been for nothing. I turn to go.

He's brave: he touches me for the second time. He takes hold of my arm and turns me back around with surprising gentleness. And it's the gentleness – plus the new look in his eyes as he studies my face – that keeps me from blasting him across the room for daring to touch me again.

The Maker is standing so close our bodies almost meet. My heart thuds in my chest, heavy and hurtful. My mage light flickers and goes out, but there's moonlight from the barred window. It's bright enough.

The Maker reaches up a careful hand and pulls the scarf from my head. He stares at my hair as it tumbles down; stares at my face, at my mage marks, his eyes searching, his whole body tense with the strain of keeping hope at bay. 'Who are you? What's your name?'

I am still a fool. I tell him: 'Zara.'

'I'm Aidan,' he says. 'Son of Fergal the Clockmaker. Will you help me, Zara? Will you help me get home?'

8

We sit side by side on the narrow bed and his story is whispered to the dark.

'They sent my brother to find me. Donal.' The moon is setting, but there's still enough light to see his scowl. 'Donal's the soldier.' Aidan shrugs. 'I'm apprenticed to Father. I'm good with machines and Mother didn't want me going to war. I'm still an apprentice but I'm already the best horologist in the city.' There's no pride in his voice; he sounds like he's swearing. 'I don't want to be a clockmaker! I want to be an engineer.'

He darts a quick look at me from under frowning brows, then smiles ruefully. His smile lights his face and my breath catches in my throat. I turn my head away, aware that I'm blushing.

But he's speaking again: 'I'm tribute.'

As he pronounces the word, the moonlight framing Aidan seems to shimmer. The Maker dissolves away and in his place I see a small figure with hair like dark wings. A head, turning slowly towards me, as though submerged in black treacle. A pale face shining; dark eyes lifting.

The vision cracks and floats away like fallen leaves on a stream. I stare at Aidan and my heart stutters with the heavy, slow rhythm of that old pain.

'Are you all right?' The Maker is watching me, eyes suddenly wary.

'You said "Tribute".' My voice is hoarse. Did I see her? Was it my mind, playing tricks? Or Swift's ghost?

'It's our word for a hostage.' Aidan says. 'Why?'

I hesitate, still dazed. 'It means something different here. A Tribute is a slave.'

Should I tell him? He hates mage-kind already. *Demons*. What will he think of us – of me – when he knows the truth? I have to trust him enough to tell him. Trust that he will understand.

I begin: 'Each non-magic family must give their firstborn to us – to the mages – the year the child turns five. It's a tithe the kine pay to their mage overlords – a human tax. It provides us with free labour, but it's also an insurance against insurrection. We have their children.'

I see the horror in his face. I don't want to say more, but I must. I owe it to Swift. And the brutal truth is probably the only way to finally reach this boy – to make him understand that this isn't just about him.

'Each autumn,' I continue, 'a new crop of children is harvested. They become servants in our houses. At twelve, most are sent to join the Tribute army – to fight on the Maker Wall and die there. A few of the five-year-olds are chosen for special training and become guards, like those in this prison. As well as guarding the city, they oversee the Tribute army. And each archmage picks one guard to be their own Guardian – their servant, shield and assassin. Guards and Guardians alike have had their minds . . . cleansed . . . so that they will

65

be totally loyal.'

He stares at me. Even in the faint moonlight, shock and disgust are plain on his face.

'We don't all want it to be this way!' I cry. 'I don't!'

He swallows and the revulsion fades a little from his face. 'Because of your mother?'

'Partly. But . . .' I've never spoken of Swift to anyone. Not since Gerontius – and I never really talked about her to him: it hurt too much. But I have to make the Maker understand. I take a deep breath and begin. 'On my fifth birthday, I was given a Tribute child by my father. To be my personal servant. I loved her. She was like a sister to me. She died. She was murdered.'

Speech has left me. Tears run down my face.

I feel the horror in Aidan's soul give way to tenderness. He wipes my tears away with a gentle hand. Where he touches my skin, his fingers leave a glowing trail of warmth. The Maker looks deep into my eyes. 'I'm sorry for your loss,' he says with quiet formality. 'What was her name?'

'Ita. I called her Swift.'

'Who killed her?'

I stare at him, my mouth open. I shake my head. I can't tell him who I am – that I'm Benedict's daughter, the daughter of Swift's murderer. And now I'm crying properly. Deep, wrenching sobs that feel like they will tear me to pieces.

'Oh, *shit!*'

If I wasn't so upset the panic in his voice would be funny. But I can't stop sobbing long enough to laugh.

'Look. If this a trick . . .' He groans. 'Just, don't get the wrong idea, all right?'

A hesitant arm goes round me. Then another. Aidan holds me awkwardly, then he relaxes and pulls me close. He stinks of sweat – both boy and horse – and he's squeezing me too tightly. But instead of the awkwardness and anger I expect to feel, a sharp but sweet pain kindles beneath my heart.

My misery loosens. I lie against his shoulder, shuddering as my body quietens. And think: *How strange that the first person since Swift to hold me like this should be a Maker.*

In the quiet and peace, I sit up and look into his eyes. His arms immediately unwrap themselves and he slides a little way away from me on the bed. I'm shocked by how bereft I feel.

He watches me warily. Still, that doubt. Does he trust me at all?

'Sorry,' I say. 'I almost never cry. But I don't talk about her.'

'S'all right.' He looks even more uncomfortable and suddenly I feel too big for my skin, all elbows and knees and stupidly long legs. I wrap my arms around myself.

'You said you were given to the Archmage as a hostage?' I make my voice business-like.

'Yes.' He shrugs.

'But . . . that means there really was some sort of parley between Benedict and your people.'

'There was a parley. The Archmage sued for peace. We're not at war now. So Benedict says. So my father believes. Our spies report that your army has withdrawn to camps a few miles away from the Wall.'

'I wish I could believe in the peace, but I don't!' I shake my head in frustration, searching in vain for an explanation. 'There's something we don't know. The Archmage hates the

Makers. All mage-kind fear that ki— . . . that the non-magic will someday rise in rebellion as they did on your side of the Wall. Brokering a truce would be political suicide.'

'I don't believe it either.' The look he throws me is full of the pain of betrayal. For a moment, I glimpse the boy of ten, secure in a childhood where love existed. The lost boy.

'It's obviously a trick of some sort.' Aidan shrugs, a faint sneer on his face. The boy has disappeared. 'I told them so! But my father didn't want to believe me. Every family in Gengst has lost someone on the Wall. We've been trapped in the past by the Mage wars for generations. Those who should invent and build the future die fighting your kind. My father wants peace more than he wants to kill mages. And the Council didn't think they had anything much to lose. Only an apprentice clockmaker.

'Give him his due – my father had a really hard time.' Aidan grinds out the words: 'He sacrificed the son he had trained up to take over the family business, but at least he's guaranteed his political career. He'll be Council leader for the rest of his life. Whether I live or die, he's always going to be the man who gave his son for the city.'

He sits hunched on the bed, lips tight and thin, eyes full of cold misery. I know he's watching the death rites of his childhood. There's nothing I can say. No comfort I can give. We all face the truth alone.

I hear myself sigh with relief as the wave of pain crests and falls back. I say: 'The Archmage wants you to fix our clocks.'

He nods. 'And make new ones. And train up some of your slaves as my apprentices. They told me your Clockmakers' Guild died out a generation ago.'

I decide this probably isn't the time to tell him that our clockmakers were murdered for rebelling against their overlords.

'I'm to be the master of your new Clockmakers' Guild.' His laugh is dry and hard. 'As long as the peace holds, I live. Until I've taught what I know. And then . . .' He stares at the floor. 'My people sold me, sacrificed me like a sheep to the winter sun.'

'And you want to go back to them?'

'Anything is better than being a slave to a filthy . . .' He breaks off with a wince.

'A filthy mage. You can say it.' I shrug, hiding my desperation: I don't want him to see me like that. Perhaps that's what makes me say it – the need to prove to him that I'm different – to prove it to myself. 'I know people who can help you get home. I'll find a way to get you to them.' It's a rash promise and even as I make it I realise the odds are impossibly long.

'Who?' His slumping body straightens at once. He leans towards me.

'I can't tell you yet. It isn't safe for you to know. I have to talk to them first. Make arrangements. But I promise – I won't stop until you are free.'

His eyes capture mine, full of hope. My heart flutters, begins to race. Suddenly I feel like I'm back inside the hawk, soaring high above Asphodel. I reach out and take his hand. His fingers tighten on mine. He shakes his head as though seeing something strange, incomprehensible.

'Are you real, Zara? You're not like anyone I've ever met.

'Nor are you,' I whisper.

'Will you really help me?' His eyes search mine, wanting

to believe. But still I feel doubt threading the dark edges of his mind.

There's a twisting pain in my chest. But still I say it: 'I swear!'

I've sworn and am like to be forsworn – helping this boy will almost certainly kill me – or worse – but I don't care.

He shakes his head, holding my gaze. 'How long?'

'I don't know. I can't tell you that. I'm sorry. You'll have to be patient. For a little while.'

'I'm not going to repair the clocks!' Aidan drops my hand, turns away. He stares into the dark, chin jutting stubbornly.

'You *have* to. He'll make you!' I grab his arm, feel the living warmth of his skin, the strength of his muscles. And know the strength is an illusion. My father could break this boy to pieces with a single thought. 'Just play along with the Archmage for now,' I urge. 'Why not? You don't want to risk . . . he can do horrible things! You won't prove anything . . . you'll just suffer.'

'*I'm not a slave!*' He remembers to whisper, but the blast of pain and anger batters me. 'My whole life, people have decided who I'm to be, what I'm to do. But this . . . *no!*' Aidan draws his arm away, stands up. He takes deep breaths, forcing himself to calm down. Without looking at me he says: 'Thank you, Zara, for promising to help me. But I think you should go now. I need to think. And . . . you should just leave.'

I'm a mage again. No longer an enemy perhaps, but not yet a friend. I suddenly feel tired to my very bones. I nod. I walk out of the cell, close the door and lock it behind me, and leave him alone in the dark.

9

It's days before I see him again. Days spent avoiding Otter, placating my tutors, staying out of my father's sight. I don't dare return to the prison. The risk isn't worth it – Aidan has told me all he knows and it's not enough. I have nothing to offer the Knowledge Seekers. Bruin gave me a job, and I've failed. As for the Maker boy's bravado – his threat to withhold labour – I have to trust that somewhere in that thick head he has a degree of self-preservation. He will have to work. He is the Archmage's creature now, whether he knows it yet or not.

With every day that goes by without a glimpse of the Maker, the pain in my heart sharpens. Why? I'm not sure I even like him. But his face, with those wounded, bright eyes shining resentfully at me, haunts my dreams both awake and asleep.

I get up before time and dress in the cold, clear light that finds my window earlier each morning. Spring has come at last. My white student robes are not the best colour to wear when spying, but I'm only Benedict's problem child. No one – from the high adepts who sit on the Council of Mages to lowly administrative mages – takes me seriously. In the hour before lessons, I wander the palazzo almost unnoticed, listening to gossip, looking for any sign of the Maker.

A week passes without success. Then one day as I trot down the marble staircase that circles up and up on its iron balustrades, the twisted spine of my father's house, I glance to the floor below and catch sight of a scarlet jerkin and cropped blond head. I grab the banister – surprise has turned my knees to butter – and watch him disappear around a corner. Otter walks slightly behind the Maker, his bulk too quickly blotting Aidan from view.

I reorganise my legs and slip quiet-footed after them, careful to keep out of sight. Two sets of boots clump ahead of me, down the corridor then up the servants' stairs at the back of the building. I trail them all the way to the attics.

Spying on Otter is almost as terrifying as eavesdropping on my father so I keep well back. When I open the landing door and edge around it all I see is an empty corridor paved with dusty terracotta tiles and lined with a row of plain doors. Storerooms, I guess. I've never had reason to come here before. Why has Otter brought the Maker here? They must be in one of these rooms. There's no place else for them to go.

I'm about to follow when I hear something. Halfway down the corridor, a door opens and a Tribute guard steps out. She closes the door with quiet efficiency and turns towards me. I back up so quickly I nearly fall on my behind. *Did she see me?*

Almost frantic with fear, I gather my magic and half fly, half glide down the stairs, following the twisting stairwell to the floor below. I slip through the landing door, close it behind me and crouch there. Blood pounds in my ears. What if the Tribute wants this floor? But I'm trapped now.

The steady clump of her boots follows the stairs down. Closer and closer. I hold my breath, but the boots pass on without a break in rhythm. A wash of relief. I'm trembling slightly as I frown into the silence. The guard must have come from the room where Otter has taken Aidan. But why she was there, waiting for them?

In less than a minute, I'm back on the floor above, encouraging my feet to silence as I approach the door where the guard appeared. I was right. They *are* in there. I hear raised voices from inside the room. Actually, one raised voice. The other is low and quiet. I recognise them at once: Aidan and Otter.

'. . . *go and get stuffed!*' Aidan isn't shouting. His voice is too full of concentrated scorn for that.

'What kind of man are you? You haven't even got a proper name – you're called after an animal, for fuck's sake. You're nothing but an intellectual eunuch – doing that monster's bidding. Why don't you slaves join together and fight back? He can't kill all of you. You're a coward! I'd rather be dead than be his creature.'

'You won't be given the opportunity to choose.' Otter's voice is still quiet, but there's an edge to it I've never heard before. The Maker has got under the Guardian's skin, something I've never managed to do.

'The Lord Benedict has been extremely patient with you, Maker.' The Guardian's voice is heavy with threat. 'But his patience is at an end. This is your workroom. It is equipped with every tool you might need. You will repair the clock shrine waiting on the work table. You will start immediately.

Or you will be punished.'

I edge closer to the door. I need to see inside. It's tiny magic: even an adept would hardly notice. The door latch is made of oak, a stubborn wood. But I convince the wood fibres that they want to float on the thickening air. Slowly, carefully, I lift the latch with my mind, push the door open as far as I dare and peer inside.

The Guardian is looming over Aidan, trying to intimidate him physically. The Maker is a head shorter and half as wide. Otter could break him in two with his bare hands and they both know it.

Damn Aidan! Why is he doing this? Why can't he just repair the shrines? Pride? Sheer stubborn stupidity? Partly, but I think he doesn't know what he's facing. He doesn't know my father.

I start to call out, then press my hand over my mouth. I can't help Aidan. I have to trust that Otter won't actually kill him. If I interfere, Benedict will find out I've disobeyed him and probably put me under full surveillance. I can't afford that now. Not when I might at last be of real use to the Knowledge Seekers.

The emotion swirling around the room is making me dizzy. *Two people?* I never sense the Guardian – Otter is a blank. That means there's a third person in the room. Someone terrified, almost to the point of collapse. I edge sideways until I see him cowering a few steps behind Otter – a little boy dressed in the black tunic of a Tribute. A thin child with bushy white-blond hair. His face is white with horror. His mouth is open as though he's crying out, but he makes no sound. I hear it though – his unspoken scream. It wails inside my head.

'Your apprentice is waiting.' Otter's voice is hard. 'Your tools are ready. Start working.' The tension in the air rises like steam.

I bite my lip, heart thudding. *Please, Aidan! Do as you're told!*

But the Maker raises his chin, blue eyes narrowed and glinting. 'Get stuf—'

Otter's hand lashes out and slaps the word from Aidan's mouth. The force of the blow lifts the Maker off his feet and sends him flying sideways. He crashes to the floor but staggers up immediately. Blood trickles from a cut lip. He shakes his head to clear it and smiles at Otter. 'Having fun?'

I groan. The attitude, the anger – the sheer, stubborn determination not to give in. It's all still there, stronger than ever. Aidan's just upped the stakes. I'm going to have to stop this. But I can't! My mind freezes. I don't know what to do.

Otter is watching Aidan. His calm control is back and he gives a short, chilly laugh and shakes his head. 'You're a little cracker, aren't you? Tough boy, eh?'

'Tough enough.' Aidan wipes the blood from his mouth with the back of his hand. 'I've been beaten up by better men than you. We know how to fight, our side of the Wall. You're a coward, or you'd be dead before you'd work for these blood suckers.'

'You don't know what you're talking about.' Otter nods his head, as though he's come to a decision. 'But I wonder how tough you'll be after a taste of this. I've got to know you a little bit now, Aidan of Gengst, so I had the prison guards bring me one of their favourite toys. Especially for today.'

The Guardian walks out of my line of vision. My mouth is dry, my heart pounding. Then Otter reappears. He's carrying a whip made of nine leather thongs with metal tips. The prison torturers call it 'the Persuader'. Applied skilfully, the metal tips slice skin. Cut through flesh and tendon to bare white bone. *Oh gods! He can't mean it!*

But the Guardian doesn't approach the Maker. Instead he walks to the child, takes him by the arm and drags him forward. The boy makes no sound, but his face goes even whiter and his whole body shakes. My stomach twists inside out. I look from the boy to Aidan. The Maker's cockiness has disappeared. There's only shock and dawning horror in his blue eyes.

'Not you, Maker.' Otter's face is blank, empty. 'We need you whole and in one piece to do your work. The boy. If you don't pick up your tools and repair this clock – properly, no messing – I'll flog the boy. There's not much flesh on him. He might die, which would be unfortunate. We'd have to find another apprentice and do it all over again. So what say you now, Aidan of Gengst?'

Aidan stares back, eyes dark with hatred. His chest is heaving, almost as though he's sobbing. But he doesn't speak. I can feel his horror as strongly as my own. And his desperation. 'No.' He shakes his head. 'You're bluffing. You wouldn't!'

Otter's expression doesn't change. His grip on the boy's shoulder is the only thing keeping the child on his feet. 'Are you willing to risk this boy's life that you're right? This city rests on the ashes of dead children, Maker. Your people have seen them die in their hundreds and thousands on your Wall. Do you think the Archmage will give this child a moment's thought? You're the only one who can save his life. Your choice, Maker. Does he live? Or will you watch him die, just so you can prove how tough you are?'

Aidan's mouth opens. His face is chalky. He's gasping. 'Bastard . . .' he breathes. And then he closes his eyes and his whole body slumps.

Thank the gods! He's giving in!

'You win.' Aidan has opened his eyes and the person looking out is years older. 'I'll do what you want. I'll work. Let go of the kid, you . . .'

Tears trickling unnoticed from his eyes, the Maker marches on the Guardian, who steps back. Aidan gently takes the boy by the shoulders. He squats down until their faces are level. 'It's all right, kid. You're my apprentice now. Hey . . . come on, stop crying. He didn't mean it. I'm looking after you now. No one's gonna hurt you. I promise.'

I back away from the scene, my body convulsed with sobs I don't dare release.

I turn to run, but a hand grabs my shoulder and tugs me around. Nearly seven years ago, Otter came to the palazzo as my father's new Guardian. Since then he has never once dared to touch me. Now he holds my arms with stone-hard hands. He glares down at me and his eyes – always so empty, so unreadable – have come to vivid, furious life.

10

'How dare you!' My outrage is only partly feigned. It is a capital offence for a kine to assault a mage. Physical contact without permission costs a hand. Otter's daring is more frightening even than the look in his eyes. There's only one explanation: my father has given his Guardian permission to touch me! My heart is racing and I feel sick. The need to get away from this man is overwhelming. I can't bear his closeness. '*Let go!*'

'Not yet.' The light brown eyes staring into mine are cloaked once more but he's holding me too close. It's unnerving: his strength, the size of him. My blood pounds, my knees go weak. The sense of physical danger is overwhelming. Desperate, I reach for my magic.

'I wouldn't, Zara.' His voice is as quiet and controlled as ever. 'Not unless you want the Archmage involved.' His eyes are still locked on mine.

Unless . . . ? 'Let go of me! You have no right –'

He pulls me inside the workroom. Kicks the door closed with his heel. Anger. I can't feel it – Otter's emotions remain as blocked off as ever, but there's no mistaking the body language. I've never seen the Guardian angry before. I didn't think it was possible. That alone keeps me from blasting him across the room. Just.

I glimpse Aidan's startled face. And the child, eyes wide in surprise and fear as he stares at me. Alarm grows in the Maker's eyes. I look away. I've compromised him. I'm supposed to save him, and now . . .

Otter releases one of my arms. It throbs. He's hurt me. I try to pull the other away, but he shakes his head. 'Not until you tell me why you're here, Zara. Idle curiosity? Would you like to explain to your father why you're spying on us instead of attending your lessons at the Academy? I know you were forbidden to see the Maker. I don't think the Archmage would –'

'*Father?*'

Oh gods. I look over Otter's shoulder and see understanding grow in Aidan's eyes. He stares at me. I see it in his face and feel it in his emotions: mistrust. Betrayal. My heart contracts with fear.

No, Aidan! Don't say anything! Please trust me! Don't . . .

'Your father is the *Archmage*? You're Benedict's daughter?' Aidan shakes his head in outraged disbelief. Anger blazes across the room; I wince. But feeling his pain is far worse – he's hurting.

'He *did* send you that night.' The Maker's voice drips contempt. I feel his anger slide into loathing. 'I was right all along. Was it funny? Did you go tell Daddy and laugh about it afterwards? About how you fooled the stupid Maker? Is that how you demons get your jollies? Was it fun, tricking me into trusting you? *You lying, conniving bitch!*'

Aidan is physically shaking with the desire to hurt me in return. But he can't. He turns his back, goes to stand at the

79

workbench arrayed with tools and a shrine clock awaiting his clever hands. If only he knew how much I am hurting already, he would be pleased. I open my mouth . . .

'You broke into the *prison*?' The Guardian's voice isn't controlled anymore. His grip on my arm tightens painfully. 'For a sweet little chat with a Maker? You *idiot*! Do you have any idea of the risk you took? How did you get in?'

I look from him to Aidan. The Maker stands with his back to us both. But he's listening. I feel his sense of betrayal. Of outrage. Worse: of hope sliding away and despair gathering.

'My father didn't send me, Aidan. You can believe that or not.'

I look up into the Guardian's face.

The worst has happened. My father will find out about my night-time visit to the Maker's prison cell and the interrogation will begin. He invaded my mind once in order to catch me in a lie; I don't doubt he will do it again if I can't convince him that today's spying on the Maker – and my visit to his cell – were motivated by simple curiosity.

If.

I close my eyes as nausea sweeps over me at the memory of what he did to me that night. Sweat beads on my forehead, my upper lip. I swallow hard, struggling not to be sick.

Even if my father believes me to be merely disobedient, even if the secret of my heresy is safe for a while longer, the punishment for disobedience will be severe. At the very least I will be kept under constant watch for weeks and months. My usefulness to the Knowledge Seekers is finished.

'Zara?'

I draw myself up. Lift my chin to look into the Guardian's face. 'I'm sorry.' I choose my words with care. I have a slender chance. Do I?

Otter watches me, his face once more unreadable.

'I was stupid,' I say. 'I've heard about the Makers my entire life. I just wanted to see one. I'm sorry. It won't happen again. Please . . .'

This is so hard. I'm not used to pleading. And it's useless anyway. I don't know why I'm bothering – Otter belongs to my father, mind and soul. But I ask anyway: 'Please, don't bother my father with this stupidity. He has important work to do and doesn't need to be distracted with this.'

'I promise nothing, Lady.' Inscrutable formality. His hand relents at last and releases my arm. I feel another bruise throb into life and rub at it vaguely as I peer up at him, trying to read my fate. There is nothing in his face to give me hope.

'A warning, Lady.' The Guardian's voice is cold certainty. 'If you dare visit the prison at night again your father will find out. He will not be pleased. I suggest you hurry to attend your remaining lessons and think very long and carefully before you do anything quite so stupid again.'

I back away, slowly; unsteady on my feet. I don't know what, if anything, the Guardian has just offered, but every fibre of my being screams to be out of here, away from him. In the corner of my eye, I see Aidan turn around, surprise and confusion on his face. His eyes catch mine, then widen as he realises how close he came to betraying us both. Then, as that shock lessens, I feel his hope return.

I turn my back and run. Out of the attics, down the servants' stairs and out of the palazzo, my robes flapping behind me like broken wings. Terror of Benedict nips at my heels. But even in my fear, the image of the Maker comforting the Tribute boy is branded in my mind.

Don't hope, Maker! I'm useless now. I've failed you. Failed Swift. Failed the Tribute child who stood beside you, his huge grey eyes mournful as he gazed up at you, but still full of the hope that children never quite relinquish.

11

Nearly a week later and no summons has come. I've been a model student: arriving promptly at the Academy each morning, attending every lesson, paying attention to my tutors. Nights are spent half-awake, dread flaring at every noise or shift of light.

I haven't seen Otter since that day in the attics. I shudder at the thought of him. But he can't have told my father. If he had . . . but why has the Guardian kept silent? Unless Benedict knows. And is waiting. Waiting to catch me out. Waiting for me to visit the prison again.

Another week passes. I see Otter in the distance. Once, I catch a glimpse of Aidan being ferried to his workroom by a trio of guards, his apprentice trotting at his heels. I'm still too frightened to attempt to contact the Knowledge Seekers.

A third week and, as the spring sun grows warmer, my courage returns. No one seems to be watching me. I must act or give up on all my hopes and accept that I will never keep the promises I made to Swift and Aidan, or to myself. I visit the market, speak with Bruin. And am given my orders: I am to find a way to talk again with the Maker. But how? I can't risk another night-time trip to the prison. And Aidan is guarded in his workroom. And then I remember: there is one clock too big to be taken to the attics.

It's the time of the famine moon – a friendly time for spies. I sneak through pitch-dark corridors to my father's library and inspect his diary. Swift was right: Benedict notes down everything. In a few days' time, Aidan will start work on the Great Clock.

On the appointed day, I rise early and slip into the Council Chamber before dawn. The throne of the Archmage – made of ancient oak the colour of tar – sits in the base of the clock itself. Marble pillars either side soar upwards to support the round face of Time, golden and unsmiling. A single, enormous wrought iron hand marks the hours. The mechanism is powered by a bronze pendulum that hasn't moved for more than a generation.

The twelve seats of the Council face the throne, raised upon a semicircular dais. In between dais and throne, piercing the centre of the stone floor, is a circle of oak. I slide the oaken lid away and stare down into a pit, three feet wide and six deep, its curved walls lined with black marble.

The prisoner pit. Where unwise or unlucky mages end their days. Where those accused of sedition, treason or heresy stand as their crimes are read out and judgement passed. My mother must have stood down there, craning her neck to see the man she once loved condemn her to death.

How many decided to die fighting rather than submit to the inevitable? No mage, however powerful, has left this room alive after the sentence of death was passed upon them. My mother? Did she fight, or submit? I'll never know.

My stomach churns at the thought of what I must do now. I crouch down quickly, before I can change my mind, and lower myself inside. When my skin touches the cold marble, I cringe. Once I'm standing, heart banging against my ribs, staring up at the circle of light above me, I want to jump out at once. Instead, I reach up and drag the lid into place.

It clunks home and I feel a wave of panic sweep through my blood. I hate the dark as much as ever I did. But I'm not a child of nine any more. I need to speak to Aidan and find out if Benedict has talked to him again; told him the true purpose of the truce. My father would enjoy tormenting any hostage, but most especially a Maker.

The oak lid is cracked with age and, as my eyes adjust to the dark, I see thin lines of light raying overhead. It's cold in the pit and I'm shivering by the time I hear the door open and the murmur of voices. Feet tramp over the wooden cover and I clamp my hand over my mouth to stop a nervous squeak. I sense Aidan's presence, and the boy. No one else.

Ordinary Tributes keep watch over Aidan now – not Otter. Otherwise I wouldn't risk it. The Tributes will stay outside, guarding the door to the Council Chamber. The Maker must be the first kine in a generation to be allowed in this room.

I don't want to use magic and risk attracting the attention of a passing adept, so I slide the oak lid off inch by inch, grab the edge of the pit and struggle to haul myself up and out. Only my arms aren't strong enough and I slip and fall. The breath slams out of my body with an *oooff!* and I lie at the bottom of the pit gasping like a stranded fish.

When air returns to my lungs I wriggle upright, aware of a painful bump hatching on the back of my head. I give it a rub and look up to see Aidan standing over the pit, a large wooden mallet in one hand, ready to give me another lump on the head. He's frowning, mistrust battling hope in his face. I watch him make up his mind.

'Want a hand?' He drops the mallet, grabs my wrist and pulls me out before I can answer. The toe of my boot catches on the lip of the pit and the Maker grabs my arms to keep me from falling. We stand face to face, our noses nearly touching, and I lose my breath for the second time in less than a minute. Then Aidan releases my shoulders and steps back.

'I thought you were never coming again.' His whisper is harsh with accusation. 'Or that you were just playing with me and you didn't mean it after all – promising to help me escape. You might not be working for your father, but you could still be having a bit of fun with the stupid Maker.'

'I wouldn't do that.' I look at him until he drops his eyes. 'It's almost impossible to get near you!' I'm still angry. 'Especially after Otter found me in the attic. If you had said one more word – told him that I promised to help you escape . . . that I've talked to people in the city about you . . .'

'Sorry. But how was I to know? It looked bad and . . .' He frowns with embarrassment. Then gives me a sideways look and slow smile. His eyes are ridiculously blue. Aidan steps towards me, eyes holding mine, still smiling. He slowly raises his hand and runs a finger down the side of my face. My legs seem to melt. 'Forgive me?' The smile warms. Everything warms. I start to step back, remember the pit just in time and lurch sideways.

'It doesn't matter now!' I snap. 'Forget it. But I have to be careful. If I get caught I'm no use to you or anyone else. I know it's hard, but you have to trust me!'

'I don't trust anyone. You should have told me who you were when we first met.' His face grows stony again, almost sullen.

'Oh!' I stare at him. I've never met anyone so obstinate! 'I tell you I'm Benedict's daughter, and you instantly trust me. Right! That was never going to happen. And try to realise that the more I tell you, the more we're both at risk. I don't even know that you're worth any of it, Aidan of Gengst!'

'Want to find out?' His eyes sparkle wickedly. They travel over my face, my hair, my body. I feel myself blushing. 'You look different in daylight. Prettier.' The corners of his mouth lift in another beguiling smile.

I give him look for look, noticing the soft-straw colour of his clean hair, the shape of his mouth without the blood and swelling, the thin white scar that runs from under his fringe and divides a sandy eyebrow, a scar previously hidden beneath a layer of dirt. I raise my chin, pleased I'm as tall as he is. 'And you don't stink any more.'

Aidan's eyes grow light; he laughs.

'I have news,' I say. 'The people I told you about – the ones who can help. They've agreed to try and get you out of here.'

'When?'

'I can't tell you that. We're working on a plan. Be patient. Keep doing your work and don't attract the Archmage's attention!'

The shutters come down again. His face is thundery. 'I'm doing the work. For the kid's sake. But as little as I can get away with. Look, Zara, I don't know how long I can keep this up. You need to get me out of here quick or I'll find my own way!' It's a threat. An empty one, but he doesn't know that. I can feel his outraged pride. His frustration. He's bubbling away like a pot about to boil over.

And I finally lose patience. 'Look!' I reach out and grab his arm, shake it. 'I'm risking *everything* to help you! And what's the point, if after all this you're going to do something stupid and get yourself killed? You might spare a thought for the people who've agreed to help you. They're gambling their lives and those of their families.'

He frowns, but he doesn't draw away. 'That's fair,' he says slowly. The frown fades. Aidan carries on peering into my face as though someone has given him a problem to solve and he's determined to find the solution.

I can't pull my gaze away. Something stirs in the depths of his eyes – surprise. A growing wonder. A strange feeling warms the pit of my stomach. I jerk my hand away from his arm and step back, heart thudding.

I sense someone watching us and turn to see Aidan's apprentice. The child stares at me, huge grey eyes solemn beneath his shock of white-blond hair. He's reed-thin and his hair so bushy that he looks like a dandelion clock waiting for its seeds to be scattered on the wind. He suddenly smiles and shyly tilts his head. It's like he's waiting for me to say something amazing.

'Hello.' Hardly amazing, but all I can manage. 'What's your name?'

'He can't tell you.' Aidan goes to the child, smiles down at him and ruffles his hair. 'He's my little chick. He's a good boy, but he can't talk. Or won't.' The Maker glances up at me, his face suddenly serious. 'Something's happened to him.'

'What? Worse than being a Tribute?'

Aidan shrugs. 'I only know I'm to train him up as my apprentice. And he's a clever little chicken, this one. Here, lad.' The Maker tugs a slender tube of wood out of his pocket – a simple flute. The child takes it with careful fingers, obviously delighted. 'Go on. Sit over there and practise the song I taught you. I'll come join you in a minute. I need to talk some more to this lady.'

The boy gives me an enquiring look. I sense he expects something more from me, so I smile and nod in encouragement. His gaze lingers a moment longer, then he scurries over to sit on one of the wooden scaffolding planks, puts the flute to his mouth and begins to blow. Soft, reedy notes – almost a tune – rise into the air.

'I made it for him,' Aidan says, turning back to me. 'I thought, if he could make music then at least he'd have some way of expressing how he's feeling. Poor little sod. I don't know what your people have done to him but . . .' He breaks off and watches the child. 'You know. There was something that bastard Otter said . . . I never thought about them before. The Tribute army, I mean. All those kids dying on the Wall. We kill them. Have done for generations. And . . . I just never thought about who they were.'

The flute's voice floats on the chill air, higher and higher, until it touches the stone roof arches. I think of my mother. This room has heard weeping, pleading, screams, the silence of dumbstruck horror. But never music. It feels like a splinter of black marble from the pit is pushing into my heart. Something is happening to me.

I feel Aidan's desire to save the boy . . . his anger. Anger at Otter, at Benedict, at himself. And I remember two small girls, each sworn to protect the other. One dead; one alive but forsworn.

Aidan looks up and catches my eye.

I know what he wants, and the heavy pain grows in my chest. Suddenly, I'm afraid. It's an old, familiar enemy, this fear – one I thought I'd never face again after Gerontius died. But it seems I am beyond stupid. I have allowed myself to care for the Maker. *What have I done?* I don't want this again – this fear of loss. But it's too late.

'You all right?' The Maker frowns at me. 'You look a bit off. Did you bump your head bad?'

'No . . . no, I'm fine.'

'I *am* grateful.' His voice is hesitant – I don't think he's used to apologising. A few minutes ago I would have found the pained expression on his face funny. 'And I'm very grateful to you and these mysterious people who are going to get me out of here. But I can't leave without the boy.' The Maker's eyes fasten on the child.

'Yes . . . I know. He'll go with you. I promise.'

He reaches out and takes my hand. His fingers wrap round my palm, warm, callused, strong. He leads me to the scaffold plank and we down sit side by side, looking at each other. *Time's grace!* I don't need this now – this emotion and the fear it brings. *I don't want it!*

90

Aidan smiles. His eyes grow warm, almost gentle, and I forget to be afraid. I reach up a finger and trace the scar that slices through his left eyebrow. 'How did you get that?'

'Fighting.' He shrugs. 'You know . . . you get a bit drunk and stuff happens. Someone hit me in the face with a beer bottle.'

'That's not a new scar. Weren't you a bit young to go drinking and fighting? Don't your parents mind?'

'My father doesn't care what I want, so why should I care about what he wants?' An old anger, an old hurt.

'And your mother?'

His face softens. 'She tries to understand. But it's hard on her, yeah. And now . . .' His eyes darken with misery. 'When they came for me they gave her poppy juice. Locked her in her room. I never even got to say goodbye. *Bastards!*'

'I'm sorry.'

He nods. 'It'll be all right. You're going to get me back home.'

Reluctantly, I say: 'I need to hide again. But we must find out why Benedict has pretended to make peace with your people. Have you seen him again?'

The Maker nods. He swallows twice, quickly. 'Three days ago.' For the first time ever I see real fear in his eyes. The sight of it makes me feel ill.

'Did he say anything . . . give any hint about what he's planning?'

Aidan shakes his head. His lips are pressed together.

'Then all you can do is to keep your ears open and wait. The Knowledge Seekers will find a way to get you out of here.'

'Knowledge Seekers? Who are they?'

'Rebels. I've been spying for them since I was ten. They're

ordinary people. Guildspeople who want the freedom to learn, to work for themselves – not their overlords. They want to build machines, to learn to read and write. To find out. They seek knowledge because knowledge is freedom. And most of all – like me – they want to stop the Tribute tax.'

'You mages will never let that happen!'

'The rebels know they'll have to fight for their freedom. As your people did long ago. You won. It's why mages hate and fear Makers.' I'm whispering. My heart is racing and my hands are cold and clammy. These words hold such danger for us both. He won't even begin to guess how much. 'You must *never* mention the Knowledge Seekers! If the Archmage thought you knew –'

'Don't worry!' Fear clouds his eyes again. 'I won't let on. And the lad can't say anything. But tell your Knowledge Seekers that when I leave, the boy comes with me.'

'Yes. I promised, remember? When are you going to trust me?'

For a moment he stares at me. Then he reaches out and touches the mage mark on my right cheek, my mother's mark, tracing its curves.

'Mages may fear us, but we Makers believe you to be demons.' He smiles into my eyes. 'I would never have believed a demon could be so beautiful.'

12

The street children of Asphodel play a game, kicking a ball made from a goat bladder inflated with air. The atmosphere in the palazzo feels like one of those balls filled to bursting point. Something is going to happen. But what? Perhaps I'm imagining the feeling. I can't stop thinking of Aidan. But I don't dare try to speak to him again because Otter has started keeping watch on me. I fear he somehow knows I managed to talk to the Maker again. And that he has told my father.

A guard boldly follows me each morning as I leave the palazzo. They wait outside the Academy and trail me back in the afternoon. I can't even slip away to the market to warn the Knowledge Seekers that something's in the air. All I can do is hope I'm wrong, dutifully attend my classes, and wait for my chance.

Swift haunts my dreams, as do Aidan and his apprentice. As each day dies without contact with the Knowledge Seekers, I fear the Maker must once more believe that I've forgotten him and my promise. I can think of nothing else, and the dreams become nightmares.

Then one night I'm woken by a hand pressing on my mouth.

My first thought is that my wards haven't worked and I will have to strengthen them. Next, that I've never killed anyone before and don't want to start now. I harden the air next to me into a shield and use another layer of air to shove the intruder away. The hand peels from my mouth and I hear my attacker crash to the floor.

I sit up in bed and kindle fire in my right palm, lifting it high. This is no mage. Could Aidan somehow have escaped his prison room? If so, he's taking a huge risk. I send the fire to hover over the head of the intruder, who's groaning and struggling upright.

'Twiss!'

I see her nod of approval as I whisper her name, rather than shouting it. For a second annoyance overwhelms any other thought. Does Twiss really think me such a fool? But I shove my irritation aside. The thief wouldn't brave the palazzo unless something was badly wrong.

As quickly as I can, I soundproof our conversation, hardening the air around us into a translucent shell, like shimmering mother-of-pearl. It takes longer than it should: fear makes it difficult to concentrate.

'Why are you here?' I demand. 'What's happened?'

The thief eyes the air-shell with suspicion. 'Bad news.' Her harsh voice sounds rusty. For a moment, her face twists with grief.

'The foundry?'

'Gone. They came for us.'

I'd known it must be this, but it feels like someone has kicked me in the stomach. 'Casualties?'

94

'All dead but one.' Again, the contortion of grief, quickly mastered. 'They took Bruin.'

Twiss's voice is monotone but I can see the child shaking. Oh gods, not this! Nausea rises in my throat and I shut my eyes for a moment. If the blacksmith is lucky, he'll be dead now. But he will have told . . . oh, everything. And he had much to tell. The news couldn't be worse, and it means my own situation is desperate.

'You have to help him!'

My eyes flick open in amazement. Has the thief gone mad?

'No one can help him. You know that.'

The child's mouth grows mulish. 'I'll take you to Bruin. You have great powers . . . Lady.' Twiss almost snarls the title. 'You can save him if you will!'

'And I will not. I'm sorry, Twiss, but if Bruin's not dead, he will be soon. The prison will be crawling with mages. I can't fight them all: I'd be caught or killed. And they would find out about me all the sooner.'

'They'll find out anyway!' The child's eyes glitter. 'The guard are out. They've arrested many Knowledge Seekers. Even without Bruin, your secret won't last the night. My guild can offer you shelter, Lady. But only if you help me find Bruin. If you don't, I'll leave you to the mercy of your own kind. What will they do to you . . . Lady?'

The thief watches me. Her face is impassive but her voice taunts. It feels like being slapped. I take a deep breath. I didn't know till now that Twiss hates me.

'Will they kill you for playing traitor?' The child's voice hisses through the darkness.

'Squash the air from your lungs or suck the water out of you so you die slowly, twisted up in pain like a cockle-fish? Heat the bones in your body so you cook inside out? Peel your skin layer by layer?'

'They won't kill me.' I fight to stay calm, but I feel the blood drain from my face, leaving me giddy and weak. I've rehearsed this moment, but pretend is never the same as real. Twiss is right: I can't stay in the palazzo. But I can't rescue the blacksmith. Or Aidan!

At the thought of the Maker, my heart begins to thud painfully. I'm abandoning him and his Tribute child. But I have no choice – I'm his only chance. I must escape, find the remaining Knowledge Seekers, get help. If I'm caught . . . The feeling of helplessness shreds the last of my self-control. I'm near to tears.

'I *cannot* help you.'

'Then die!' The child spins on her heel.

I stop her mid-stride, fastening the girl's bare feet to the wooden floor with a swift thought.

'Devil's spawn! Mage!' Twiss struggles, spitting with fury, but her feet remain stuck.

How can I convince her? I take a deep breath. 'I'll bargain with you.'

The child glares at me with suspicion.

'I will mind-search for him. See if he's alive. But that means I'll have to leave my body. You'll have to guard it. Can I trust you?'

'Find Bruin!'

'This is dangerous. I could be detected.'

96

'Then be careful!'

With a sigh, I release the thief. 'Very well.'

I settle back onto my bed and stare at the marble inlay of the high ceiling, trying to ignore the chill of the room and compose myself. I never enjoy sendings. There's always the chance that my consciousness might get lost and never find its way back. Pushing the thought away, I shut my eyes and concentrate.

With surprising ease, a thread of awareness floats free and pauses for a moment, observing my body lying on the bed, watched over by a frowning, dirty child. I concentrate on my memory of Bruin and direct the sending towards the prison. If the smith is alive, he'll be there.

Nothing. Well, I hadn't expected it. Bruin is probably dead. The thought fills me with sadness, but I push the emotion away. I can't afford the distraction. And I don't want to think about him as a person I liked and admired when I'm going to have to go now and look in the torture rooms. I anchor one end of my mind even more firmly to my body, then stretch myself thinner and thinner, until I become a slender wire of thought slicing through space, air and stone into the dark, airless cells of the prison.

I whip through room after room, stretched so thin that I observe their contents without emotion, almost without thought. At last, I find Bruin . . . what remains of him. I check to make sure, then return to the child.

I lurch upright, shaking with such violence that the bed shakes with me. My heart pounds and I gasp for air as though I've been swimming underwater. It isn't only the strain of being out of my body. Now that my consciousness is unstretched, my head is full of what I've seen – pictures worse than my darkest imaginings. It's all I can do not to be sick.

I clench chattering teeth and watch Twiss. There's no way to break the news gently and this child wouldn't know what to do with gentleness anyway.

'He's dead.'

Incomprehension on the girl's face.

'I touched him with my mind.' I speak slowly, watching for understanding. 'No life remains.'

Twiss hugs herself, her face crumpling over and over while she struggles not to cry. 'I don't believe you! I'd know if he was dead. I'd feel it . . . I'd . . .'

I look away. I can't bear the naked agony on the girl's face.

'What did they do to him?' The thief's voice is thick and slow with shock.

'I can't tell you that.' I swallow, shudder. 'He's dead. He's not suffering now. You've done all you can for your friend. Now guide me to sanctuary.'

'No!' Twiss collapses onto her knees. She begins to sob uncontrollably, rocking back and forth. Her pain fills the air, sharp and fierce.

I lean forward and put my hand on her shoulder.

Twiss jerks away. She lurches to her feet and stands glowering at me, hiccuping with fury between sobs. 'You're a mage, like the rest of them. You deserve to die! I ain't taking you anywhere.'

There's so little time. I have to escape and for that I need Twiss. But I won't use mind-control. I'd rather die. I have to convince her.

'You want revenge. So do I. Yes, I'm a mage. That makes me

the most powerful weapon you have. Can you afford to throw me away? What would your friend Bruin do?'

We stare at each other. My shivering eases, but as shock recedes a cold, deep fear seeps into my bones. I need to be out of here. Now.

Twiss sniffs, swipes at her nose. She frowns mutinously, then shrugs. 'Come on, then. But hurry!'

I jump out of bed and begin to rifle through my wardrobe, pulling out last year's robes, ones no one is likely to remember when they search my clothes. I dress myself quickly, my mind on the escape plan I worked out months ago. Last of all, I take the wallet holding Swift's letter from under my pillow, slip the leather necklet over my head.

'Quickly!' urges Twiss. 'Come now.'

'No.' I shake my head. 'I have to do a little magic.' I watch the girl's eyes widen in disbelief. 'It's necessary. The Archmage won't stop looking for me, so we must convince him that I'm dead. I've made preparations. A few minutes, only.'

The thief's hiss of anxiety loud in my ears, I set about what I have long practised. I lay my nightclothes upon my mattress and, reaching up, pluck a slender, very sharp knife from the air. I hid it in a fold in the air months before, but I don't have time to explain to Twiss and she allows a cry of amazement past her lips.

Of course she's shocked: it's unheard of for a mage to possess a knife. Why would we need one, when we could do the work of a knife with our minds?

'This is why.' I answer Twiss's unspoken question as I saw off a small hunk of my hair and place it on my pillow. It's joined by a fingernail paring. And then . . . I take a deep breath, hold it, and press the point of the knife into the skin of my forearm. It hurts, and I'm surprised how difficult it is to force myself to keep pushing until bright red blood wells up and splashes onto the white sheet. When there's enough, I pull the knife out and keep it clenched in my fist as I quickly knit my flesh and skin back together. A trail of blood would give away my trick. I could have extracted the blood painlessly with magic, but I need bloodstains on the knife. And the pain is a promise.

I kneel and hold out the knife towards the hidden shrine where a small pendulum clock ticks. Out of the corner of my eye, I see Twiss shrink away, making the sign of warding.

Lord Time, accept my blood as a willing sacrifice, and grant me success. Confound my enemies. I concentrate on the ticking of the invisible clock, visualising the swing of the tiny pendulum. Steadied by its rhythm, I stand and begin. I've never attempted anything so complicated. This is adept's magic. I stare at the strands of hair, at the blood soaking into the sheet, and demand that they grow. Increase, change, fuse.

It's hard work, but slowly, a semi-human shape grows upon the bed. It's not alive in any sense of the word. But it has substance. I find that when I raise the knife over my head and plunge it into the place where a heart should be.

Twiss gasps.

I leave the knife embedded in the figure, raise both hands, and kindle fire. The fire flows from my hands onto the bed and the thing it contains. It puddles on the bed, lapping merrily, flickering upwards, consuming. Little will remain. But there will be enough to lead the searchers to believe that Zara, only child of Benedict, Archmage of Asphodel, is dead.

I dissolve the soundproof shell and nod to the thief. Twiss stares at me, eyes wide with superstition and fear. But she turns at once and leads me out of the room.

13

Twiss disappears. The child seems to melt into the very stones of the palazzo. I gape at the spot where she was standing a moment ago, then jump as a hand grabs my wrist. The thief's face looms in front of me and I flinch in surprise.

Twiss bares her teeth in a mirthless grin. She lets go of me, jerks her head and slinks away, keeping low and creeping along the wall. She stops to glance back. The message is clear: follow and keep up!

I try to copy her movements but my arms and legs feel even clumsier. I ease round a corner to find I've lost her again. Nothing but shadows and cold dead stone. Torchlight flares at the end of a corridor and I freeze. Someone yanks me sideways into a cross passage. Mouth dry with fear, I squeeze against the wall beside an annoyingly calm Twiss as a group of guards pass, wooden batons drawn, escorting a huddle of kine. Guildspeople . . . almost certainly Knowledge Seekers. As the guards and their prisoners disappear from sight, Twiss turns her head and spits. Otherwise, during the entire journey, she makes no sound.

I make too many. I clench my teeth as I graze a wall with my shoulder. My boot scuffs the floor with a clunk that makes

Twiss turn to glare at me. The thief seems able to turn invisible just by the way she moves, stands and breathes. Although it's heresy to think that a kine might be able to do magic, I can't explain it otherwise.

By the time we reach the cellars, her every movement expresses contempt. I've had enough.

'Hang on!' I hiss and conjure a finger of mage light. It flickers, pale blue, above my head. I'm tired of travelling blind. The cellars are surely safe – the guards have no business down here, but neither do we. Why has the thief led me here? Twiss twirls around. Even in the dim light, outrage is plain on her face. I ignore her gestures to be silent. I want answers before I take another step. 'Where are you taking me?'

'I ain't tellin' you that,' she hisses. It's a secret between us thieves. I never even told Bruin. Now shut up and keep up or I'll leave you behind!'

I glare at her, at the end of my patience, then freeze in astonishment as she screams and rises into the air, twisting and winding like a ball on the end of a string.

'I hesitate to interrupt, but I fear I *must* enquire . . .' The voice comes from a darkened doorway directly in front of us. I don't need light to know who it is. I know that voice only too well. '. . . what you, Lady, are doing in the cellars at this time of night. And in such company.'

Red mage light rises in the air over our heads, and in its lurid glow, Aluid's face leers out of the darkness. The bottle of wine tucked under one arm explains his own presence here – my tutor has taken a break from the night's activities to raid the wine cellars. His puffy eyes blink and he smiles. Like a cat tormenting a mouse.

Twiss screams. She dangles in mid-air and my heart lurches as I see the child's arms and legs folding up as though an invisible force is pressing them into her body. I can just see the sheen of hardened air encircling the girl. Aluid is crushing her.

'Stop that!' My breath is coming fast, my heart racing. I have never battled another mage in a real contest. I have no idea if I even have the power to fight a fully trained adept. Perhaps a fight can be avoided: I'm Benedict's daughter. That must count for something.

'I order you!' I try to say the words calmly and quietly, mustering as much authority as I can.

Aluid ignores me. He splits his mage light into three and hurls the fireballs across the room to light three wooden torches suspended in wall brackets. He takes a moment to enjoy the effect before turning to me. Even in the flickering torchlight I can see he looks amused. He can have no idea of my connection with the Knowledge Seekers or he would be appalled, infuriated, sickened – anything but amused. He's thinking, I can tell, how best to turn the situation to his advantage.

'The creature touched you, Zara.' Aluid glances up at the writhing, moaning Twiss. He sneers in distaste. 'And look at it – it's doubtless a thief. Possibly one of these outlaws we are rounding up. I'll take it to join its friends in prison. But thank you: you're right to stop me killing it. The thing may have useful information.'

I can't help it: my eyes flick up to Twiss. The thief's body is compressed into a foetal position, but the crushing seems to have stopped. I take a deep breath and compose a cold and unconcerned expression for Aluid.

'But . . .' he continues, narrowing his eyes, '. . . you still haven't explained why you are in the palazzo cellars in the middle of the night. And why you were talking – actually talking – to this creature.'

'You will address me as "Lady".' I give him my haughtiest look. 'And it is not for you to question my actions. You will release that kine to me. I am following my father's instructions. Do you question the will of the Archmage?'

'I think . . .' Aluid advances towards me. I dislike people standing too near and have to fight the impulse to retreat. 'I think,' he continues, 'that we'll go and ask your father what he would like done with it. Doubtless he'll be delighted to have a chance for a chat with you. I know how close the two of you are.' He smiles.

My heart pounds in my ears. This is it, then. A shame he isn't as stupid as I'd thought. I smile back at Aluid, sharpen my will into a shiny blade and cut through his magic with a single swipe.

Twiss drops to the floor like a stone. I back away from Aluid, away from his heavy face twisting with shock and outrage as he realises what I've done. As I gather my magic for the first fight of my life, I hear the sound of feet, running away. Twiss has deserted me.

'What in the name of Time . . .' My tutor advances on me. He sends a jolt of magic to slam both doors of the room shut.

'I asked you not to interfere!' I step back. I try in vain to stop myself retreating. Of all my tutors, I loathe Aluid the most. Even for a mage, he is arrogant. And his breath stinks of fish.

'The thief is a plant!' It's a desperate lie, but I have to say something. 'She's spying on the Knowledge Seekers for us. I'm controlling her mind.' One look at his face tells me he doesn't believe a word.

'It rather looked like she was controlling you.' Now that he has caught me out, Aluid stops stalking me. He twitches his robes into more elegant folds and smirks in triumph. 'And how do you know about the Knowledge Seekers? Lord Benedict didn't tell you. He gave strict orders that you were to remain in ignorance of their activities. I think your father will most certainly want to talk to you.' Aluid raises a hand. I feel a hysterical desire to laugh. He always uses the grandest gestures for the simplest magic. Doesn't he know it slows him down and makes him look an idiot?

As he draws breath, I strike. I stick his feet to the floor, fasten his eyelids together and give him a nosebleed. Nursery tricks, but something in me baulks at the idea of killing – even Aluid. His yell is more outraged dignity than pain, but I don't take time to enjoy the sight of my tutor flailing his arms and toppling over. I hear the bottle of wine smash on the floor as I race for the sealed door, rusting its iron hinges and nails so that the whole thing collapses into a heap of wood. A sudden silence alerts me. I whirl around in time to see Aluid, free and no longer bleeding, stagger towards me, a deadly look in his eyes.

'Childish tricks belong in the schoolroom, Lady,' he pants. 'And children who choose to fight with grown-ups can get badly hurt! I just hope your father allows me the pleasure of questioning you myself!'

A sphere of crystalline air forms around me and begins to

close in. He might stop short of squeezing me to death, but the look in my tutor's eyes foretells pain and humiliation. The air-ball shrinks rapidly until it shimmers a few inches from my face.

Aluid raises both hands and slows the compression to a snail's pace. 'Let us see just how small a space you can fit into.' He smiles, showing yellow teeth.

'You smell like a pile of rotting whitebait, Aluid!' I only hope he can't see how frightened I am. 'Since you have a swamp for a mind, I suppose that's not surprising.'

I reach out a finger and touch the cage. It feels cold and hard as ice. Focusing all my concentration, I extract heat from the air inside the ball and use it to conjure fire. The sudden drop in temperature inside my cage makes me gasp in pain. Shivering uncontrollably, I release the fire. A blue, hot flame spews from the tip of my finger, fanning out until the entire air-cage is alight. Its heat sears and for a moment I think I've killed myself, but the ball flares red and is consumed, leaving nothing but a shimmer of warmth.

Before Aluid can react, I turn the stone floor beneath him to slurry. He sinks with a squelch up to his neck, and I harden the stone around him. I can feel his will fighting mine but, as often as the stone begins to soften, I harden it again. I'm panting, sweat dripping down my face and off my chin.

Fire consumes air; water consumes fire; earth consumes water; air consumes earth. The litany runs through my head, but I find no inspiration. I'm reaching the end of my strength. I can keep Aluid trapped in the stone, but not for much longer. And I don't have enough strength left to walk out of the room. If I move a foot he will overpower me. We're both trapped.

A dark shadow flickers in the corner of my eye. Creeps along the edge of the far wall.

'You can't keep this up.' Aluid grunts as he speaks. He looks like a decapitated head, his long, yellow teeth bared, his eyes glaring in a blood-stained face. 'Your father won't kill you, I suppose, although he would be wise to do so. You are working with those scum, aren't you? You're a traitor to your race. Degenerate!' Spit foams down his chin.

I close my eyes. My legs are shaking uncontrollably. I recognise the signs: I've nearly used up my store of energy.

'You're finished!'

I can shut out the sight of his face, but not his voice. It rages on and on.

'By Time's grace, I'll be out of here within seconds. I'll deliver you up to your father. How proud he will be to welcome such a daughter. Benedict will cleanse your mind until it's as empty as a walnut hull. There'll be little of you left when he's done. Does the thought frighten you, Lady?'

My legs collapse. As I fall onto my knees, my concentration breaks. With a cry of triumph, Aluid shoves my mind away. I grapple with him but feel the stone begin to soften. He's won. I fall forward onto my face. Nausea floods through me and I feel myself slipping into unconsciousness.

I'll kill myself. I'll never let them take my mind. Darkness swirls behind my eyes. As I fall into it I hear a crack, like the sound of a bat hitting a ball, and Aluid's voice stops.

Silence.

108

14

My flesh, my heart, my very bones are freezing.

'Wake up! Wake up now, or I'll leave you to die!'

Twiss's face fades in and out of view, scowling down at me.

'C-c-cold . . .' I can hardly get the word out. I'm lying on a stone floor and my body is shaking uncontrollably.

'Get up!' No sympathy in her face – Twiss's expression is the one kine always wear when you catch them unaware. Hatred carved into the flesh, as if their faces are made of centuries-old olive wood, smooth and polished.

'If you don't get moving, you'll die.' Twiss grabs my shoulders and tugs me up to sitting. 'Get on your feet! Come on. I ain't staying here to get caught. Not with him.'

Him . . . Aluid. I can't spare the breath to ask. I hold onto Twiss and try to rise to my knees but I can't. I'm sinking into a sea of ice, the cold crushing my will. This is too hard; I'm so tired. Why have I left the darkness where nothing matters? Not my father, not the mages, not Swift . . . I shut my eyes.

Pain burns the top of my head and jerks me back to life. Twiss has grabbed my hair with both fists and is doing her best to pull it out.

'Stop it!' My lips are so numb I can barely form the words but pain gives me strength. 'Let go!'

Twiss climbs to her feet, still holding on. I have no option but to stagger up as well. The thief grunts with effort, but she's strong. She tows me from one side of the room to the other, back and forth, like a farmer leading an ox. I stumble behind, bent over, shouting at her to stop.

'Shut up! Do you want them to hear? And come and find him?'

Him. Aluid's face fills my mind. Then Benedict's, his cold control dissolving to fury. The thought of what he will do to me makes my stomach turn over. I stop shouting. Twiss lets go at last and I straighten up, rubbing my scalp, blinking back tears of pain.

'Stay on your feet and keep moving.' She watches me with narrowed eyes, ready to pounce. 'You used up too much of yourself. I've saved your skin three times now.' The girl jerks her head towards the centre of the room and I look at last.

The sight makes me shudder harder than ever. Aluid clawed halfway out of the stone before he died. His eyes are open, his blood-stained face purple with rage. Beside him, in a puddle of wine that looks horribly like blood, lies a plank of wood from the demolished door. I swallow my nausea, shocked to find that my only emotion is relief. The cold seems to have lodged in my heart.

'You may have saved my life . . .' I drag my gaze from the dead man to confront Twiss. '. . . but I've saved yours too. You couldn't have killed him on your own.'

'Nor could you.' The thief's lip curls in contempt. 'But you're the only mage we got. Come on, we have to get out of here.'

'And just leave him to be found? It's obvious a magic user killed him.'

'*I* killed him!'

I ignore the remark and close my eyes for a moment, preparing. Do I have enough strength to do this? I'm still shivering from cold and exhaustion. But there isn't any choice. If Aluid's body is found, Benedict will realise who helped kill him, and he won't stop until he finds me. I sit down to conserve energy and focus my mind. Precision is important.

I steady my breathing and set about transforming the stone surrounding my tutor's body once more to slurry, drawing water from the air and pushing it into the stone. Slowly, Aluid settles and begins to sink. I'm shaking with the effort when his glaring face finally disappears from sight and the floor closes over him with a soft, sucking sound.

I pause, dizzy. But my work is only half done. I try to ignore the chill creeping through me as I struggle to return the water to the air. Slowly, the floor hardens. As it does so, I force the stone to reform in quarried chunks, painstakingly realigning seams of mortar. It takes all my concentration. I taste stone, smell it, hear particles of limestone grinding together. Afterwards, it's a quick business to tidy away the remaining broken glass and spilled wine before covering the floor with a layer of dust and grime.

I sit, shaking, out of breath, staring at the empty floor. It's hard to believe that Aluid is dead, that his body is entombed in this small, dirty cellar. I crave warmth; desperately need sleep and food.

Hands grab me under each arm and pull me to my feet. Twiss slings my arm over her shoulder and lugs me across the room. We stumble over the remains of the door and through the opening into a narrow corridor. It is darker than midnight here, a clammy dark that presses on my eyes and heart. I long to conjure a finger of mage light to push away the darkness, but I haven't even the strength for that.

Twiss seems to find her way by instinct, like a mole. She's half carrying me, but the child is so strong she might be made of bog oak. The thief's breathing hardly quickens at all as she leads us through the twisting and turning corridors, pausing to open doors, stopping only to push me through low doorways before dragging me through the dark, on and on.

My legs move by themselves, now. It feels like being out of body again, watching myself stumble and crawl through the darkness. I'm still cold, but I've stopped shivering. I feel drugged with exhaustion, but part of my mind chatters with the irritating persistence of a magpie.

We can't be beneath the palazzo any more. These must be the catacombs. I can smell the earth, the age, the dust of dead bodies. There will be bones . . . and skulls neatly stacked on earthen shelves, grinning at us in the dark. We're under the city. Where is she taking me? She hates me. How can she see in this dark? Even a mage cannot see in the dark. She hates me . . . she saved you. Perhaps she will kill me . . . she didn't save you in order to kill you. Where are we going? I hate this place – the dark, the smell of death. Are there any Knowledge Seekers left?

Without warning, Twiss stops, dragging me to a halt. There is a solid wall in front of us; I can feel the deadness of it inches from my face. Twiss fumbles at the wall; metal clicks; hinges groan. The darkness opens and she pushes me through a narrow opening into blinding light.

I fall on my hands and knees onto an earthen floor. Before I can coax my eyes to work or get any sense of where I am, different hands grab me, fling me to the ground. A thin strip of sharp metal presses against my neck and I feel something trickle down my neck. *Blood! A knife!*

My reflexes take over. I harden a fist of air and crash it into the person holding me. A cry, and the knife drops away with a clatter. Still half blinded, I find the blade with my mind and destroy it, shattering the iron into infinitely small particles. Quickly I form an air-shield. Sheer terror has given me energy, but I'm exhausted now and maintaining the shield takes all my strength. I lever myself up onto one knee and crouch, panting with effort.

The oily light is coming from smoking lamps hanging from the walls of a small, cave-like room. Of course! It's so obvious that I feel a crazy desire to laugh. The thieves have their headquarters in the catacombs! It's perfect, and explains why my father has never been able to root them out – and why Twiss dared not tell even her beloved Bruin.

This room has been made semi-habitable: a few rough benches and a table. A door stands opposite, fitted with bolts and locks. Some sort of stronghold, or guardroom perhaps? A boy in his teens is helping a young woman to her feet. She wears a leather belt with an empty knife-shaped holder. Anyone would recognise them as thieves: the woman is tall, the boy short, but they are both slender and muscular with

113

close-cropped hair, their clothing tight-fitting and dark. And they are shouting at Twiss.

'She's a mage!' The woman shoots me a venomous look, wiping away blood dripping from her nose. The air punch was a facer. I feel considerable pleasure at the fact and am immediately horrified. What's wrong with me? It's like my response to Aluid's death. I frown, trying to clear my head, to think, while the woman shouts: 'You brought a mage here? Are you mad?'

The boy carries a long wooden stick with a sharp, pointed end. He keeps jabbing it towards me, his eyes averted. He shouts: 'We need to kill her! Quick, while she's weak!'

I reinforce my air-shield as much as I can but it feels patchy. My heart beats faster and I try to calm myself, concentrating on the deep, slow breathing that gathers strength from the air itself. I can defend myself for a while longer, but if I don't rest soon, find something to eat, I'll collapse. Was this the sanctuary Twiss promised?

Twiss grabs the boy's arm. '*No!* She's working with us. Touch her and I'll skin you. And so will Floster.'

'"Mistress Floster" to you, middling!' The woman's hand keeps straying to her empty knife holder. She watches my every movement with a predator's gaze, the desire to kill shining in her eyes. Unveiled hatred of such intensity is terrifying. My breath control breaks. I begin to pant and shiver with fear. I want to shout: *I hate them too! I'm not like them!* But I can't waste strength speaking. And is it even true? I am a mage.

'Go fetch the Mistress, you rattle-skull.' Twiss looks furious. 'You know I work with the Knowledge Seekers. So does this mage. They know all about her.'

The woman shakes her head in disbelief. 'She's mind-controlling you!' She grabs Twiss's arm and starts to twist it behind her. Quick as a ferret, the child slides out of the arm lock. A vicious elbow to the woman's stomach sends her gasping to her knees. The boy looks on, open-mouthed, rotating his stick from me to Twiss and back again.

'No one has ever got in my head, Ferring,' Twiss spits, narrowing her eyes in disgust. 'No one ever will; I'll take my spirit into death before I let a filthy mage touch my mind!' She pauses, gasping for air as though drowning, then shouts: '*Bruin is dead!*'

Twiss's cry is swallowed by the earthen walls without even the faintest echo. But the pain in the girl's voice penetrates my exhaustion and fear, and I wince. Twiss stands silently, fists clenching and unclenching, mouth convulsing. Then: 'I'd kill her myself if she weren't of use.'

The woman kneels, gaping at Twiss. 'I didn't know.'

'There's lots you don't know. Stop being a fool and go fetch the Mistress. She –' Twiss jerks her head towards me – 'ain't going nowhere. I got news and the Mistress won't be pleased to be kept waiting.'

The woman jumps to her feet, shoots a last, hungry look at me, and runs from the room.

'S-sorry about Bruin, Twiss.' The boy looks shocked.

Twiss doesn't answer him. She turns to face me. The child's eyes are dark and hard as obsidian. Whatever is going on behind them is hidden, but I can imagine it only too well. Twiss's pain has rekindled my own. I settle more comfortably on the floor

115

and stare straight ahead, waiting for what will happen next and thinking of Swift and how I failed her. And of the Maker. I am forsworn. Unless I can find help soon – here in the city of the dead – I will have abandoned Aidan to whatever fate my father intends for him.

15

I stagger to my feet as a bone-thin, grey-haired thief enters the room. I don't need to be told that this is Floster, Mistress of Thieves. Hard eyes cut through me as though trying to slice open my head and heart to see what is inside.

She gives me a moment's consideration, then speaks: 'If you want to live, mage, do what I tell you and stay where I put you. Poke so much as your nose outta your cell, the middlings'll tear you apart. I've no time to deal with you tonight. We'll decide what's to be done with you soon as may be.' Her eyes narrow to shining slits. 'Benedict's own daughter.' She smiles and my stomach squirms at the sight. 'A rare bounty he'd pay for you.'

She turns her back and strides out the door, grabbing her torch from the wall and holding it high over her head. The guards hustle me after her, poking me in the back with their wooden staves. I stumble through a maze of turnings and junctions. After several minutes, the Mistress's torchlight melts into a brighter glow and the tunnel opens into a large, echoing cavern. A frail cobweb of wooden beams and stone columns holds up the earth overhead.

The room boils with scurrying figures. Fear curls my stomach as I see them: leather-clad and countless as wood ants. Almost all are children. These must be the 'middlings' Floster spoke of. A handful of adults stride in their midst. Where are the parents?

I glimpse small clumps of Knowledge Seekers scattered in dazed huddles, looking nearly as terrified as I am. Thank the gods – I'm not totally alone with the thieves; others have made it to safety from the city. The Seekers' confusion and fear fogs the air of the cave. *I'm like you!* I want to shout. *My enemy is your enemy. I've lost everything too.*

My feet slow as I stare. A sharp poke in the middle of my back sends me stumbling after Mistress Floster. The next moment a young thief notices my mage marks, my grubby white robes, and a howl goes up. On every side, children gather, their eyes eating into me. They flinch from my gaze, fear battling hatred in their faces. And now they begin to hurl curses and taunts along with bits of wood and stone. Something hits me in the face.

I clap my hand over my cheek and my fingers come away wet. My blood is wine-dark in the smoky light. I stare at it in shock. *How dare they?* A surge of anger gives me the strength to heal my face. I refuse to die here, mauled to death by a pack of grubby brats! I can't die before I've avenged Swift and Gerontius, before I've rescued Aidan! As I search for the strength to fight back, another stone hits me in the forehead.

'Leave her be!' With a growl of warning, Twiss launches herself at a boy who raises a stone-filled paw. She has him down in a moment, though he is twice her size. The Mistress strides to the the squirming, punching tangle and yanks Twiss off the boy.

'*The mage is safe-sworn!*' Floster's voice rings out and all sound and movement in the cavern stops. Shock and disbelief rinse death-lust from dozens of dirty faces and I feel a mad desire to laugh as mouth after mouth gapes in surprise.

Groups of Knowledge Seekers turn to stare at me, curiosity diluting the hatred in their faces. I see Tabitha the silversmith, an island of calm in the bedlam. Her beautiful grey eyes are red and swollen, her face grief-stained. She must have lost someone she loved. For the first time since I've known her, she gazes at me without flinching and I see a flicker of something . . . sympathy?

Twiss squirms out of Floster's grip. Her nose is bleeding: the boy got in at least one punch. She swipes the blood away with the back of her hand and looks from Floster to me and back.

The Mistress speaks again, her eyes pressing the the mob to stillness: 'The mage works for us. Touch her, any of you, and I'll skin you myself. Here's my mark: my safe-sworn.'

Floster takes a pendant from around her neck and tosses its leather thong over my head. I flinch as a circle of green jade thuds onto Swift's letter. I feel like I've been marked as a possession – a thing. I want to tear it from my neck, but I don't dare. Hundreds of disbelieving eyes glare at the pendant. A hiss of frustration circles the cavern.

Floster stands stone still, her will beating them down. 'You've all got jobs to do. Get on! And you . . . ' She raises both eyebrows as she turns to Twiss. 'You aren't in charge of the guild . . . yet.' Her mouth twitches. It's the first glimmer of warmth I've seen in her. 'Behave yourself, my girl, or I'll serve you up a whipping you won't forget. You're in trouble already for fetching the mage

119

here without permission. My room now, brat. I want a full report.'

She jerks her head and Twiss scowls but runs off. Floster turns to the guards surrounding me. 'Put the mage in a hole,' she orders. 'And make sure she stays in one piece.'

Her eyes flick over me, then Floster turns and stalks off after Twiss. Middlings duck out of her path. She strides from the chamber like a river boat ploughing through reeds. A man, one of the few adult thieves in the chamber, detaches himself from a group of Knowledge Seekers and follows the Mistress. The way he moves – with the muscular grace of a greyhound – catches my eye. He is black-haired, neither short nor tall, dressed in dark leather from head to foot. As he passes, he gives me a look of pure speculation.

Hours later, I wake to total darkness. My heart kicks like a frightened colt. I lurch upright and instinctively conjure mage light. I concentrate on the flickering blue flame, force myself to stop gasping for air. Gradually my heart slows and panic recedes.

I remember being pushed into a hole in a wall and collapsing with exhaustion. I'm sitting on a straw pallet in a space barely big enough to hold it. Earthen walls crowd in on all sides. I bite my lower lip, concentrating on the details of my prison, fighting another surge of panic. One arm's length above me hangs a dirt ceiling, roughly whitewashed. A low wooden door faces me. Air holes pierce randomly through its planks and a small, rectangular viewing slot sits two-thirds of the way up its length. This is blinkered shut, like a blinded eye.

A prisoner of the Thieves' Guild!

Thieves. It's ill-bred to talk of them. To repeat rumours of mages found dead with their throats cut or flint arrowheads in their backs; of leather-clad skulkers who walk unseen amongst us, whose minds resist our control. But we all know the stories: they follow us through the marketplace, rest beside us on our pillows and invade our dreams.

They won't kill me: I'm too useful.

I stare at the wooden door, squinting with pain. My head throbs; my mouth is sour and my body aches. I have nearly spent myself out with magic. It will take days to recover . . . if I live that long. Even if the thieves don't kill me, my father will be on the hunt now. He'll know of my heresy, my betrayal. I can't be certain my faked death will fool him. I think of the captured Knowledge Seekers and give thanks that the thieves kept their lair secret.

The silence is absolute. It's as though I am the only person left alive in this labyrinth. My stomach begins to churn. I could tear the door to splinters with a thought, but I know it isn't there to keep me in: it's to keep those wolf-children out.

I wrap my arms around my body and squeeze until the shivering eases enough for me to notice the slop bucket. *Praise be to Time!* I stagger up too quickly and crack my head on the low ceiling – perfect! – and hunch down again, swearing loudly, using every filthy word I know. Not nearly enough! And feel oddly cheered. When I use the bucket I find that someone has provided paper and a jug of water for washing and feel a stab of gratitude.

Gratitude? This is what it's like to be a prisoner. The overwhelming vulnerability you feel when the most basic of your needs is no longer in your control. Suddenly, I understand Aidan's barely controlled anger.

Perched once more on the lumpy straw pallet, I try to ignore the stink of mildew and think. Is the Mistress friend or foe? What will she do with me? I remember the black-haired thief who followed Floster like a hound trailing at his mistress's heels. Something had been odd about him, but what? And then I realise: when he looked at me there was no fear in his eyes. Even the Mistress of the Thieves' Guild watches me as though I am a viper who might spit venom at any moment. But Floster's Hound isn't afraid of me. Like Bruin.

The blacksmith's strength, his desire for justice and strong will – I can't quite believe all of that is gone. When I was younger the thought of him was a source of comfort. Like Gerontius. Bruin barely tolerated me, but I didn't mind – not very much. I wish I could forget what I found in the prison's torture rooms. Gruesome images parade before my eyes. *Think of Aidan! Of his blue eyes and beguiling smile.* For a moment, I see him. But he isn't smiling. He stares at me reproachfully, then turns his back.

The emptiness knotting my belly finally drives away these hauntings. And I realise I've never been hungry – really hungry – in my life. Last night I ate myself up with magic and now I'm starving.

Do I demolish the door before the last of my strength fades and I'm trapped? It isn't a real choice. If, despite everything, Benedict has discovered the thieves' den in the catacombs, he could have killed them all while I was lying unconscious. The thought of bodies, broken and twisted as Bruin's, makes me shudder.

Slowly, painfully, I gather water from the air, prepare to mix it with the iron of the hinges. Then the silence is broken at last by the scrape of the door's viewing slot sliding back. The rectangle fills with flickering light. The light is blotted out, replaced with a bloodshot eyeball. It looks at me. I stare back, transfixed: is it thief . . . or mage?

'Well?' demands a familiar voice. I feel my body slump with relief. 'Open up then, don't just stand there gawping at her. Here . . . shove over, let me do it.'

My legs don't seem to work. I manage to kneel as the door swings outwards. A figure stands outlined in the flood of torchlight: small, upright, dark. Our eyes are level. Her pointed cat's face is as fierce and solemn as ever. I suddenly want to laugh. I press my lips together but can't stop a half-smile. 'Good morning, Twiss.'

The fear and panic flooding the catacombs last night is gone. Now all is purposeful. Individuals and groups pad through the tunnels and passages, faces calm, eyes intent. Disaster cannot be imminent. Fear of my father fades. He must think me dead. Will he care? Only that something he owned is lost.

Another striking change in the thieves' lair: all the middlings we pass avert their eyes or ignore me. Their faces show suspicion but not blood lust. Mistress Floster is indeed a woman to be reckoned with.

We pass through the main chamber into a different part of the catacombs. The passages are taller and wider. Oil lamps line the walls; they stink of rancid fat. The dingy yellow flames flicker constantly – the catacombs here must be well ventilated. My feet don't want to walk in a straight line and I'm staggering by the time Twiss finally stops beside one of the larger doors. Two guards have paced behind me the whole journey: a couple of the rare adult thieves. No one has spoken to or touched me.

Twiss raps on the door, pushes it open and enters. A guard jabs my back with her staff, prodding me so hard I nearly fall through the door. I'm in a meeting room of some sort: fairly large, with a rough-tiled floor and limewashed walls. After my cell it seems like a palace.

Candles are placed at intervals on a long table, casting a warm light over the seven people sitting behind it. In that moment, I plunge into cold despair. This is a Council Chamber, like the one in my father's palazzo. And I am on trial, as my mother was. All that is missing is a prisoner pit.

Out of the corner of my eye I see Twiss edge to one side and sit cross-legged against a wall. I swallow dryness and arrange my face in my best imitation of my father at his haughtiest. I gaze from face to face, assessing these people I had thought were my allies. It's as bad as I feared: I would be a fool to expect sympathy or kindness here.

Mistress Floster sits opposite me, her head with its sleek grey hair perfectly still, hazel eyes watching my every breath. I am reminded of the merlin I flew in another life. The thief and the six Knowledge Seekers remain silent, testing my nerve. One of them is Tabitha, but I gain no comfort from her closed, still face. A small fierce thrill of recklessness kindles in the back of my head. I have lost everything. Only my life is left and I'm not that fond of it. So. Let us play.

124

'I need food,' I say, staring straight into Floster's chilly gaze. 'And a chair. Or you can try to question me while I'm lying unconscious on the floor.'

Floster's eyes narrow with what might be amusement. 'Get the mage a chair. And, Twiss, bring bread and meat.'

Twiss slips from the room. I hear the door softly open and shut. Then the wall behind Floster shifts and a man steps forward. A gasp of surprise escapes my mouth. It's the black-haired thief: Floster's Hound. How could I have missed seeing him before?

He moves soundlessly around the table, brings a rough wooden chair from a corner of the room and sets it on the floor beside me. As he does so he glances sideways and catches my eye, a half-smile on his face. He is gone before I can gather my wits. He lounges against the wall, watching me with amusement in his dark brown eyes. Though he's nearly my father's age, I feel my face grow hot. The thief is handsome and knows it.

I ease myself onto the chair, closing my eyes in relief. Sleep has saved my life, but I've worked more magic than I thought possible in the past twelve hours and my body is starved. Suddenly Twiss is beside me, shoving a bowl of steaming meat and vegetables into my hands. A wooden spoon and crust of bread are stabbed in the middle of the mess. I grab the bowl, then realise with horror that I'm going to have to eat this while Floster and the Knowledge Seekers watch. My dismay must be writ plain on my face because the Hound gives a snort of laughter.

That does it! Damn the lot of them! I sit upright on the hard seat and dig in with the spoon, ignoring my audience. The stew tastes of turnip; the meat is tough and sour. It's glorious. I swallow it down and wipe the bowl clean with the bread. In seconds the bread has gone the way of the meat and I gaze at the empty bowl sadly.

'So,' says a Knowledge Seeker, a small, dumpy woman with black hair divided in the middle and smoothed behind her ears. 'Mages don't live on human blood after all.'

16

The Knowledge Seeker smiles all the time she is talking.

'I am Mistress Quint, head of the Apothecaries' Guild. And that was a joke.' She nods encouragingly. 'Drinking blood is one of the myths about your kind. We are educated folk here. We know the stories are false. But it is always useful to have facts confirmed.' She nods, smiles and rubs her hands. There is a scent of madness hanging round her.

I draw breath and tear my gaze away to look at the others.

'Let us keep to facts then,' snaps the Knowledge Seeker seated beside her – a blond man of middle years. His long face is clever; a sharp intelligence glares from blue eyes. His movements are slow and deliberate, and he wears a fine brown surcoat and frilled linen shirt my father would not have despised. This man turns his penetrating stare on me and my throat dries.

'I am Philip, known as the Nonpareil, master artist and head of the Council of Knowledge Seekers of Asphodel.'

The Nonpareil! Here? Even in my fear and anger, I gaze at him in wonder. The man is a legend – the greatest painter ever born. Feted even by mage society. It's said that his house in the artisan quarter is as large as my father's palazzo. That he lives as well as a mage. He is the last guildsman I would expect to have joined the Knowledge Seekers, let alone lead them.

Only . . . I remember the portrait of my father that hangs in the entrance hall of the palazzo. It was done shortly after my mother's death. I often look at it and wonder why my father hung the painting and not the painter. Benedict is acknowledged to be a handsome man, and the image shows a suave and elegant figure. But beneath the smooth, smiling surface – in the eyes and the curl of the mouth – the Nonpareil has painted my father's soul, eaten up with viciousness, cruelty and greed.

'We are here to decide what is to be done with you, Mage,' Philip says in his dry, precise voice. 'We face a time of crisis, and in such times the logical mind depends upon facts, not superstition!' He throws a dark glance at the apothecary, who smiles and nods happily.

'Fact: you have, for personal reasons, spied on your own kind and colluded with the Knowledge Seekers for six years. In that time you have proved trustworthy and occasionally provided useful information.

'Fact: your usefulness is now questionable, except as a hostage.

'Fact: if your father finds out you are alive and in our keeping, he will renew his hunt for our safehold with all the resources at his command.

'Fact: there are many here, especially members of the Thieves' Guild, who find your existence insupportable and desire to destroy you. Your presence here is at best a distraction and at worst a potential source of unrest and rebellion in our ranks.'

He counts off each new statement, then steeples his fingers and leans back, his eyes never leaving my face. 'So, mage . . . why should we keep you alive? Now that you have fled your father's house, what use are you?'

I don't know.

I look from face to face. The silence lengthens.

Tabitha, who has been sitting quietly at the end of the table, leans forward and glances around at her colleagues. At last, she speaks: 'This mage has served us.' Reluctance drags at the silversmith's voice. 'She has risked her life for us. She saved Twiss last night, even though it meant fighting one of her own. If we ignore those facts, we are no better than our overlords.'

There is no liking in the troubled grey eyes that flicker to me, then quickly look away. I can feel the silversmith's pain even over my growing terror. She has suffered a great loss. I try to cut off her emotions: I can't afford distractions if I'm to survive another day. *Time's grace, help me to think!*

The artist is right: what use am I to anyone? All my promises: to help Aidan, to free the Tribute children. I told Swift I would keep her safe forever. Am I going to die not having kept one of those promises?

I turn to look at Twiss. She gazes back at me, her face doubtful.

It is oddly freeing to lose all hope. I say: 'Do you value human life only if it's useful to you?'

'Are mages human?' the round woman shoots back.

I look her in the eyes. A small flare of victory lights the bleakness in my heart as her gaze shifts and drops. But then I realise – it's only because she fears me.

'I'm as human as you are,' I tell her. 'Although some mages would deny your humanity. They believe that only magic users are truly human – chosen by the gods to have dominion over animals and kine alike.'

'Don't all mages think so?' The round woman nods as though answering her own question.

'I don't!'

'And what do you believe?' Mistress Floster asks.

I no longer trust beliefs. I only have memories. I remember Swift laughing, running ahead of me down a corridor. Remember her whispering one of her stories in my ear, trying to comfort me in the dark nights of our childhood.

'I don't know why the gods gave some magic and denied it to others,' I say at last. 'But I don't think lacking magic makes you less human than me. Most of my kind have allowed themselves to believe a great evil. They convince themselves that they are chosen by the gods and can do as they wish. I want it to stop.' I pause, struggling to make them understand. 'I want a world where there are no Tribute children.'

'Why?' Philip leans forward, real interest lighting his eyes for the first time. 'The blood of Tribute children keeps you alive. Without foot soldiers to die in their hundreds on the dark Wall, the mages will lose the war with the Makers. You will be overrun, hunted down and killed until the last mage is gone from our world. Why would you seek your own doom?'

Oh, clever man. To ask *that* of all questions. The one thing I cannot answer, which has tormented me from the night my father murdered Swift. I shake my head, helplessly.

'We're wasting time we can ill afford.' The artist sighs.

130

'The choice is –'

'Anything but clear, Philip!' Floster breaks in. 'This mage helped kill one of her own to save Twiss. That's a blood duty I can't overlook. I say she can be of use. She knows her father's black heart better than any other. Knowing your enemy is the first step to beating them. My spy tells me she's nearly as talented as her father.'

Spy? Who can Floster mean? I was their spy in the palazzo. And then I understand: she must mean Gerontius. Doing me a good turn even in death.

'A bit of magic on our side for once wouldn't go amiss,' the Mistress continues. 'I'll not throw away a good weapon without a better reason than fear of Benedict! He's been hunting us thieves for years; he fears us . . . and he has reason to.' Floster smiles a cold, deadly smile and I realise she hates him as much as I do.

'And can you guarantee that your middlings will obey your orders?' This from a slab-faced man dressed in a blacksmith's leather apron. The sneer in his voice verges on insult. The man is either stupid or very brave: I would not dare insult Floster. 'Those brats of yours nearly tore the girl from limb to limb last night.' He makes the sign of warding. 'A *mage*? Here? And Benedict's daughter to boot? More trouble than she's worth. Kill the bitch and be done.' He glares at me, loathing plain in his face.

'No!' Tabitha cries. 'We are the Council of the Knowledge Seekers. We are sworn to seek truth and justice. And you are forsworn, Hammeth! You are not fit to sit in Bruin's place.'

And now I know who she's mourning. Oh gods. The

silversmith was Bruin's lover.

The room explodes with angry voices. Floster jumps to her feet, her face flushed with fury.

'Tell 'em about the Maker!' Twiss's husky voice cuts through the noise and the others fall silent, turning to look at the middling. 'Go on,' she urges me. 'The Maker. I never told 'em. You do it.'

'Maker?' Philip leans forward, his attention sharpened. 'What Maker?'

I frown in confusion at Twiss. Why hasn't she passed on my news? Whatever happens to me, the Knowledge Seekers need to know about Aidan. They're his only chance.

'My father has a hostage. A Maker.'

A gasp of disbelief circles the table. Philip sits bolt upright.

'It's true! He's a young man given as guarantee of a new truce between Benedict and the Maker city of Gengst-on-the-Wall.' All eyes are on me. I need more to tell them – I need to know Benedict's secret plan. But I have nothing. 'The Maker is young. My age. His name is Aidan and he's the son of the head of the Maker Council – a clockmaker.

'My father claims he sued for peace with the Makers, but I don't believe it. Aidan is repairing our clocks and training an apprentice. But I'm sure my father doesn't want peace. He's plotting something. Something to do with the Maker. We must rescue him!'

'A Maker.' Philip's eyes slide past me and he slumps backwards, staring into his own thoughts. His face has come alive. The change is startling; he was formidable before, but now it's as though he's woken from a half-sleep.

132

'Truce?' Floster leans forward too, but in alarm. 'The Archmage has brokered a truce with the Makers?' She frowns. 'What nasty worm lies wriggling at the heart of that, I wonder?' Her eyes, sharp as bone needles, stab at me. 'There's more to this . . .' She breaks off.

The tension in the room has changed.

'You say you spoke with this Maker?' asks Philip.

I nod.

'Benedict allowed that?'

'He forbade it. But I wanted to find out what my father was up to.'

'Presumably the Maker is guarded.'

I shrug, and see Twiss grin in approval. Philip sees her too – he notices everything – and his mouth twitches. 'Your bravery and initiative are not in question, mage,' he says. 'And why, young Twiss, did you not report the existence of the Maker to us earlier?'

Twiss's grin fades and her eyes widen in fear as she glances at her mistress. 'I . . . I forgot. Br-Bruin n-needed me to be his eyes and ears at the foundry.' She is stammering, her face stricken. 'I failed them. I didn't f-feel them coming in time.' A sob escapes her and she covers her face with her hands. Her pain cuts sharper than any knife, and I wince.

'Enough, Twiss! The smith is dead. You're not to speak of it.' Floster's voice cuts like a lash and Twiss flinches. 'You'll be punished for forgetting the Maker, never fear. But for now, I've a job needs doing and you're the only one can do it.' She addresses the leader of the Knowledge Seekers. 'You agree, Philip? The Maker changes everything.'

133

He nods. His eyes find me. 'I will want to question the mage carefully. I need to know everything about the Maker. How often did you speak to him, mage?'

'Twice.' I frown. 'His name is Aidan. And mine is Zara. I am a person, you know.'

'Are you? Are you, indeed?' For the first time Philip smiles.

'You understand?' Floster asks.

I am still in the makeshift Council Chamber. Philip and Twiss are here too . . . and of course Floster's Hound, ever watchful. All the others have left. There has been more food, and many many more questions; about my father, about Aidan.

'If I obey you, work with you to defeat the Archmage, you will let me live,' I reply, hearing the growing tiredness in my voice. 'It's not a difficult concept. You should know by now that Benedict is my enemy as much as yours.'

'Why do you hate your father so much?' Philip asks.

'My reasons are my own.' Swift is too private a pain to be shared here.

'You own nothing now,' Floster says coldly. 'Not your life, nor your past; not memories, hopes or fears. I own you and them. If you live on, you live at my pleasure, as an adopted member of my guild. None of the others would have you.'

'Should I be grateful to you?' My temper flares at last.

She smiles. 'I don't believe in miracles, child. But you're not a fool. I know you, Zara, daughter of Benedict, he who is the scourge of my guild. Your father has killed more thieves in his reign than the past ten archmages combined. Did you know that?'

She's dropped her guard at last. Emotion pounds me from across the room and I wince.

Her eyes glow with scorching hatred and I try to shield myself from the blaze. And then, like the passing of a storm cloud, the emotions shut off, and her voice becomes matter-of-fact. 'I'm giving you to Twiss to train. You will obey her in everything. And work hard, mage. Your life depends upon it.'

17

'I don't believe you forgot to tell them about Aidan.' I pause in the middle of pulling on leather leggings, balanced on one leg like a heron, and shoot a look at Twiss. 'What did Bruin say to you after I left the foundry?'

She holds out a leather tunic. I slide the leggings up over my hips and tie the lacing. My grubby mage robes lie in a heap on the floor.

'Sharp, ain't you?' Twiss growls. 'Bruin was waitin' for you to find out what your daddy wants with the Maker. Which you never done. Then he planned to set up a meet with Floster. I reckon he wanted the Maker to help with the foundry.' Her jaw clenches and she looks away.

'It ain't your place to ask me questions!' she suddenly shouts. 'You ain't "Lady" no more. You're my 'prentice. You'll give me respect or I'll have you beaten.' She looks smug for a moment, then her face crumples. 'And don't you talk about Bruin. I swore . . . and I meant it. No matter what.' She stares at me, her eyes hard and flat.

'What did you swear?'

But she shakes her head and shoves the tunic at me again.

It's patched, the leather worn to thin suppleness. 'Finish gettin' dressed.'

The tunic fits snugly over a coarse linen shift. My arms and feet are bare. Twiss frowns at them. 'You're whiter than a drowned slug.' Her nose wrinkles. She looks just like one of the scornful half-wild tabby cats that keeps the palazzo free of mice. 'No matter.' She shrugs. 'If you was a real thief you'd rub soot and oil over yourself before you went out on a job. That's what the fair ones do. Them marks on your face is what worries me. Can you magic 'em away?'

I stare at her. Count the heartbeats ringing in my ears until I can speak.

'No! . . . Magicking your own body is hard – even simple healing isn't easy. Something as complicated as removing your own mage marks? No!' I shudder at the thought of my face stripped of its marks. *Who would I be?*

'Are you born like that – with them swirls on your face?'

'The marks are put there on our naming day.' I force the words out of my mouth. 'It takes six adepts to perform the ritual. Only the parents are allowed to watch. It's very sacred. I can't talk of it to a . . . I can't talk about it.' Surely she'll stop now. Surely she understands . . .

'Are they like tattoos, then? They shine.'

The thief crouches on the floor, staring at me, asking things no kine should dare think, let alone speak of.

Strike the creature down!

I hear my father's voice in my head, demanding obedience. I wait till the urge drains away. To punish myself, I tell her as much as I can bear: 'Silver. Inlaid in my skin. Fine strands of silver.'

'Oooh.' Twiss stares at my face in wonder. But her eyes turn to flint almost at once. 'We have to hide 'em, silver or not. The Mistress says we gotta get rid of any stink of the mage about you. You wait here and don't you dare move! I'll be back 'fore you can scratch your arse.' She bounces up and races off, banging the door behind her.

I consider disobedience for all of three ticks, before settling down to wait. Twiss carries Floster's authority, and I don't feel like testing the Mistress of Thieves' tolerance of me just yet. In any case, Twiss is nearly as quick as her boast. She slams back into the room, plops down on the ground beside me and holds out a jar stoppered with a cork bung.

'Mistress Quint of the 'Pothecaries makes this herself. For folks what can afford it, it'll hide any scar.'

Quint. The mad Knowledge Seeker. The one who nods her head and wrings her hands and asks me if I drink blood.

My fingers cover my mother's mage mark. I can feel the thin silver lines . . . almost remember her face. I was three when she died. I stare at the pot Twiss holds out.

'No.' I shake my head.

Who would I be? What would I be . . . without my marks?

Twiss's eyes narrow. 'Don't fancy looking like kine?' Her nose wrinkles in contempt.

'That's not why . . .'

'Ain't it?' She shrugs. 'Don't matter. You can't live down here marked like that – middlings don't always remember to do what they're told. Best not to remind 'em what you are till they get used to you. Or do you want to die? I can't fight off the whole lot of 'em, and I ain't gonna die for a scummy

138

mage in no case.'

The hatred simmering under the surface flares once more. She's right: I have no friends here, least of all this strange girl who can't seem to decide if she wants to keep me alive or kill me herself.

But to obliterate my marks . . .

Fear. If I give in to it I lose everything. All I have is my hate. All I have is Swift. I have to live to avenge her . . . to stop what happened to her – to me – happening over and over to the end of Time.

Time's grace, help me!

I reach out without another word and take the pot of ointment from Twiss. The cream inside is thick and oily. It feels cold on my skin as I trace it over my mage marks, covering them slowly, line by line. My hand shakes.

Sometimes the child dies when they are marked. I don't remember the pain. The adepts carved my mother's mark on my right cheek, Benedict's on my left. My own mark – the symbol of my soul – sits in the middle of my forehead. I wipe out my marks and it is like being unborn.

When I've finished, I look at Twiss, happy there's no mirror in the room. The thought of my naked face makes me dizzy. I blink hotness from my eyes. Twiss peers at my cheeks and forehead. 'That's done it.' She smiles, satisfied. I see her power over me in that smile. I am a thief's apprentice now.

I am born again: new and bare and totally alone.

Nothing . . . nothing has ever been this hard. I can't do it.
  Not just the dark, although I hate the constant

gloom. The oil lamp in the wall bracket gives a grudging light.

It isn't just the smell that sits in my nose, so thick I can taste it – soot, stale air, sour bodies. And always, everywhere, inescapable – the smell of earth: of clay and worms and decay.

Dirt. I long for a bath; for clear, warm water to rinse away the stink of fear rising from my armpits and the sweat tricking between my breasts and down my backbone.

I close my eyes and once more I am flying the merlin, soaring into sharp mountain wind and the smell of cedar trees. Freedom. Time's grace, have I offended you so much? Send me courage. For Swift. And Aidan. I promised to save him. Swift is dead. Aidan, at least, is alive.

Middlings surround me, crouched on bony haunches like underfed dogs. Fear holds them back. A hand's span of air, carved like a battle trench around my sweating body, is the only thing keeping me safe, keeping me from reaching for my magic and using it to get out . . . to run back to my own kind and hope to be forgiven. Perhaps my father is right and there can never be anything but war between us and those without magic.

I sit among them in my patched leathers – hair covered, mage marks hidden, Mistress Floster's safe-sworn hanging around my neck beside Swift's letter – and feel each hating glance strike its blow. I taste their longing to tear my arms and legs from my body and scrape my eyes from their sockets. My heart is thudding as though I've been running, and sweat drips and drips down my backbone.

Watch Twiss. Listen to Twiss. Concentrate.

The eyes dart between us. Twiss, as I've discovered, is a storyteller. She has the whole cavern full of smelly, dirty little thieves drooling for her next words as though they were morsels of tender capon.

But the tale she's telling . . . The hair on the back of my neck bristles at each word.

'. . . *and the mage squeezed all the air from the Mer's body and she died with the scream stuck in her gullet. He sucked the marrow from her bones. Blood dribbled down his chin 'til his long black beard was stained the colour of rust. And that was two brave thieves dead and their middlings cryin' lonesome in the den. Only Peet was left, littlest of the three. Peet was small but she was clever . . .*'

Twiss pauses; her eyes circle the room. She smiles at the sight of wide eyes and open mouths.

'*Does no good trying to be not-seen: the mage's magic eyes sees too much, Peet thinks to herself. Does no good trying to be not-heard. His magic ears be too big. Then Peet grins to herself, for she's thought of a bang clever plan.*'

No one is looking at me now. All of us stare at Twiss.

'*So off she goes into the town and she steals herself a fine robe from the house of a counter.*'

Snorts of derision at the word 'counter'. I jerk my foot out of the way as a middling beside me spits. The gob of saliva plops onto a stone beside my foot and quivers with outrage

141

at the counters and their special privileges.

'*Peet washes up her face and hands, polishin' 'em with sand till they're smooth and fine as any lady's. Then she goes and steals a rich jewel from a goldsmith's shop.*'

Nods and mutters of approval. They know this story. Dozens of hindquarters wriggle down into the dirt. The middlings settle themselves in anticipation, like puppies waiting to be tossed a juicy scrap.

'*Off Peet goes to the palazzo of the mage. And when she gets there the ghosts of her brother and sister are screaming at her to turn tail and run. "Go on home, Peet! Our middlings got no mum nor dad now. You gotta look after 'em. Go on home, Peet. Or the mage'll suck your marrow too!" So what d'ya think Peet does? Does she turn tail and go on back home?*'

'NO!' screams the room.

Twiss smiles a slow, wicked smile.

'*Peet sings the sorrow song and sends her brother and sister's spirits off to Sanctory. Then she marches up to the front door and sees a silver death's head right in the middle of the door with eyes made out of diamonds. The eyes watch her as she reaches out and tugs the bell pull.*'

'Ohhh!' The small middling next to me stops picking its nose to sigh in delighted horror.

'*DONG! The bell rings once.*

'*DONG! It rings twice.*

'*DONG! It rings three times.*

'*A Tribute child, a poor shivery thing, opens the door and bows low to Peet, thinking her a grand lady. Peet shows her the jewel and says it's a present for the mage. Peet's took to wait in a room*

142

where the table and chairs is made of solid gold and the floor is covered with the hides of people, tanned and stitched together. When she sees that, Peet's tum goes all squirmy and she's near to puking but she just grips her hands tight and waits for the Tribute child to fetch the mage.'

'She'll smell him comin'!' shouts someone in the crowd.

Twiss glares at the culprit, hands on hips. 'You wanna tell this story, Biter?'

'NO!' scream a dozen voices, and a gangly boy with close-shaved white-blond hair winces at several well-aimed blows from his neighbours. Twiss lifts her chin and waits for silence to settle.

'Everyone knows you can smell a mage. They stink from drinking blood and their teeth is rotten from sugar cakes and plum puddings.'

The nose-picking child groans with longing.

'Peet smells Death and she knows the mage is coming. She hears silk shoes whispering over dead folks' skins and she knows the mage is outside the door. The door swings open and he's right in front of her: six feet tall with a beard long as himself and every hair of it rusty with blood. His robes is black as his heart and his eyes is silver and sparkling like the diamonds in the death's head. Peet sees those diamond eyes shining at her and she knows the mage is battling for her soul.'

Memory sweeps Twiss away and in her place I see my father, his brown eyes glistening like pebbles in a mountain stream. My blood turns to ice as his mind cracks mine to pieces like a rotten walnut hull.

I'm on my feet, pushing my way out of the cave-like den.

I dodge around some children, leap over others, ignoring the shouts of anger and threats. I'm shivering and sweating, hot and cold. It's too dark, too smelly. I can't breathe.

I shove past the taller children lounging in the doorway, careful to use my hands and not my mind. No magic. Even in full-flown panic part of me knows that if I use magic they will tear me to pieces. And then I'm in the tunnel. Running. *But where?* I don't know or care.

It's good to run. To run as hard and fast as you can. Through dark tunnels, stumbling over the uneven ground, dodging holes and broken masonry half seen in the dim light of the oil lamps. Soon my lungs are gasping for air and I have a stitch in my side. Normal, real, solid pain. The nightmare fades and I slow to a walk. That's when I hear my pursuer.

I barely have time to turn around before a body pelts into me, knocking us both down. I land on my back, painfully, and someone sits on my chest and grabs two handfuls of my hair.

'Ow! Get off, Twiss!'

'What the hell d'you think you're doing, running away like that?' She lifts my head by my hair and thunks it back onto the ground. Gently for her, but I see stars. 'You gone mad?' Twiss leans down until she's close enough to bite off my nose. Which she is probably capable of doing. 'Well? Are you mad?'

'No. Get off. You're hurting.'

'Don't care.'

'Well, I do. Get off, Twiss.'

'Promise you won't run?'

'Yes.'

She may be thin as a starved kitten, but Twiss is heavier

144

than she looks. I groan in relief as she jumps to her feet. I lay on my back, staring up at her, still dazed from the fall and head-banging. The thief proffers a hand. 'Come on,' she says and tugs me to my feet.

'How come you're so strong?' I mutter. She's half my size but I don't doubt who would win in a physical fight.

It's the right thing to say. Twiss grins with pride. 'I am, ain't I? That's working the bellows for Bruin. He used to say I was the strongest scrawny bit of nothin' he'd ever met . . .' Her voice tails off and her hand moves to grip my arm, imprisoning it. 'Why'd you leg it? That were stupid. You'd just get yourself lost down here and starve to death.'

'I wasn't trying to escape.' I sigh. 'Just bad memories. I don't want to talk about it.'

Her eyes narrow and she opens her mouth; then shuts it and shrugs. 'Just don't do it again.'

As we walk back in silence, Twiss's hand locked on my arm, I decide to ask her the question that's been nagging at me since she first brought me to the catacombs.

'Where are the parents, Twiss? All you middlings – where are your parents?'

Her fingers tighten, cutting into my bare arm, and I know I have guessed correctly.

'You lot!' she hisses. 'They died, didn't they? Mages killed 'em. Every one. Middlings raise themselves – we're mum and dad to the little 'uns and they raise up the babies in their turn.'

'Your parents?' I ask.

'I 'member my dad. He were killed when I was eight. I don't 'member my mum but . . . I miss her the most.' Her voice is

145

hoarse with longing.

My throat goes tight and I take a deep breath.

'That's stupid, ain't it?' she asks, hesitant. And I know she's never talked of this to anyone before. 'Missing me mum when I never knew 'er.'

'No,' I say. 'No, it's not stupid at all.'

We walk the rest of the way back in silence.

18

'The Mistress wants you.'

Floster's Hound looms over the middlings. We're at breakfast. I'm sitting next to Twiss with a bowl of bread and a hunk of slightly mouldy cheese. The middlings have grown used to my presence and Twiss seems to take pride in having a pet mage. But I don't think I'll ever get used to the crowded den, the noise and smell. Or to being a giant among scrawny, undersized children.

Now I blink up at the Hound. Like the other adult thieves I've met down here, I can seldom read his feelings. Not being able to sense their emotions is like being blinded. *What does Floster want?*

Her messenger points at Twiss. 'And you as well.'

Twiss grimaces and shoves the last of her bread into her mouth.

The Hound jerks his head towards the door and we scramble up and follow him out. My right foot has gone to sleep. It feels like a block of wood, then explodes with pins and needles. I stumble and nearly fall. The Hound pulls me upright. His hand is clamped around my arm and I can't pull it away. My heart lurches in my chest and my throat goes tight. I don't look at him, but I can smell him: he smells of wood smoke, earth and oiled leather . . . and danger. I sense it clearly when he touches me. Something has happened – and this man knows what it is.

'Let go.' I lift my eyes and when they meet his, he drops my arm. He dips his head mockingly.

'Apologies . . . *Lady*. Let's not keep the Mistress waiting: patience isn't her strong suit.' His face is sardonic, his eyes arrogant; every move of his body is smooth, controlled . . . threatening. It's like turning a path and finding yourself face to face with a hill leopard. As I follow him, I realise I'm frightened. I glance at Twiss, walking beside me, and she shrugs and shakes her head. She doesn't know what's happened either.

'You will tell us the truth,' says the Mistress of Thieves.

Seven faces look back at me. I feel the Knowledge Seekers' emotions; the room is full of a poisonous fog of suspicion and hatred. These people are alien and I am wholly alien to them.

Once more my father's voice rings through my head, insidious, certain, damning: *Kine are not human, Zara. Do not make your mother's mistake. We must rule over them, as the gods decreed, or their jealousy and fear would overwhelm us. Our race and theirs cannot live in peace and fellowship. To think otherwise is not merely weak, it is dangerous.*

He's wrong. I know it. But it is the hardest thing – to live among those who think you inhuman. It is beyond loneliness. The whole of me aches with a monstrous dark hurt. This place sits near the edge of madness. I must take great care not to slip over the precipice.

Twiss catches my eye and frowns her question: Do I know what's going on? I give a tiny shake of my head. The child moves closer to me. Suddenly I am in my father's library, Swift cowering behind me. I thrust away the memory and, as I do, I realise that Twiss has moved to my side not in fear, but as my would-be protector.

Tightness grows in my chest. I press my lips together and try to shut off my emotions. I can't afford distractions: something has happened and it bodes ill.

Floster sits upright at her place behind the long table. Her head with its cropped grey hair is tilted in enquiry. She hoards words as though they were gold secs: never using more than she must. She's waiting for me to speak.

The Hound glides past her to lean against the wall. He watches me too. A long knife in a leather sheath hangs at his hip, its wooden hilt wrapped in narrow bands of sweat-stained leather. My eyes keep flicking back to it. Time's grace! I'm locked in a room with a thief wearing iron. *They can't hurt me!* My mage marks are still there, under the layer of cosmetic. I am Zara, daughter of Eleanor. I'm almost an adept. Someday I will be as powerful as my father.

This is not someday.

Philip, leader of the Knowledge Seekers, sits, as before, beside the Mistress. He scares me more than Floster. His blue eyes, deep set under sandy brows, flick from Twiss to me and back, never resting.

The tension in the room is angry and vengeful.

'No more lies!' says the Mistress.

With a jolt of surprise, I realise Floster is talking to both of us. Twiss's shoulders hunch as she realises the same thing.

'Your *father* . . .' Floster glares at me, pronouncing the word as though the taste of it fouls her mouth. 'The Archfiend's latest works are true to his nature. Two hundred and thirty-seven guildsfolk murdered. Their heads decorate every gate in the city. Their houses are burnt to the ground; their children sold into slavery.'

Images of suffering form in my mind. Sickness twists my stomach. Asphodel will be a place of evil and fear for every kine now. And as I scan their faces, Death stares back at me from the eyes of the Knowledge Seekers. It seems my father's handiwork is like to kill me as well.

Floster presses her lips together. Hatred rises from her like the reek of a midden. 'Not one of them was a Knowledge Seeker, as Benedict knows full well. We got every Seeker left alive out of the city that first night. These folk were their kin: fathers, mothers, sisters, brothers. Friends and neighbours, even.'

'Our spy informs us that Benedict has called the battle mages back from the Wall, leaving only a skeleton force to oversee the Tribute army.' Philip speaks for the first time. 'These mages have been set to work terrorizing the city. Guards patrol every quarter of Asphodel; there is a permanent curfew, night and day. People are allowed out of their houses at midday for two hours only.'

I barely have time to register the fact that the Knowledge Seekers still have a spy in the city when the Mistress speaks again.

'The city's shut up tighter than a gnat's arse.' Floster's eyes grow even harder. 'But your father hasn't had it all his own way. I lost three of my best archers but they took out seven mages between them.'

Even though I'm at war with my own, horror shudders up my spine. Was it anyone I knew? An Academy student? One of my tutors? I shudder: a flint arrow in the back is every mage's nightmare. Our shoulder blades twitch with thinking of it.

'We're trapped here,' Philip says, his voice full of suppressed frustration. 'All us Knowledge Seekers. Only thieves may leave the catacombs. This city beneath a city is overcrowded and riven by fear and suspicion . . .'

But I don't hear him any more. It hits me: *I'm trapped too, like the Seekers!* How will I avenge Swift, or rescue Aidan? I promised to save him but if I'm trapped in the catacombs, I might as well be dead.

'I can help!' The words blurt out of my mouth before I can stop them. 'I can fight!'

I look from face to face, read refusal in their eyes. 'The Archmage is my enemy too!' I'm shaking with fear – but even more from frustration. These people were meant to be my allies!

'If your father got hold of you, he'd open up your head, find out about the catacombs and we'd all be dead.' Floster's voice is contemptuous.

Part of me, the part that is like Swift – keen to learn, to know the secrets of the world – that part pricks up its ears. Thieves have long been a thorn in the side of magekind. They are a puzzle, a mystery, a frustration. A mage cannot read the mind of a thief. We tell ourselves it's because they're little more than animals. But I've long known that's nonsense: we can fly with a merlin, run with a hare, hunt with the mountain cat. So why are thieves different?

'Teach me to shut my mind like you do,' I retort to Floster. 'Like a thief. I can learn: I'm an adept . . . well, almost. But I'm the only magic user you've got. I can be a powerful weapon against Benedict. Are you going to let me rot down here because you're scared? I want to fight!'

Even as I speak the brave words, a small treacherous voice in my head asks: *But, can you fight?* Aluid's face, sinking into the slurry, flashes in front of my eyes, and I shudder. I couldn't kill him. When the moment came I couldn't kill – not even to save my own life.

'At least I can protect your fighters,' I blurt, seeing Floster's mouth open to refuse. 'Or . . .' and I have a moment of inspiration, '. . . I can spy for you inside an animal – in a hawk or pigeon, for instance. I can give you hidden eyes and ears. A spy over the city . . . or in the corridors of my father's palazzo itself!' I think I see a quickening of interest in Floster's eyes, but before I can explain about mind magic, she shakes her head.

'It takes months to train a middling to be not-seen-not-heard. We haven't got months. And I doubt any other than a thief could learn. Not even an "adept".' The word is mocking in her mouth. 'You'll help in other ways.' Floster pauses. 'I can always see what your father will give me not to cut your throat.'

Utter despair as I watch my last chance slip from sight. 'He'd give you the knife!'

'I think not.' Foster's voice is coldly confident. 'Benedict isn't a god, though he wants to be. He isn't immortal and you're the only child he has. Or like to. Mages don't breed well. No, he'd pay dear to have you living so he could scour your mind

152

clean and fill it with his own thoughts.'

I close my eyes until the wave of revulsion passes. Floster is waiting when I open them, like the merlin, hanging in the air over her prey. She's scored and knows it. It's true: mages fall into and out of bed with each other as often as they change clothes, but a pregnancy is a rare and celebrated event.

'And you're the only hostage I've got. Which makes it cussedly awkward if you turn out to be the traitor.'

The word hangs in the air.

I stare at Floster, and feel understanding fall into place in my brain with a clunk.

'*Traitor?*' A husky young voice grunts the word in disbelief.

I'd almost forgotten Twiss. Now she lurches towards Floster, her dark eyes wide with shock.

'Someone ratted . . .?' The child freezes. Her face turns the colour of greystone. 'Who?'

'That is what we intend to find out,' Philip says. 'Today our spy in the city managed to contact us. They confirmed what we had suspected – the foundry workers were betrayed. It would seem that there is a traitor amongst us. It can't be one of those who knew about our pet mage or she wouldn't be here now.' He considers me. 'Unless . . .'

Eight pairs of eyes stare at me, foreign as the eyes of reptiles or birds. With a shock that makes me sway I realise that Floster's comment wasn't a joke. They think I have betrayed them to my father!

'I . . . I . . .' All blood seems to have evaporated from my legs but I'm the only mage in the room so that can't have happened. 'I've worked for you for years! I want my father dead. Why

153

would I tell him about the foundry?'

'When you were a middling, you joined us because you were mad at your daddy. But you're older now. You realised it wasn't play-acting.' Floster sounds like one of my tutors explaining elementary magic to a rather dim student. 'Bruin's foundry was going to give us iron: swords, knives, pike ends. When it came to it – to letting us live or your own kind die, you went back to blood.'

My mouth drops open in stupefaction at the wrongness of it all. For a moment I can only splutter at her calm matter-of-factness.

'Well, that's convenient!' I manage at last. 'Did your spy accuse me? Have you got any actual proof?'

Floster's face might have been carved from stone. She doesn't answer because she can't. They have nothing but hatred and suspicion. I look from the Mistress to Philip, sitting upright and watchful beside her.

Bitterness wells up. 'Of course! So much easier if I'm the traitor rather than one of your own.'

Something flies at me. Screaming and hissing, Twiss jumps on my back and wraps a rope-like arm around my throat. It tightens into a noose. I can't breathe. I stagger and drop to my knees. Fingers claw my hair, yank my head back.

'Filthy, lying mage! You never tried to help Bruin! You set him up!' Twiss is shrieking in my ear. She gives me no air to answer.

Floster is shouting but I can't hear what she's saying over Twiss's screams and roaring profanities. I only hear blood drumming in my head. Time itself slows to watch me die.

Someone is tugging at Twiss, lifting us both off the ground. But the girl holds my neck with Death's own grip. She means to kill me. Thank Time she hasn't got iron, like the Hound, or I'd be dead already. Stars explode in my head but the pain begins to fade. I'm dying.

I can stop Twiss with a thought. But it might kill her. I don't want to die . . . do I? If I die now I fail Swift again. I abandon Aidan. I hear my Tribute child's voice in my head, calling me to protect her . . . to save Aidan. But I can't . . .

The strangling arm loosens, is tugged away at last. Twiss wails in despair and takes a fistful of my hair with her. I gulp air and it feels like swallowing coals. I gasp and retch, my sides heaving.

The sound of a slap concusses the air and leaves sudden silence, broken only by a horrible rasping noise, which I realise is me, trying to breathe. I kneel, head bowed, every muscle in my body quivering. I've never been nearer Death and she retreats reluctantly. Almost, I wish to call her back. To rest. To stop. If Twiss, who knows me better than any other kine, believes I could betray those people to their deaths, what point is there?

The floor is amazing when I finally open my eyes. Every particle of dirt vibrates. Every grain of mud – a hundred distinct colours of brown. I raise my head on a stiff, reluctant neck and look at Philip and the other Knowledge Seekers, their faces showing a range of emotions from shock to enjoyment. Last of all, I look at Twiss.

The Hound holds her wrapped in strong arms. Floster must have climbed right over the long table. Her eyes bulge dangerously. Her hand is raised to strike Twiss again, but the child looks the most shocked of all . . . although I cannot see myself, of course.

The young thief stares at me, her face a mask of loathing. 'Filthy mage! Murderer!' She mutters the words over and over.

'I didn't betray them, Twiss!' My voice is hoarse. It hurts to speak. 'It wasn't me!'

She doesn't believe me. I see it in her eyes.

'I promised,' she whispers, looking mad.

'Shut it, Twiss!' Exasperation in Floster's voice. And worry. 'You dare go against my safe-sworn? I'll beat the disobedience out of you myself! I should never have let you near the blacksmith once I saw how things were.' She looks at the Hound. 'Thieves can't afford to love!' she says. 'Not till the mages are driven from Asphodel.' Her eyes return to Twiss. 'Bruin would be ashamed of you. Ashamed!'

This last pierces the child's madness. She gasps and grows silent and unresisting. But her eyes never leave my face and they speak of hatred and revenge. I have a new enemy: Twiss, the mage-killer.

19

'You didn't kill her. Why?' Floster is seated once more at the table. Her face is stony.

I groan in frustration, wondering at the ability of kine and mage alike to only hear what they wish to hear. And say again: 'Twiss saved my life.'

Floster shakes her head in exasperation. 'A mage, attacked by a thief? She should have been dead in an eye-blink.'

I look at Twiss, standing quietly beside her mistress. The girl stares back with brown-stone eyes full of hatred. The sight is surprisingly painful. I shrug. Floster can believe me or not – I don't care any more. 'I can't hurt Twiss – she saved my life. Besides, she's a child.'

Philip barks. It takes me a tick to realise he's laughing. 'You are barely more,' he says.

'I haven't been a child for years.'

'Your father killed your mother, they say.' Floster's voice is tinged with smugness. She thinks she knows why I turned traitor to my own. She's wrong, but it doesn't matter.

'Twiss has lost the person she loves too,' Floster continues. 'She's not a child either. However . . . I think I must believe you.'

The flare of hope startles me with its fierceness.

The Mistress of Thieves looks at Philip, conferring: 'I was wrong. It seems the mage hates her father more than she hates us. The traitor must be a Knowledge Seeker.'

'Or a thief!' Philip lifts an eyebrow. 'You cannot guarantee that Benedict has not bribed one of your own.'

'It won't be a thief, Seeker.' Floster's voice is soft and deadly. 'Our fight with magekind is to the death. It's one of you guildspeople. If they still live I'll sniff them out and make such an example of the bastard that middlings will scare themselves silly with the tale for generations to come.'

'*No!*' Twiss grabs Floster's arm, tugging it frantically. 'She's fooling you, like she did me! Mages are pure evil. Her heart's black with Bruin's blood. I should have left her to die.' Twiss breaks off and steps back. She glares at Floster, who seems, for once, lost for words.

Twiss whirls around to shout at the Hound: 'You know I'm right. Tell the old fool!'

The words have hardly left her mouth before the leather-clad man lunges forward and slaps her face. Hard. Twiss flies backwards and sprawls on the floor. I freeze as Floster lifts a warning hand.

Twiss lifts her head and I see blood trickling from a cut lip. The Hound scoops her up with one hand, dangling the unresisting child by the scruff of her neck. He looks a question at his mistress.

'No,' Floster says, weariness heavy in her voice. 'Don't beat her. Just get her out of my sight. And Twiss, disobey me once more . . . dare to attack the mage again, and it won't be a

158

beating you get from me. She wears my safe-sworn. You will be cast out.' Her face, her voice, are bleak.

Twiss's mouth falls open. Her bleeding lip quivers. The Hound drags her to the door and thrusts her out; turns and stands, his face once more wearing its sardonic mask.

The Knowledge Seekers shift in their chairs, glance at one another. The air is full of uncertainty.

'Nothing's decided!' A bullish voice breaks the silence. 'And in any case she'll not last a day down here now.'

It's the blacksmith, Hammeth, Bruin's successor. His hair is plastered to his broad forehead with sweat and dirt, and the smell of frustrated inactivity comes off him like the stink of a polecat.

'Your cubs'll tear the bitch to shreds and eat her.' He smiles a nasty smile but his face remains carefully averted from mine.

Coward! I stare at him, daring him to meet my eyes.

'And best thing too!' His voice grows louder, belligerent. 'The traitor's not yet been caught. And that's because she stands before us bold as brass, with her red hair like the devil she is. She'll sell us to Benedict, Floster, and you're an old fool!'

A movement behind Floster, of violence suppressed. I can almost feel the Hound force himself back into stillness. Floster herself ignores Hammeth. Her eyes are fastened on me. I see speculation in her face. 'You said you could spy for me inside an animal. What did you mean?'

The flood of relief almost washes away the pain in my throat. 'It's called mind magic. I can send part of my awareness – my consciousness – into an animal. I can make it go where I want it to, listen and see through its ears and eyes.'

'Mind-control!' growls the smith. 'That's what she's talking about.'

'It would help us if you could control your tongue, Hammeth.' Philip turns his head to spear the smith with a chilly look. 'Continue . . . Zara.' His eyes are speculative.

The smith subsides, muttering and throwing dark looks in my direction.

'Any animal?' asks Floster.

'Yes. Although I have the most experience with birds. Hawks. But a cat . . . a rat, even. They get everywhere in the palazzo.'

'Places our spy cannot go.' Philip's eyes kindle. 'I like it. Mistress, what say you?'

This is it. My life depends on this woman and her next words.

The Mistress of Thieves stares at me. Her face gives nothing away. At last, she speaks: 'I'm sure in my mind that this mage is not the traitor. But happen I'm mistaken, Marcus will have his instructions.' The smile she gives me now is cold as death.

Marcus? Who's Marcus? And then I realise: *She means the Hound!*

'Marcus will be her "Guardian",' Foster continues. She pronounces the mage word with dark enjoyment. 'He'll not leave her side.'

I stiffen. Before I can stop them, my eyes dart a glance at the Hound. He's watching me, his face unreadable.

'Even the redoubtable Marcus is no match for a mage!' A plump man in the pale blue tunic of a counter speaks for the first time. 'Whether or not we can trust the female, disaster might strike at any moment. Do we imagine that, at the point of capture, the mage will offer her neck to your man's knife? We must weigh the risk against possible advantage. Put them into the scales and see which weighs heavier.' His stubby-fingered hands mime the action, eyes narrowed in calculation. 'Our lives depend upon secrecy. If the Archmage should decide to investigate the catacombs . . .' He shudders. 'We'd be as rats for the slaying.'

'Rats give a nasty bite in the dark,' Floster says. 'Benedict would find flushing us out harder than you or he can imagine, Barnum. Do you think I've no defences? But if the Archmage knew about catacombs he would have attacked by now. The traitor's a Knowledge Seeker, as I said. Someone who knew about the foundry. And they're either still in the city or among the dead.'

She shrugs. 'But the war continues. You guildsfolk cannot go back, cannot live in the city again until we defeat Benedict. This mage offers me a way of getting vital information. Do you want to return to your homes, or do you want to run to the Maker world, hoping the mages don't slaughter you as you attempt to cross the plains? Even supposing the Makers would take you in.'

'I am eager to make an expedition to contact the Makers as soon as may reasonably be undertaken.' Philip leans forward, his eyes alight. 'But that is not possible yet. Mistress Floster is right. Our options are limited. Time is running out. Benedict will find us sooner or later. I prefer to carry the fight to the Archmage, and this girl is our main hope of that. I think we have no choice.'

Tabitha the silversmith has been sitting silently this whole time. I had thought her in a dream of despair, unaware of the arguments around her. But now she leans forward.

'Mistress, a word. I have known the mage, Zara, longer than any other in this room. I was her primary contact in the city. I cannot say other than the truth. You know, all of you, I have reason more than most to hate the traitor.' Her voice is quiet. 'It was not this girl. That is what I believe.' She slumps back in her chair again, into silence.

'A vote, then.' Floster's voice rings out. 'I move that the mage, Zara, be allowed out of the catacombs to work under my orders. I take full responsibility for her safety and the safety of the community. If I fail, I will submit to the appropriate punishment.' She raises her hand.

One by one, other Council members lift their arms. Philip is first. Tabitha puts her hand up slowly, her eyes focused elsewhere. Mistress Quint bounces in her chair like a smug black cat, nodding and smiling, as she lifts her hand. The counter holds his hands before him like the scales of a balance, a frown of concentration on his face. Then he too, raises an arm. Five votes for yes. The blacksmith scowls from his chair. The last member of the Knowledge Seeker Council is the head of the Tailors' Guild. The woman shakes her head in worry. Then cries: 'I don't know! Oh very well. If the rest of you . . .' And reluctantly lifts her arm.

'Six for. One against. The vote is carried.'

I barely hear Philip's voice over the roar of the blood in my head. I am to live!

'You're fools, the lot of you!' The blacksmith pushes back from the table, sending his chair flying. 'I'll have nothing to do with it.'

162

'Concentrate on making spear points then!' Tabitha snaps. The silversmith is transformed. Her blonde head lifts and her eyes burn, lit by a silver fire. 'It's all you're fit for in any case. Do your work so we can get out of this hellhole someday. If the mage can help us return to Asphodel then I will give her whatever support I can.'

Her eyes meet mine. Taken unprepared, I'm defenceless as her emotions blast me: a flash of stomach-twisting revulsion, followed by such guilt and despair it's like being burnt. I look away, shaken.

The blacksmith glowers for a moment, then stamps from the room.

'Well,' Philip says after several ticks of silence. 'I'd best take charge of the mage. The further she's kept away from Twiss and the rest of your middlings the better, Mistress. Zara can lodge in my quarters and help with my studies on the Makers.'

'Very well,' says Floster. 'I'm trusting you, Zara, daughter of Benedict. Mind you honour that trust. Marcus!' She keeps her eyes locked on mine as she gives her orders. 'If she tries to escape the catacombs, kill her.'

I tear my gaze away and stare at the Hound. His expression hasn't changed but something in his eyes makes the hairs on the back of my neck stand up.

'It will take time before we are ready to test your abilities,' Floster says to me. 'We need to contact our spy in the city, make our plans, get a suitable animal. Stay with Philip and do as he tells you until we're ready. Then you can prove whether or not you're worth your keep.'

She strides from the room. For once, the Hound does not

163

follow her. He waits as the remaining Council members drift from the room one by one. Then he hooks a chair with his leg, draws it beneath him and slumps into it. His eyes never leave me. My mouth grows dry and I find it hard to concentrate on what the Nonpareil is saying.

'You also have work to do with me,' Philip continues. 'I want to know all you remember about the Maker and what he told you of his world. You must teach me about your magic and the weaknesses of your tribe. And of any books you may have read in your father's library.' His eyes grow eager. 'Especially those about the Maker world: their machines. The old war. Oh yes, and you can tutor me on my reading and writing.'

Shocked, I can only stare.

'I've taught myself the rudiments, from books the thieves have stolen for me. But I'm not fluent yet. I am convinced you will make an excellent tutor.'

I look at this tall thin man, peering at me like an eager child. The hunger for knowledge blazes in his eyes. It's too familiar. I both love and fear that hunger. It's as vast and all-consuming as the ocean.

'The last person I taught to read died,' I say. 'The Archmage killed her.'

20

I'm not free yet. Mine is a prison of candlelight and mirrors. As well as me, it holds paper and quill pens, detailed drawings of gears, wheels and levers scattered on every surface . . . and a strange man. Philip the artist is unlike anyone else I've ever met. His cleverness shines like mage light behind his clear blue eyes, but it devours him as it burns.

I watch him now, bent over a drawing of a monstrous mechanical bow, a machine of diabolical cleverness, and shudder at the horrors the human mind is cable of inventing.

Philip works surrounded by candles. Their holders have curved backs of silvered glass which collect the light and reflect it onto his table. It's a clever idea, like all of his inventions. Including the one he draws now: a bow held sideways in a wooden frame, the bowstring bent not by the strength of an archer's arm but by a wooden screw. An arrow shot from such a bow could pierce armour or shoot a mage in the back from hundreds of feet away.

Philip glances up, brushing his hair back from his forehead in a gesture which I've learnt means he is impatient with some imperfection in his work. Before I can turn away he catches the expression of horror on my face.

'We *are* in the business of killing, you know.' His smile is both gentle and wry. 'There is no pleasant way to kill another human being.'

'I know.' My voice is a whisper. I force myself to think of the mother I don't remember, who died fighting for change. Of Swift. Of all the enslaved Tribute children in the palazzo and city – those I noticed and those I didn't, because before Swift I never thought of them as human at all. Of the child soldiers who die every day on the Wall. Of the public executions of thieves or kine convicted of capital crimes, where mages bet on how long the victim will survive as their bones are slowly heated inside their flesh, or their skin peeled from their bodies layer by layer, like an onion.

I do hate my father. I want him dead. But the rest? Must every mage die? My mother wasn't evil. And she was not the only one.

'In my father's library . . .' I begin.

Philip drops his pencil at once – as I knew he would. He drains the cup of sweet-smelling mead that always sits beside him. 'Tell me,' he asks. 'Please.'

As I talk, he begins to draw once more. The point of his pencil is made of pure silver. It leaves faint lines on the paper, lines that will grow darker and stronger over the coming days as the silver tarnishes. I touch the mage mark on my right cheek, feeling, beneath the thick paste of cosmetic, the lines of silver laid in my skin. I trace the swirling pattern that was the soul-sign of my mother and am calmed.

I tell Philip of the writings I found, records of rebellious mages exiled or put to death. Tales of the Maker cities, of the ancient war there. Of the world when mages ruled every country and land. Of the great rebellion. Of the massacre of the mages and the death of magic. Of the Wall and the rise of the Makers. Of their infernal machines and devices of war. Of the extermination of engineers in our own world.

The candles flicker and go out, one by one. I kindle mage light. It shines down upon us as I talk. I talk and the Seeker listens long into the night, until dawn chases the darkness from the unseen city overhead.

Hail. Beating on the roof of my bedchamber. The percussion of ice shattering on tile: brittle, sharp. The rattle grows to a hammering, a pounding, a drilling. It hounds me from my sleep. And with a lurch in my belly I realise, yet again, that I'm not safe in my bed in the palazzo, but huddled beneath a scratchy blanket on a straw pallet in a corner of a damp, chill cavern in the catacombs beneath Asphodel. Far beneath. Out of reach of hailstorms. So what . . . ?

I push upright, tug aside the curtain hung round my bed. The pattering noise continues. The door! It's under attack, pelted with what sounds like . . . small rocks? Mud? And now the sound of voices, human wolves: '*Come out, mage! Traitor! Filth! Blood sucker!*'

My throat dries to choking; it's like Twiss is strangling me all over again. The mob has come. Is it her voice I hear beneath the shrill cries of the younger ones? Tears burn in my eyes and I shake them away. Why should I care if Twiss hates me?

I jump to my feet, conjure a ghostly finger of mage light.

167

'Zara?' Philip lurches from the other chamber, his bare white legs and feet extending stork-like beneath his nightshirt. I want to laugh and cry.

'What is it, Zara?' He looks terrified.

'Middlings,' I say. 'Twiss must have convinced the whole tribe that I betrayed the foundry workers.'

The door is shaking on its hinges. The shower of pebbles has been replaced by a pounding thud. A battering ram! I gather my thoughts; I have not done proper magic for so long. But it's easy. I send a thought, find the slender pole of pine and in a moment the wood is decayed and crumbling. The middlings' howl deepens in fury. Dozens of voices rise in a scream that seems to come from one throat.

My stomach turns over. 'It's all right,' I say, not believing it myself. 'I can hold them off, and Floster will stop them soon. Won't she?' I glance at Philip and he looks back at me with troubled eyes.

'She must! You're far too valuable.' Outrage in his voice. Valuable. That's all I am to the Seeker: a useful tool.

Another sound outside: the scuffle of bare feet running away. And then a new knocking on the door, but a human fist this time.

'Zara? Philip?' It's the Hound. His voice is unmistakeable, rich and dark as winter honey. 'They're gone,' he says. 'They won't bother you again.'

Philip stumbles to the door and unlocks it. He eases it open, struggling against some obstruction. A rattling, crunching sound as the Seeker pushes the door wide. And now I see what has made his shoulders stiffen beneath the nightshirt. Although

168

I avoid touching the kine, as they do me, I push Philip gently to one side and step out into a scene from my father's book of the Underworld.

A skull grins up at me, its lower jaw torn away. It lolls, king of the hill, atop a tumble of human bones. Creamy-white in the blue flare of my mage light: leg bones and arm bones, shattered, amputated by battering on the door; skulls dinted and cracked by impact.

A hailstorm of bones.

I'm not horrified or frightened or disgusted. The emotion that seizes me is blacker than any of those. Despair is a bottomless pit and I feel myself tumbling.

A hand grabs my elbow. The Hound holds my arms and gives me a small but sharp shake. 'That's enough of that, girl. You'll see worse before this is over. But you're not a quitter nor a weakling. Do yourself honour. No one else will.'

His face is inches from mine and, as my head stops spinning, my chest tightens. I'm breathless as I stare at him.

The sternness in his eyes softens. 'You'll do now,' he says and lets me go. Almost, I see him smirk. The bastard! He's used to eliciting a response in females, I can tell. And enjoys it.

I snuff out my mage light to hide my burning face. I washed off Quint's cosmetic before retiring to bed so my embarrassment is as plain to see on my cheeks as my mage marks.

The Hound watches me in the light of the torch he must have brought with him. He lifts it from the wall bracket and turns to me, an amused smile hooking one corner of his mouth. 'Go back to bed. I'll stand watch tonight. I recognised a goodly number of the little arsewipes and they'll not dare come back when Floster and I've done with them. Nor will the others.'

His smile turns grim and he's suddenly terrifying. I shudder and hope that Twiss isn't one of the middlings who will face Floster's wrath tomorrow.

'Please talk to the Mistress, Philip. She must have forgotten about me.'

A sevenday has crawled into Time's belly since I have been allowed to leave these two small rooms. I live on morsels of information and rumours teased from Philip. Things are bad in the city. Raids, intimidation, daily executions. I wonder if my father intends to kill all the kine. Even he cannot want such a thing, surely. Who would do the work? The catacombs have been silent as Death since the night of bones. I asked Philip if Twiss was one of the mob, but he shrugged and said our time is too precious to worry about such things.

'Zara.' Philip frowns in irritation at my pestering. 'The Mistress will tell you when you are needed. Until then you are to stay safely here and help me. You have not finished recounting the aftermath of the Maker war. I need to know about their machines, anything you remember. I don't understand why you did not question the young Maker when you had the chance!'

I can't help it: I burst out laughing at the idea of Aidan and me sitting on his hard, narrow cot in the prison and discussing what war machines his ancestors built three generations before.

'I don't see what is so humorous.' His voice is peevish.

'Sorry, Philip. But does Mistress Floster really understand that I can enter the mind of any animal – a hawk, a bat or even a rat? That I can see what they see, hear what they hear? Think of the places I could go, what I could overhear, if I shared the mind of one of the palazzo rats.'

He frowns. His eyes shift and slide away, back to the wooden model of a catapult he's testing, using lumps of clay dug from the walls and flinging them at a target. He makes an adjustment to a wooden cog, shaving off a paper-thin curl of wood.

'But it would be very dangerous, and you have become useful to me.' He's pouting like a stubborn child. My heart sinks. He won't remind Floster about my mind magic. Not yet. Not until he's drained my memory of the knowledge he seeks.

I press my lips together too. I won't plead again. But nor will I tell him more about the Makers. I ignore the Seeker's increasingly irritable questions and at last he falls silent. I retreat to my bed, draw the curtains around it and begin to plan.

Philip has a sweet tooth; he is never without his cup of honey-mead at his elbow. I have noticed that it is not only honey he craves, but the mixture from the smoked glass bottle in the locked cupboard. Six careful drops he adds to his cup. If he is tired or work is going badly, he will add three more. Syrup of poppy. It's only a guess, but a fair one. Many, many mages are poppy addicts. Those who find the luxurious ease of their lives has become tedious; and tormenting kine, eating and drinking and bedding are no longer enough.

After our evening meal, taken in awkward silence, I unlock the cabinet, extract six drops of liquid from the bottle and enclose it in a capsule of crystallised air. It is such pleasure to use magic again!

Philip sits quietly at his table, reading a book the thieves stole for him. I clear the remains of our dinner and smile at

171

the irony of the child of Benedict performing the tasks of a house slave for a kine. And as I remove his empty dish, I drop the capsule of poppy syrup into his cup of mead. I soften the crystallised air and mingle the syrup with the liquid in the cup. Philip will sleep deep and long this night.

When I go to bed, I don't wash the cosmetic from my face. I keep my leather tunic and leggings on and sit upright behind my curtain wall, waiting until the light in the next chamber goes out and the darkness is broken by the sound of slow, heavy snores.

I set mage light flickering to light my way and send a tendril of thought out into the corridor, searching for middlings. But the one I truly fear is the Hound. Will I feel him if he's there? 'Not-seen, not-heard', they call it. Thieves . . . they are uncanny. I'll have to chance it: I'm going to remind Floster of her promise to use me as a spy. To convince her that I am too useful to leave rotting down here in the house of the dead.

I unbar the door and slip out into the corridor. From the other side I find the stout oak bar with my mind and make myself invisible hands of thick air to lift it back into place. I turn to face the silent maze of catacombs, half expecting to find the Hound's lean shape rear out of the darkness to confront me, a contemptuous smile on his lips. But I'm alone.

Emotion rises in my head like wine vapour and I grin at the darkness before me, feeling my chest swell with excitement. My heart is thudding and my hands are sweaty, but I could laugh out loud with joy. It's like the times I hurried through the markets of Asphodel, spying for the Knowledge Seekers. I feel alive again.

Philip's lodgings in the catacombs lie only a few twisting corridors from Floster's chamber. I think I know the way, but I keep careful track of each turning in case I'm wrong. I don't intend to take any chance of getting lost in these endless tunnels. The corridors are lined with shelves, resting places of the city's dead. The bones of kine shine in my mage light, the skulls grinning at me.

I can't help you, I whisper to the bones as I slide along the corridor, trying to imitate Twiss's way of moving silently. I can't help Swift. Where do her bones lie? The thought squeezes my heart.

It's stupidly easy. Almost before I can see past my dark thoughts, I am entering the long, curving earthen tunnel that leads to Floster's chamber. It should be dark as a womb, but as I edge round a bend I see the smoky orange-yellow glow of torchlight!

I lunge behind one of the ancient oak supports holding up the ceiling. My mage light pops out and I stand listening to the silence, heart thudding. Nothing. Perhaps Floster always keeps torches lit in her corridor. Perhaps the Mistress of Thieves is scared of the dark. I clap a hand over my mouth to stop a nervous giggle. And then all desire to laugh drains as a man veers into sight. He is outlined in smoky orange light: broad shoulders, long, strong legs striding swiftly towards me.

He pauses, only feet from my pitiful hiding place, and wrenches one of the torches from the wall. And as he does so, I press my hand against my mouth until it feels my teeth will break. Am I mad? It can't be him, but it is.

Otter, my father's Guardian. Otter, creature of the Archmage.

Here, in the catacombs.

He's dressed like a thief, in dark leggings and tunic. His hair is hidden under a leather cap, but I know his face too well to be mistaken.

I'm frozen with shock. It must be that stillness that saves me. That and my dark clothes. Torch in hand, Otter strides past, a thoughtful frown on his face. A moment later I realise that if he had glanced to his right he would have seen my staring eyes, their whites glowing in the torchlight. But it isn't until my father's man has vanished into the earth maze that I think to close my eyes. Twiss would scoff in scorn. Twiss . . . Floster; they belong here in the darkness. But Otter? My legs give way and I slide down to sit slumped against the wall.

Is Floster the traitor?

The idea is unthinkable, but once thought, I can't shake it off. What other answer can there be? Otter was visiting the Mistress. He came from her chamber. A meeting in the night; a meeting hidden from the community; a meeting of conspirators. It can't be otherwise. Slowly it comes to me: *I'm in deadly danger.* If I'm found here . . . if Floster were to suspect what I know . . .

I'm running down the corridor towards Philip's rooms before I have even thought to get to my feet. *Who can I tell? Who will believe me?* I'm trapped now as I have never been! Dead and buried underground.

I hurtle on, only half aware of where I'm going until I outrun panic and slide to a stop. I'm panting, sweating. And a new fear slides like a cold knife into my stomach. I've taken a wrong turn in my headlong flight. I've strayed. And am lost.

*Swift wasn't frightened of the dark. She would crawl
into my bed and patiently hold me until my shivering
faded and I drifted off to sleep. The only thing she
feared was my father. Swift was the strong one. The
good one. I should have been the one who died.*

'How far do you think the catacombs go, Swift?' My voice is
a scratchy whisper, but it sounds loud in this dark, winding
tunnel.

I've walked for miles. For hours. Time's grace knows how
long. Wearily, I recall my first terror, the heart-thudding, choking
fear, when I realised I was lost in the catacombs. But extreme
fear can't last. I didn't die of fright. No . . . I shall have to
stumble on and on through the winding labyrinth, my only
company the grinning skulls and dismembered bones stacked
in the cubbyholes lining the tunnels, until I die of thirst.

I tried sending a thread of thought to explore each passage
I came to, but the magic ate up my energy too quickly. So I
decided to simply turn right at each junction and hope to
eventually find a way back to the thieves' den or out of the
catacombs entirely.

My feet are cold, slippery with blood where flints embedded
in the dirt have cut them. My mouth feels like I've swallowed fur.
The walls around me gleam damply in my mage light, but the
clay smells sour and I shudder to think I may soon have to try to
suck the moisture from it. The ache in my legs becomes pain, but
I don't dare sit down to rest in case I fall asleep and never wake up.

'Shall we turn right for a change?'

Swift doesn't bother to answer, let alone laugh. Well, it was a poor joke. We stumble into yet another tunnel.

Part of the wall detaches itself and reaches out dark arms to catch me. I dodge and smash at the creature with a fist of air. It's a golem, animated clay, come to smother me. My father has sent it. And I'm hallucinating. But mad or not, I shan't let it catch me. And I run on stumbling, wooden feet.

'Zara! Stop!'

The voice sounds familiar, but it's a trick and I wobble faster. Not fast enough: inhumanly strong arms grab me from behind. Panic gives way to fury. 'Let go!' I bellow and reach into my magic to blast the creature.

It flies away, but its arms hold me in a death grip. The tunnel shakes with the force of our collision as we slam into the wall. Somehow, in the moments of shock and pain, I realise the body I'm sprawled across is warm. I have a second to think: *How strange!* before I slip into silk-cold water. The water spins faster and faster as it slides down an endless drain of darkness, taking me with it.

21

I wake to two nagging certainties: my head hurts and I need to pee. But if I stand up to search out a chamber pot my head will most definitely explode. So I have to lie here and cross my legs. And try to remember . . . and then memory drops back into my head with a kick like a donkey and I groan and wish I could forget again.

'She's awake.'

'Go get the Mistress.'

I don't open my eyes. As long as I keep them shut, nothing can have happened. But that is foolish. I'm nearly seventeen, not seven. And I'd rather face Floster with an empty bladder and some dignity. I crack open one eye, then the other. The light hurts. My head feels like someone has played courtball with it.

A woman stares down at me. Mistress Quint. Her black-bead eyes shine with curiosity and a possessive satisfaction. 'There now,' she says, rubbing her hands together and smiling. 'I told the Mistress you would wake, and with nothing more than a headache for your trouble. Hurts, does it? But you haven't split your skull, just given yourself a bad bump.'

I lever myself up on my elbows and wince at the pain

stabbing my head, my neck. 'Ow!'

'Oh, good!' She sounds so happy I squint at her in amazement. '*Good?*'

She nods, swaying back and forth like a child's wobble doll. 'I've never had the chance to attend a mage. It's selfish, I know, but I can't help feeling it very fortunate that you hurt yourself. Not seriously, of course – just enough so I can study you. And good, yes . . . good because your blood and humours seem to work just the same as those of human beings. And so I can confirm that you are *not* a demon. No . . . not at all. Despite the old tales.'

'Never mind that.' The woman is mad but I have my own urgent preoccupations. 'I need to use a chamber pot. If . . .'

'Excellent! Please, let me assist you.'

She holds my arm as I sit up and slide my legs over the side of the bed. I close my eyes until the wave of nausea passes. When I stand up, Quint steadies me, keeps me upright as I hobble to the curtained cubicle, which hides the chamber pot in its wooden chair.

'I can manage, thank you,' I say firmly as I detach her arm. The look of dismay on her face startles a painful splurt of laughter, for it's as plain as her nose that the apothecary wants to watch me pee to make sure I do it the same as kine. I draw the curtain with a shaking hand, and when a few ticks later I push it open, Quint is standing in just the same spot, frustrated curiosity all over her round plump face.

Before she can rush past me to examine the contents of the pot, the chamber door opens and Mistress Floster sweeps into the room like a winter wind. I look into her eyes and any desire to laugh dries. Oh dear Time. She comes with a guard of two thieves. Both are armed with iron.

'Get her back in bed. She's about to fall over.' Floster's words are cold and calm and her eyes never leave mine. They are full of careful, directed fury.

What happened in the catacombs? Does she know I suspect her . . . that I saw Otter? How can she, unless he was the one . . . *Time's grace!*

Quint pushes me back onto the bed and wraps a woollen blanket around my shoulders, tucking it under my chin and chucking like a mother hen. For I'm shivering violently. Who was the man I attacked in the catacombs? Was it Otter? Is he dead?

'Well?' Floster stands at the foot of my bed, staring down at me with unforgiving eyes. What does she know and what does she guess? I decide the safest thing is to pretend to have forgotten everything. Then I can't have seen Otter.

'I don't know what . . .' I begin. 'I-I don't remember very much.' I can see she doesn't believe me.

'Then I'll have to explain. You left these rooms against my orders. You then went off and lost yourself in the catacombs and when Marcus attempted to rescue you, you attacked him.'

Marcus? It wasn't Otter. Or a golem . . . although that might have been better. I have used magic on a thief! On Floster's right-hand man no less! I put a hand to my aching head and groan.

'I-I don't remember,' I lie. 'Just something horrible, coming at me out of the dark. I panicked. I'm sorry . . . is he . . .?'

Her jaw tightens and she looks at me like she'd like to grab the pike from her guard, spit me on it and roast me for her supper. 'He's not hurt . . . much. He always did have a hard head.'

A fond, slightly sad smile flickers over her face and disappears as quickly as it came. I can almost see her push her feelings aside. Her cold eyes consider me and I'm very, very relieved she doesn't know that for one brief tick I read her emotions. She loves him! Floster and the Hound. Oh Lord Time. No wonder she's furious with me. I not only disobeyed her, I nearly killed her lover.

'I remember leaving –'

'You wear my safe-sworn, mage. But I can take it back. Why did you disobey my orders?'

'I'm wasted locked away down here!' I sit up, ignoring the pain in my head. 'You've had time to plan, to get an animal. Why are you waiting? I've told Philip everything of use I know. He doesn't need me now. I wanted to find you. To convince you that I can work as a spy without endangering anyone.'

Reluctantly, I add: 'I needn't go into the city. The closer I am to the animal the easier, but I don't need to be in the same place. I might even be able to do something from the part of the catacombs nearest the palazzo.' As much as I long for a sight of the sun, for the touch of a mountain breeze on my face, the important thing is freedom to fight – to save Aidan. 'When I'm above ground you can post a guard with me. If there was any danger of capture they could . . .' I wince.

'Cut your throat.' She smiles. 'Yes, I had thought of that already. But . . .' Her eyes narrow. 'The survival of my tribe depends on the catacombs remaining a secret. You might not, when the time came, want to die. You might prefer your father's mercies. You might kill the guard or turn the iron to rust. The instinct to live is strong, often surprising even the one on the point of death. And . . . mages are not to be trusted. Therefore I'll choose the time and place carefully.'

I sense freedom slipping away and grow reckless. 'Or do you have another reason for the delay, Mistress?'

'What do you mean?'

'Call Philip here. I will explain my meaning in front of him.'

'What do you know, mage? What have you . . .' She breaks off. I see realisation dawn. Oh Time, will she kill me out of hand now? Before I can tell her secret? Surely not in front of Quint, who stands to one side, nodding her head to and fro, watching us with shining button eyes.

'Welter, find Philip the Seeker and bring him here.' This to one of the guards, who turns and leaves at a run. 'No one else, only Philip,' Floster says to me. 'When Philip arrives, Mistress Quint, you're to go and tend Marcus.'

Quint pouts, but leaves without fuss when the door opens a few minutes later and Philip enters.

'Ah, you're awake, Zara. Good. You have worried me. Most irresponsible.' But he smiles, looking down at me with something I'm shocked to see is akin to fondness. Or perhaps only the possessiveness a Seeker shows towards his tools. But even so, the artist is genuinely pleased to see me alive. It's so unexpected that I feel oddly close to tears, so I turn and look at Floster.

'Well,' she says. 'Go on. Tell the Seeker what you saw last night. The thing that made you run away like an unbreeched

181

middling and lose yourself in the tunnels.'

'Someone visited you,' I begin. 'Someone who should not be here.' I'm confused now. Surely Philip can't be part of the conspiracy. Is Floster innocent after all? But then, what was Otter doing outside her chamber? I rub my aching neck and frown at the Mistress of Thieves. And she nods and raises an eyebrow.

'Otter. My fath— Benedict's Guardian. I saw him in the corridor outside your chamber. Dressed in thief's clothes, but it was him. I wasn't mistaken.'

'You weren't. It was Otter.' Floster seems to enjoy my confusion.

I stare at Philip. He frowns and sighs. 'Well, that is unfortunate.'

'Unfortunate?' My mouth drops open. Doesn't he understand? 'Otter is my father's man! Guardians are trained . . . if you can call it that. Their minds are invaded until they lose themselves. They become an extension of the will of the mage they protect. If Otter was here . . . if he was meeting with *her* . . . then, don't you see? She must be the traitor.'

'Someday I must tutor you on deductive reasoning, Zara.' Philip's voice is abstracted, as though everything I've just said is unimportant.

'I don't understand . . .'

'Otter works for me,' Floster says.

'No, Mistress.' Philip shakes his head. 'The Guardian works for himself. But he is our ally.' This to me.

'I don't believe it!'

I look from Seeker to thief. They're convinced they're right.

But I know Benedict. My father's machinations run deep. What can he mean by this? Otter is his creature, I'm sure of it. I am a mage; I know what they don't – the horror that is the life of a Tribute child picked to be trained as a guard. The cleansing of young, flexible minds. The harshness of the physical training. I know how many fail one or the other and are culled, like runts in a litter of piglets.

But Otter found you with Aidan, a voice in my head argues. *He didn't betray you then. Perhaps Floster is right.*

No! Otter is my father's Guardian. That's all I need to know. 'You can't trust him!' I cry. 'My father has planted him here. I know it. You don't understand. Guardians can't betray their mage. It's . . . impossible. They would die, or go mad. It can't happen!'

'If you're right, Benedict knows about the catacombs. So why hasn't the Archmage sent his army to wipe us out?' Floster shakes her head. 'No, mage. I am not mistaken. It isn't Benedict who holds the upper hand here – it's me. Otter will help me drive the fiend from Asphodel!'

Her voice rings loud and harsh; I wince as the noise pounds my aching head. I was wrong: Floster isn't a traitor. So I will live . . . for now. But what of Otter? And does he know I'm alive?

'Don't tell him . . .' My voice fades and I lean back, wincing. The pain in my head beats like the drums of a hundred troubadours inside my skull. Why hasn't my father invaded? Too many questions . . . and I'm too tired to make my fuzzy brain work.

Suddenly Quint is back in the room. 'She must sleep. You've overtired her!' The apothecary's voice is querulous and bossy. I

22

Two days later my head no longer seems about to explode like an over-ripe pumpkin, but I still don't understand why Otter was in the catacombs, or why Floster is so certain she can trust him. So I wait for something to happen and do my best not to go mad.

I read Philip's small collection of books, trying not to think about Aidan, who fills my thoughts more and more each day. He must believe I'm dead. Does he care? Does he think of me at all? Has he given up hope of escape? Is he even alive?

I lurch out of bed, then wince as my head reminds me that sudden movements aren't a good idea. At least I am standing up when the door to the chamber opens without warning and the Hound enters.

I haven't seen him since the night I lost myself in the catacombs. And I didn't really see him then. His left eye is bruised a rich purple and yellow beneath his brown skin, and his expression as he looks at me is sour. I guess that a black eye is the least of it, and his head is probably even sorer than mine.

'I . . . I'm sorry . . . I didn't know it was you.'

His face remains carved from wood, the expression

unchanging. I push aside a flare of irritation. 'I panicked!' I say. 'I behaved like a fool. There. I've said it.'

The Hound smiles . . . I think he smiled. It's gone too quickly to be sure. But the wood seems to soften to clay.

'You're wanted.'

'That makes a change!' I snap before I can stop myself.

The Hound's eyes narrow in warning. 'Mind your tongue, Zara.'

I'm briefly, irrationally pleased that he never calls me 'mage'. I'm a person to him, even if not one he likes. Then all thoughts fly like swooping bats out my head when he says: 'The Mistress don't have a sense of humour where you're concerned, so keep a civil tongue in your head. I'm to take you to her now. She's gonna give you your orders. You and I have work to do.'

The brazen disc of the sun hangs in a white sky. Grey-green cedar trees crawl up the slopes of the nearby mountains. I stagger out of the darkness of the cave that serves as a back door to the catacombs, and raise my face like a blind kitten, basking in the warmth, thinking of nothing but the touch of the sun on my skin. The wind carries the scent of warm cedar. Of thyme and wild rosemary. Of growth. Of life. After an eightweek in the house of the dead.

'So beautiful.' I haven't seen the face of the earth for a lifetime. I'd forgotten.

'Yes.' The Hound stands beside me at the lip of the cave. He's staring down at the valley spread before us, waiting, I realise, for me to recover. Now he places the cage on the ground in front of us. The sparrowhawk inside shifts from foot to foot, shaking its hooded head irritably. 'Life ought to be enough, I always think.' He opens the cage, lifts out the bird on a gauntlet-clad hand and stands with a thief's uncanny stillness, stroking the bird's chest with a finger. 'But it ain't. You can ask your daddy why, sometime. Then you can kill him.'

Our eyes meet.

'You don't think we'll win.'

'We might.' His voice holds no belief. Before I can protest, the Hound speaks again: 'What matters is fighting.' He jerks his head towards the cave. 'I like living with the bones back there. Reminds me dead is dead. It's how you live that's important. Fear has kept us slaves for longer than the oldest of them bones can remember. But we're fighting now. Fight and win or fight and die. Either way, it's better.'

He points across the valley towards the largest of the foothills on the city's edge. 'Reports say they're gathering at the mages' temple.'

'The Temple of Time.'

He shrugs indifference. 'Must be important if Benedict is worried about spies in the city. The Council of Mages.' A hungry tone in his voice. His eyes fasten on mine. 'You go and listen, little bird. And come back and tell us what you hear.' He's holding the hawk tightly under one arm. 'Ready? Got your bearings?'

I nod. Every summer solstice I can remember, I have attended the sacrifice to Time's grace. Already, in my mind's eye, I see the place. The wide path leading to the round white temple waiting on the summit of the hill. The dust of the marble paving where I stood on aching legs as a small child. The sound of crickets. The grove of gnarled olive trees encircling the hilltop like sentinels. That is where I'll go. The olive trees.

I gaze across the valley. 'Ready,' I say. And sit cross-legged on the ground. I separate out a narrow thread of consciousness and wait, heart thudding in anticipation.

Marcus lifts the hood from the sparrowhawk. In that moment, I enter the hawk's mind.

Airborne. We scream in defiance as we unfurl our wings, slash the air and soar up to greet the sky. Higher and higher, until the sky grows brittle and we can see the earth curve to meet the distant sea. We stretch our wings flat, and circle. Seeking. There. That place. Fold the wings, swoop. Feet tucked, head swivelling, eyes scanning. And there: prey! A rabbit scuttles and the hawk folds its wings to dive.

Ruthlessly, I wrench the creature's mind away; our flight stumbles. For a moment, the air refuses us and we fall. I stretch our wings. Two strong beats and we are once more flying towards the olive trees.

I see them coming as we approach the hill. Seven archmages approach the hill from seven directions, on horseback. Following each is a small phalanx of Tribute guards, bronze helmets shining in the glare of the midday sun. They have been height-matched, like carriage horses. Male and female, they march in perfect step, shouldered pikes rising and falling rhythmically. I hear the sound of their sandals slapping the earth like the beating of a drum.

I must make haste. Our wings beat ever faster; we whip through the air, circle the hilltop once, spying out the temple. It sits in solitude on a circle of marble paving broken by Time

188

and colonised by basking lizards. They scuttle to safety as the flying arrowhead of our shadow touches them. I keep the hawk's mind and choose the tree. That one. Its arthritic limbs sprawl towards the temple, offering shade. Flap, glide. Alight. Grasp the branch with strong talons, balance, edge close beneath sheltering silver leaves. And wait . . .

The sound of marching ceases. The guards have been left halfway up the hill. Kine are not allowed in the temple precincts. Our sharp hawk's ears listen as one by one, the archmages mount the path to the temple.

My father comes first. And I am grateful for the alien nature of the hawk's mind. Even so, the rage of the child Zara flares and runs through us like wildfire. It takes all my control to keep our body silent and still. Our talons ache to tear. To pierce his cold lizard's eyes and tear the heart from his body. We shiver and settle, ruffling our feathers, our hawk's eyes staring, watching. And thankful that even an adept cannot sense another mage in the body of an animal. I am free from threat of discovery. As long as none of the mages attempt to use the hawk themselves. So best if they do not know we are here. I tighten my control on the hawk.

My father occupies the tallest bit of ground, directly beneath my tree. He places a wicker basket beside him and stands silently watching his fellow archmages approach.

I recognise them all. Merze, the youngest. A tall, intense-looking woman from the north, her hair the flaxen colour common in that region. She nods at my father, a slight smile passing over her face as she notices how he has positioned himself. She turns and watches as Goddart and Tressam appear, heads bent in animated discussion. Gossipy, plump Goddart used to be one of my favourite visitors to the palazzo. He always had a sweetmeat for me, and a kind word. Tressam, in contrast, is narrow and hatchet-faced. A thin, dour man.

The last three stroll up the path. Wonset, the oldest archmage and my father's predecessor as leader of the alliance. A frightening woman with the hunched back of age, her hair white as bleached linen and eyes the eerie blue-green of glacial ice. She always looked at me with ill-disguised loathing and I knew, without having ever been told, that she hated my mother.

Falu, on the other hand, is straight as a willow tree. Tall and dark-haired still, though older than my father. With a quiet strength of will like a deep drowning well. Lastly, thin-lipped and silent, Aris.

Aris the Blood-Drinker, the kine call him. I believe him to be mad. Notorious even among mages as a killer of kine, a rapist and torturer. Evil rises from him like the stink of decaying corpses. As the mages gather in a circle, facing my father, I notice those nearest move away from Aris, as though from a corpse suspected of harbouring plague.

'We shall make offering before we begin, to ask Time's grace to aid our aims and confound our enemies.'

My father lifts the wicker basket from the ground beside him and the hawk hears the fluttering of a bird within. It will be a white dove. At the thought of the blood about to be spilled, we pant in hunger and lust. Nearly, the beast slips from me. I wrest control of the bird's instincts with a cruelty I've never used before. I'm sorry for it, but too much is at stake here.

The mages filter into the darkness of the temple and I take

the opportunity to shrug the ache from our wing muscles, to shift our feet and settle our feathers. Then the scent of blood enters our nose, carried on a stray breeze, and once more I'm battling the hawk. Forcing it into stillness. I succeed just in time as my father reappears, cleansing the blood from his hands with an elegant blast of magic. I taste his strength. Watch his every movement. Hating. Fearing. A sudden flicker in my thoughts, a mental hiccup, warns that my struggles to control the hawk are draining me. I'm tiring.

'A report, Benedict.' Wonset rests her hands, twisted with arthritis inside fingerless lace mittens, upon the silver head of her cane. Her voice is querulous. 'Have you rooted out the last of the vermin? Have you traced the source of it? It must come from the Makers! We must stamp it out. I'll not have these, these "Seekers" spreading their poison in my city. I hold you responsible! Eleanor's legacy! If you had –'

'Enough.' My father barely raises his voice, but the old woman falls silent. No one mentions my mother. Even I am shocked that Wonset has broken the tradition of silence. 'The Makers are not involved. This rebellion is home-brewed. There are no Seekers left alive in Asphodel. And soon I will exterminate the last of the verminous animals, the thieves.'

'Others have made that claim before you,' Tressam snaps, with an irritated wave of his hand. 'Thieves breed and spread like rats. Kill one and two spring up in its place. Control is all we can ever hope to achieve. But thieves do not threaten our existence. The Makers –'

'Don't believe it, Tressam! I've told you before that the thieves are organised and in league with the Seekers.'

'You give them too much credit, Benedict.' Aris's voice slithers into the air. 'Thieves cannot *think*.' His laugh is chilling. 'Set traps and snap their heads off! But worry about them? I think not. Sport, dear fellow. That's all they are.'

My father makes a gesture of impatience. 'I haven't called you here to argue about the intellectual abilities of kine. The Seekers are finished. I'll gather in the last of them soon enough . . . when I'm ready.'

I remember Otter. Does Benedict know about the catacombs after all? Has he been waiting for the right moment to come in and wipe us out?

My father's voice breaks through my thoughts: 'I have been playing with the rebels for some time now, but I have decided it is best to cleanse Asphodel of the infestation once and for all before I destroy the Makers.'

'Very grand, Benedict. The blonde Merze laughs. 'You've never lacked ambition.' She has been his lover, I realise with a shock. And resents him.

But now Falu speaks, and the dark woman's intense voice commands attention. 'The Maker whom you hold hostage. He is the key? You're a clever man, Benedict. But I fail to see how one boy can destroy an entire city.'

'The key. An appropriate analogy, Falu.' My father's voice takes on a respect I've not heard him use with any of the others. 'After generations of war we are no closer to destroying the Maker cities. The Maker kine breed like rats while our numbers decline with each generation. So I have fashioned a key which will open a door in the Wall. Once their defences are breeched we can take their cities one by one. Final victory awaits! We merely need reach out and take it. Think, friends, of the immortality that will be ours when we rid the world of the Makers and their infernal machines forever!'

'So.' Tressam's voice is sour. 'You want us to commit to all-out war. To offer up our warrior mages and Tributes to your will. I warn you, Benedict. I will need to hear much, much more before I agree to any such thing.'

'You will have to explain, Benedict,' Falu agrees in a quiet voice.

'Blood sport, Benedict.' Aris laughs, steps towards my father. 'I can hardly wai—'

As he speaks, my hawk's ears hear a distant twang, and Aris chokes on his words. A slender, flint-tipped arrow shaft protrudes from his throat. I hear a horrible gurgling and the man totters and falls face down on the stones. A feathered shaft sticks up from the back of his neck, the feathers swaying in the breeze.

Silence.

And then, in a swirl of black, my father is airborne. One by one, the mages fly up, robes flapping black, crimson, blue, gold. Circling the hilltop. Human eagles, hunting. I shiver and hunch deep in our feathers. The hawk is disturbed by the scent of human blood. It longs to escape. But I dare not fly now. I should break the connection and return to my body . . . but I must know what happens. It should have been my father lying there dead. If only Aris had not stepped forward . . . Please Time, let the assassin escape! Is it the Hound? Surely not. He is with my body. He promised . . .

And then, before I can decide to go or stay, I see the mages circle low and descend in a flock. They disappear into the olive trees on the far side of the hill. And a human cry: a roar of frustration and rage. My father's voice.

I wait. Fighting to hold on as the hawk struggles to regain its will. I grip its mind desperately and . . . there. They emerge from beneath the trees. My father stalks ahead, eyes blazing. In front of him, floating in the air, is a thief. A woman. It only takes one glance to know she is dead. And suddenly I understand. Mistress Quint must have supplied her with poison. The assassin killed, then killed herself. Oh ye gods. My heart swells with so heavy and sore a pain I fear it will break inside my chest.

As the lifeless body is flung on the ground near me I see a young woman of no more than twenty-five. Once she was pretty. Now her features are twisted in agony. Whatever Quint gave her, it wasn't an easy death. I look at my father's face and rejoice at the bitterness I see there.

I will pay you out, dear Father. For this and so much more.

'You see?!' Benedict is raging still. 'A thief! Lying in wait. They knew of this meeting. Now do you doubt me? The thieves are our greatest enemies. Aris thought them animals. Well, they may be, but that animal killed him.'

His teeth are bared in rage. And fear. Joy! The great Benedict has felt Death's kiss. He knows who was meant to die today. I look down at the dead thief. Sorrow for her death. For her bravery. But Aris, at least, will never murder another kine.

'It isn't safe to remain, Benedict!' Goddart wrings his hands in fear, watching as the guards scour the olive grove, allowed this once into the temple precinct. A group of them draws near. Soon the hawk will be discovered. I must leave. But . . .

'We will need to meet in safer surroundings. May I suggest indoors?' Wonset's voice is acid.

The guards draw near, stabbing the low bushes, poking their pikes into the tops of the trees. I see Otter, and wonder again where his loyalties lie. Did he know of the assassin? Does he know I sit here, inside the hawk?

'You must accept my hospitality tonight,' says my father. 'We will continue our meeting after dinner. No one, I promise, will disturb us.' Benedict's voice is chill and calm again. But I feel his rage vibrating in the air. 'Aris will have to disappear. We can think up a reason later but it cannot become known that an archmage has been killed by kine. Wonset, deal with his people. We'll send an emissary to his city. But this assassination did not happen.'

Deal with his people? I look into the old woman's face and read the answer. Horror loosens my grip on the hawk. The bird screams, flaps its wings and takes flight.

I hear Falu's voice: 'What is that? There in the tree! I'll take it . . .'

I spin into darkness, rewinding the thread of my consciousness. Fainting, shivering, I fall back into my own body.

When I open my eyes, I am weeping. I look at the Hound and cannot speak. He reaches out and holds me tight. I cling to him, shaking, crying. Then fall head first into a deep white nothingness of exhaustion.

23

'Give her more, Mistress Quint.'

I've never liked mead. Quint pushes the cup of golden liquid into my hands. I frown at it.

'Drink, Zara. There isn't much time.'

I look at Floster. My heart feels frost-blasted. 'Who was she?'

The Mistress's face softens with sadness. 'A good, brave girl,' she says. 'And I need you to make sure she didn't die for nothing. Come on, Zara. You have to be strong enough to go into the palazzo tonight. We must know what they are planning.'

'All those Tributes. Aris's guards. They . . .'

'You can do nothing for them. Only for others. Or it will never stop. You know this, Zara. This is why you chose to join us. Don't give up now.'

'I can't . . .' I take a breath. Of course I can. I must. It's true I'm tired to the point of exhaustion. That my body is still shivering. But the mead brings a welcome numbness. It gives me the courage to finally ask: 'Did you know Benedict would kill the guards?'

'It was Benedict who should have been lying with an arrow in his throat. Mirri was my best archer.' Floster's voice is dry.

She sighs. 'At least the other Tributes will survive. It was only Aris's who had to be silenced.'

'Otter. He was there.'

'Yes.' Floster's eyes and voice give away nothing. 'Concentrate on your job, Zara.' She gestures at the rat winding round and round inside the cage sitting at the Hound's feet. I look up into his brown eyes and thank the gods that if I have to do this thing, at least it's this man who'll be my companion. I know, now, why Floster depends on him so fundamentally. He is like an oak tree. He gazes back, unsmiling.

'We need to go,' he says. 'Wrap her up warm. The tunnels are cold, and the girl goes very chill when she's in the beasts. Don't stay too long out of your body tonight, Zara, or I think you won't be coming back. No good if you find out what the bastards are up to but die before you can tell us.'

'Off with you.' Floster hesitates, then seizes my hand in a brief, crushing grip. 'The gods look after you, Zara, daughter of Eleanor.'

The Hound and I sit in the guardroom I stumbled into that first night: the night Twiss brought me here. It's the closest we can get to the palazzo without leaving the catacombs. I'm wearing a thick woollen jacket over my leather tunic. The rat is twitching and pacing inside its cage. It senses something is about to happen: everyone says rats are clever. I don't like rats.

'It's time, Zara.' The Hound knows I'm frightened. But I don't mind. I can trust him to kill me. Which suddenly strikes me as so funny I laugh out loud.

'You all right?'

I've worried him. I just grin back. That old feeling of reckless excitement is sweeping aside fear. It's time. I glance from the Hound to the thief whose job it is to take the rat into the palazzo cellars and release it. A woman in her thirties, not a middling – I suspect Floster doesn't trust them where I'm concerned. She's quiet and so still that if I didn't know she was there I wouldn't see her. Again, I wonder about this talent thieves possess . . . and firmly push aside the distraction.

I nod at the Hound. Take a deep breath, gathering my will, concentrating. And it's so easy. I was born to do this. It feels so right . . . perfect. Doing magic cannot be evil. It can't. Only people are evil. Magic just . . . is. It's the last thought I have in my own body.

Good dark. Stay in the dark, deep places. Creep along walls; hide in corners. And sniff. Smell my way. Sharp, rich, rotten, sweet. Stone, dead and cold. Wood, dry and chewy. Gnaw it bite it. No time. Want to chew. NO! Up. Up to the place where bigs live. Smell beetle! Pounce. Catch it catch it. Hold it tight. Wriggly. Crunch it up. Snick-snack chewy sharp-sweet. Swallow. Lovely . . . More beetle. NO!

The rat is tricky. Wily, slippery. Far the cleverest animal I've ever mind-controlled.

We crawl. Rat-Zara. She makes us go up and up, skittering on our feet on the cold earth. Smelling the dust of the stones. Through the lovely, kind dark up to where the bigs lie in wait to trap, to knock, to hurt. With their dogs and firewoodsticks killing dark. She won't let us go back to the dark smelly places where safe dark lovely smelly rotten. On. Light. Ssssssss. Lash tail. Light kills. Smell it out. Curvet tumble slither slide creep crawl run and run faster than bigs can. Through caverns of cold stone and stickfires. Stinks of fire of bigs.

The rat fights me to the last, lashing its tail and chittering as I force it to slink along corridors, creeping along the line where wall and floor meet, scurrying from shadow to shadow. Closer and closer to my father's library.

The palazzo buzzes with activity. High alert. Guardian and Tribute slaves rush to and fro. But none see us. Finally, the rat's blurry, weak eyes show me the door I seek: the door to my father's library.

No light seeps under the door. The corridor is empty except for the regular pacing of the guards on their rounds. The archmages sit long over their dinner. But it is here they will discuss the dark thing my father is planning. There are too many ears in the dining hall. Servants' ears, kine ears; and my father has new proof that he is spied upon. This room – his inner sanctum – this is where he will bring them.

Squeeze, wriggle, ooze. Our bones shift and soften and we push and scrabble beneath the door, feeling in front of us with wriggling whiskers. Lovely dark. But . . . we hiss and the fur on our neck and shoulders bristles in fear and hate. There has been a catbeast here.

And suddenly I have a fight on my hands. The rat twists and turns, thrashing on the floor as it fights to rid itself of my presence. It's taken me by surprise; nearly, I lose my hold. But this is the library. This is where Swift died. All the black fury of that night returns, and I bear my will down on the beast. And it is stilled. I loosen my hold just in time, before I crush its mind altogether.

Whimpering, the rat scurries into the place I have chosen: beneath the clock shrine. The shrine is made of oily cedar wood. Carved feet lift the base two inches from the floor. More than enough room for a small rat. The smell bites our nostrils, but will cover our scent as well. We swivel our head from side to side, peering through the dark at my father's chair. We are a few feet away, but see only shadowy blue, purple and grey blurs. I doubt that there will be much improvement when the candles and oil lamps are lit. Our sharp, clever ears are our weapons tonight, not our weak eyes. And despite the loud ticking overhead – Aidan's work – we will be able to hear any word spoken in this room.

We crouch on the cold stone floor. The rat pants in distress and shivers, but no longer fights me. I feel a stab of self-loathing. I'm doing exactly what Aluid wanted; what I refused to do, what I've always hated – crushing the will of the animal I'm controlling. But I have no choice. For Swift. And Aidan. Tonight I will learn why my father took him hostage. Tonight I finally keep my promise to try to help him.

Even with the ticking of the clock overhead, I lose all track of time. It seems hours before footsteps approach and light spreads like water beneath the door. Our heart pounds in our chest and our neck fur bristles as the door swings inwards. My father's voice, translated through the high-pitched hearing of a rat, booms and cracks through the room. It takes minutes of struggle and panic before I adjust my brain to the sounds and hear words rather than concussions.

The mages lounge or perch on the chairs set out for them, doing their best to ignore the fact that my father's chair sits in front of his desk, facing them, like a throne. And that he sits in it like an emperor. Even through the rat's weak eyes, I can see the arrogance of his posture. His voice makes it even clearer. Benedict is ordering minions, not discussing plans with equals. Aris's assassination seems to have knocked the fight out of his fellow archmages as thoroughly as I have overwhelmed the rat.

As my hearing adjusts, I listen to a conversation already well begun:

'... but we have no guarantee that the Makers will collapse in confusion as you suggest. So we kill the Council? So what? There will be other politicians. And don't forget the soldiers. They're the ones who matter.'

'The head of their army will be present, Falu.' My father's voice is patient, but I can hear the irritation behind the calm tones. 'And you underestimate the impact on the city when the entire Council is wiped out in their own chamber. At the same time, we mount our attack. We will have cut the head off the body; the arms and legs will be leaderless. Yes, they will fight. But not long or effectively. Our warrior mages and Tribute army will wipe the city of Gengst-on-the-Wall from the earth. And with the Wall breached, the most powerful of the Maker cities in ruins and every last soul killed. Well ...' His laugh twists even the rat's strong stomach. 'If we work together, we will exterminate the Maker race within weeks.'

'And who is the adept you've chosen to inhabit the hostage Maker's body? They will need to be impeccable. I know few who I would trust with such a task.'

In my shock I barely recognise Wonset's cold, quivering old voice. *Aidan!* This is why my father brought him here. Benedict

201

plans to wipe his mind and send his possessed body home, hiding the mage who inhabits it. There will be nothing left of him! Of the thing that makes him himself. It's worse than death! Aidan will be a golem made of flesh. A golem holding the will and magic of a mage bent on murder.

Bile rises in the rat's mouth. We shiver. The rat whimpers. I'm too stunned to notice the animal's distress as my father's voice booms and echoes bizarrely through the room.

'Why, I myself will inhabit the Maker.' Benedict's voice is rich with anticipation. 'Who else?'

Laughter. Laughter from half a dozen voices.

'And who will repair the clocks when they break again?' This from Falu. 'If you kill all the Makers, who will repair Time's shrines?'

'The Maker is training an apprentice. They have nearly finished the repairs on the Great Clock in the Council Chamber. When that is done we are free to proceed.'

The rat and I crouch, shivering and shocked, staring into a blurry blankness of evil. Aidan. Oh gods, Aidan! Then the rat squeaks and races like a lightning flash for the door. Before I can think; before I can stop it.

A grey monster armed with gnashing fangs and slashing claws jumps out of the dark. Attacks. We veer, dart. We scream. We whirl, run madly one way and the next. The voices of evil roar and cheer.

POUNCE! Sharp claws dig into our back. Stabbing pain, unbearable pressure. Our spine snaps and the agony stops. Now there is only a quick suffocating darkness. So this . . . this is Death.

24

'Clever puss.' The human's voice purrs. It is pleased with me.

Hands stroke me, lift me up to sit on a warm lap. I press my nose into the hand. Fingers rub the special spot behind my ears and I shiver in ecstasy. They have taken away the rat. I wanted it. I lick my lips, savouring the taste of rat, then curl up on the human's lap.

Voices float above my head. Back and forth. Distracting. Keeping me from sleeping. I open a sleepy eye, and . . .

. . . *I am Zara!*

The cat-me body stiffens, spine arching, claws unsheathing, digging into . . . my father.

'Ahh!' An ungentle hand scoops me up, throws me. I arch and twist in mid-air, land sliding and skidding on all four paws, and run for the door. It opens before me. One of the mages, Merze, I think. I get a whiff of her delight at my father's discomfiture as I wheel out the door into the corridor, running for my life.

My life.

I was in the rat. And then the cat . . . *this cat* . . . attacked without warning. It must have been in the library the whole time. The rat knew. And I squashed its will, didn't listen to its instinct to flee.

Stupid. And so I wasn't prepared for the cat. I remember desperately trying to detach myself from the rat as it died. Flinging my consciousness free from the dead pathways of its brain before they dragged me into death. But I had no time to find my way back to the catacombs. I was disorientated and floating. *Free floating!*

Inside the cat, I shiver with horror. So close to disembodiment . . . and the Hound's reluctant knife.

I must have somehow found the strength to transfer to the cat before I floated away entirely. I've never heard of any mage managing such a feat, not even my father. Another time I would be pleased. But I'm simply terrified. And desperately worried.

I'm growing weaker. The cat is easier to control than the rat, but even so it takes many ticks before I can slow its headlong flight. I encourage it to hide, flanks heaving, heart pattering, in a corner. I must think! It's so hard. I'm tired. I want to let go . . . I need to return to my body. I know where it is now. I sense the connecting thread of consciousness. Dwindled, but there. I should go now, before it's too late, before the thread weakens, thins, and snaps like the rat's spine. Floster and Philip must learn of Benedict's plan. We have to stop him.

But first, Aidan. I must tell Aidan. Now.

Ignoring the numbness chilling my consciousness more and more each minute, I tighten my grip on the cat. And we run. Run and run through corridors, sliding on the marble as we turn – right, left, right. Dodge through a half-open door under the feet of a cursing guard and on into the courtyard. And now. Slow. Pad on unconcerned paws to the entrance of the prison and saunter in. The guard barely gives us a glance. Dozens of cats and kittens prowl the palazzo, ratting and mousing.

So easy. Hope lightens our paws. Scamper up the stairs, ears flattened, tail streaming behind. And smell him almost at once. The part of me that is Zara senses him immediately; as clearly as seeing. He is asleep, on that small bed. Behind the door . . . the door . . . the *locked* door. *Oh, pestilence!*

I growl and scratch at the wooden barrier separating us. Furious. Furry and furious. And am struck by a sudden image of how we must look; a small fluffy lilac-grey cat spitting and clawing at a prison door. If a cat could laugh, we'd be howling. Instead, we sit, curl up a hind leg and lick it furiously, soothing our embarrassment at having been ridiculous.

And then. Narrowing our eyes to slits, we peer past our leg at the door. We slink into a waiting crouch, as though yet another juicy rat sits quivering its whiskers in front of us. And I open the door. The fragment of my consciousness inside the cat finds the strength to command the iron of the bolt to unstick, to shift, to slide backwards. And the latch of the unbolted door to lift. We shoulder the door open and slip inside.

He sleeps. We jump up onto the bed, crouch beside him. Watching. The dark is not dark to us. In the half-light, the starlight and the light of the new weakling moon shining in at the window, we see him. Relaxed in sleep, Aidan is surprisingly beautiful. His hair is corn-coloured silk, smooth as the pelt of a hill leopard. His mouth curves, full lips soft and tender.

Slowly, we balance on his chest, rising and falling gently under the blanket. He is naked. He smells . . . oh, he smells of wonder, of spices and secrets. Of boy. Of man. We reach out a gentle, soft paw and pat his cheek. He sighs. Snores.

Aidan! Wake up!

He groans. And snores on.

We unsheathe our claws. Only a fraction. And . . . pat!

'Ow!'

We leap back as the boy jerks up in the bed, clutching his face. A bit too much claw, then.

'What the . . .' He breaks off and stares at us, befuddlement giving way to confusion. His head jerks around. He stares at the open door and his mouth drops open. It's funny. I'd laugh if I could. Instead I wait as he climbs slowly out of bed and then do my best to trip him up by winding in and out between his feet.

I wish I could take him with me now. Lead him out the prison and float him magically to the catacombs on the same strand of consciousness I must soon follow. But I can't. All I can do is warn him.

Aidan stares down at me. And I see wariness turn to fear in his eyes. He reaches out a shaking hand and pushes the door closed. He retreats to his bed and sits on it. 'What are you?'

I open my mouth. And miaow. Oh, why can't animals talk? It would make life so much easier! Slowly, I shake my head back and forth, showing my inability, and Aidan's fear grows in his blue eyes. He guessed . . . and now he knows. Knows a mage is in his room wearing the body of a cat.

His fear makes me nervous. He might do something foolish. And I am nearing the end of my powers. Strength to concentrate is fading. I need to warn him and get out. My eyes search the floor, find a patch of dirt in a puddle of moonlight. I trot to it. Turn and look over my head at the boy until he slowly gets to his feet and reluctantly joins me.

I reach out a paw, and write in the dirt.

DANGER

He drops to his knees beside me and as he reads the word, his eyes grow huge. I pat the dirt with an awkward paw. He catches on quickly, smooths the dirt in readiness and I write again. Nine more times I write with a clumsy, slow paw. And each time Aidan wipes the words from the dirt, hands shaking as the meaning of my message is revealed.

BENEDICT

TREACHERY

BIG CLOCK

WHEN WORKS

YOU DIE

DELAY REPAIRS

WILL RETURN

FOR YOU

ZARA

As he reads the last word, the fear in his face is replaced by wonder. Then a new horror wipes it away. I flinch back as Aidan leaps up with a strangled cry to grab the blanket from his bed. It's not until he wraps it around his waist and hips that I realise he's mortified that I've seen him naked.

The cat and I sit back on our haunches, too tired even to think of laughing. Our head drops. We are shivering with exhaustion.

'Zara? Are you ill? What's wrong?' He kneels, reaches out a tentative hand. I can almost feel him wondering if he should pet me or not. So I lift my head and touch my nose to his. A cat's kiss. I give him a brief, tired purr. Then turn and walk to the door.

Obediently, he opens it. 'I know you'll come back for me. I trust you, Zara.'

I give him one last look. He is frowning after me, worry dark in his eyes. But he knows what he must do. He shuts the door behind me. And I perform the last job of the night.

It's killing me. I'm nearly spent. But the door must be re-bolted. Scraping, slow, heavy, the iron bolt slides home. And in that moment, I release myself from the cat, struggle, weak and fainting, up and up, seeking the slender thread of consciousness. Find it at last. So thin. So worn. Winding like a single strand of gossamer silk out of the prison, through the palazzo. A frail thread, rubbed to the point of breaking by Time.

I'm so tired. I watch the thread of my mind twisting its way on and on. I pull myself along it, hand over hand. It hurts. Not with the sharp pain of a burn, but the deathly deep ache of tiredness. And with a sudden despair I realise I can't do it. I've waited too long, outlasted my strength. It's too far, too difficult. I haven't the strength or the will. No one can do the impossible. Let me give up. Please. Let me rest.

Time for me to die. Time for the Hound's gentle knife.

I let go.

Oh, the relief! Just slide away. Fall . . .

I feel the Hound willing me to come back but I don't listen. I can't do it. I'm too tired. I've fought for so long. Let it stop now. Let someone else do it.

I trust you, Zara.

Oh, it hurts. I didn't know anything could hurt so very much. But what can I do? So many he's trusted have let him down.

He needs me. Swift needed me and I failed her. I can't – I won't – do that again.

I wind the slow path of agony home to my cold body.

25

Time passes. I'm indifferent to the god's presence. But I am sometimes aware of Mistress Quint nodding and bobbing beside me, of Philip's voice in the background. Why is he so sad? Something is worrying him.

I cannot seem to get warm. Quint keeps a hot brick wrapped in flannel at my feet, covers me in a mountain of blankets, and still I shiver. I drift in and out of strange dreams. Swift visits me. And Aidan. And the Hound. But . . . where is Twiss? I miss her scowling face.

'She keeps asking for a cat,' says the apothecary's voice.

'Get her one, then!' Floster sounds angry. She frightens me. Is she the traitor? Almost, I am interested enough to open my eyes; to come out of the hidden place. But then the dreams beckon and I drift away.

When I return there is a kitten curled on my chest, purring. I reach out and pull it to me, snuggle it beneath my chin. The kitten's soft fur and hot, sour breath warm me. At last, I begin to thaw.

'It wasn't this cat. It was another.'

Mistress Quint is, for once, elsewhere. The Hound is my nurse today. He sits in the apothecary's chair with its flowery cushions, looking extraordinarily out of place. But unworried. Little worries a man who takes Death as his companion.

'Which cat was it then, Zara?'

'I've told you.'

'You've told us nothing. You've been Elsewhere, child. I never thought mages could go there. Guess I was wrong.'

'*Elsewhere?*'

'It's where we thieves go when we don't want to be seen. Or heard. Mostly we go shallow; sometimes deep. Go too deep and you never come back.'

I frown at him, understanding none of it. But it doesn't matter. Nothing matters but Aidan, and Benedict's evil plan.

'What do you mean, I haven't told you? You have to know! About Aidan. About the Makers! We have to stop my father . . .'

I struggle to sit up, dislodging the kitten, which squeals as it slides down my chest, roly-poly. Then rights itself and scampers down to attack the moving mound of my feet beneath the blankets. 'I must have told you . . .'

He shakes his head. 'You said stuff but nothing that made much sense. Who's Swift?'

Horror rises up my body like chill water.

'How long have I been like this? How long since I went into the rat?'

He watches me, eyes cautious. 'Three days past. You nearly died, child. I told you not to stay so long.'

'Three days . . .' I whisper the words, too horrified to shout. 'I need to talk to Floster. And Philip. *Now!*'

'Calm down! They're coming. I sent Mistress Quint scurrying off after 'em when we saw you'd come to yourself at last. How're you feeling?'

'Well enough!' I pull myself up to sitting, irritated by the weakness that leaves me breathless, heart pounding after such a slight effort. The kitten growls and tries to kill my toes.

The door to the sick chamber swings wide and Mistress Floster stalks in, closely followed by Philip. No sign of Quint, I notice. Good. I don't know who the traitor is or was. But what I have to say now is too important to trust to any beyond these three people.

'Benedict is going to attack the Makers,' I say as soon as the door is secured behind them.

Floster halts at the foot of my bed, eyes gleaming. 'Go on.'

'The Maker hostage, Aidan.' As I think of him, panic attacks: my heart doubles its efforts. I take a slow deep breath, and the room stops spinning. 'As soon as he finishes repairing the Great Clock, Benedict will pretend to return him to his people as a sign of goodwill.'

'Ambush?' Philip guesses.

'No.' I swallow, pushing down the tide of nausea. 'The boy will be a golem. An empty hulk controlled by an adept. My father intends to wipe his mind completely and enter into him himself. And then after Aidan is welcomed back into the city, Benedict will chose his moment and kill Aidan's father and the rest of the Council. Then he'll go after their military leaders. At the same time, the combined warrior mages of the seven cities will attack Gengst-on-the-Wall along with their Tribute armies.'

A sharp intake of breath from Floster. She's guessed what I will say next.

The words burn my mouth: 'Benedict will murder every soul in Gengst and raze the city to the ground. Total destruction. Then they will move on to the next city. He believes that once Gengst is destroyed, the resulting panic and confusion will make the smaller cities easy to pick off, one by one. Until the whole of the Maker world is . . . gone.'

I'm shivering. 'He'll kill them all – every man, woman and child. No Maker will be left alive. He plans the death of an entire people.'

Floster's eyes narrow, grow calculating. Now it's Philip who looks shocked. The Hound nods, as though he expected such horrors all along.

'We have to stop it!' Their slowness irritates me.

'We will.' Floster sounds doubtful.

'I don't see . . .' Philip is frowning, struggling to solve the problem.

Only the Hound understands. 'And how do you expect to get the boy out, Zara? Magic him?'

'I can.' I search from face to face, willing them to believe me. 'I told Aidan to sabotage the repairs to the Great Clock. Delay. So we have some time. Hou – Marcus and I can sneak into the palazzo. We can –'

'A good thief could get in and out of the palazzo in the old days. Before Aris took your father's arrow in his throat. Now? With Benedict jumping at every shadow thinking it'll be a thief trying to kill him? Difficult.' Floster shakes her head, her mouth tight and grim. 'And you? You're not a thief. You can't

213

do not-seen-not-heard. You wouldn't get five yards. And then we'd all be dead. No. We have to do it another way.'

'But the boy must be rescued.' Philip's face is pale with excitement. 'He's an engineer as well as a clockmaker, Mistress! The knowledge, the power that boy could give to us. The weapons he and I could make together . . .'

'There's no way of getting the lad out. I'm sorry, Philip. The risk is too great. Even Marcus can't prowl the palazzo safely these days. NO!' She hits the post of my bed with her fist. A blast of frustration blares from her, then dies as she regains control. The Mistress of Thieves shuts her eyes and looks, for the first time since I've known her, close to tears. 'I wish to the gods we could save him. But what we *can* do is stop Benedict returning the Maker to Gengst. We'll have to ambush the convoy taking him back. Kill them. Kill the boy. What's left of him. And most importantly, kill your bastard of a father.' Her eyes stare at me and I see no way out. She will not change her mind. Aidan will die.

'You're in love with him.'

The Hound isn't asking. We're alone once more. Have been for nearly an hour, and for an hour I've sat and stared ahead, not seeing, not caring. They're going to let Aidan die. And there's nothing I can do. I've failed him. Like I failed Swift. I'm left with nothing but hatred. I'll make my father pay for this. I'll make him pay if it's the last thing I ever do.

'You love the Maker.'

Why does he keep saying that? What business is it of his?

'So what?' I snap. 'You love Floster.'

214

He nods, his face impassive.

'You'd kill for her.'

'Have done,' he says.

'You'd die for her.'

He shrugs. 'We all die sometime. Best if you can put dying to some use.'

'Well then?'

'Ain't just you, is it?' He lifts his eyebrows and gives me a searching look. 'Not just your life at stake. Or the Maker boy's. It's all the folk down here. And those up top that'll have no chance in hell of a better life if we lose this fight. I feel for you, Zara. But we gotta do the best thing for everyone. And if that means the boy has to die . . .'

'Would you leave *her*? Would you leave your love to have her mind invaded and crushed by my father? Would you leave the little bit of her that's left alive trapped inside the shell of herself with him, tormented past all imagining as long as her body lives? Would you really leave her? Or would you try anything . . . *anything* . . . to get her out?'

The thief frowns. He drops his eyes, rises from the chair and leaves the room. He doesn't answer. But I know the truth. And so does he.

26

In the morning I dress myself. My leggings and tunic hang off me and I'm pleased I have no mirror to testify to my resemblance to the long-term residents of the catacombs.

Quint ordered me to rest in bed, but I haven't time. I pace up and down the sickroom, counting my footsteps. On my first attempt I stop after fifteen tottering steps. Soon I can walk for thirty. By lunchtime I make fifty and retreat to my bed, childishly pleased with myself.

The door opens; it's the Hound, carrying a tray with a bowl of meat stew. My mouth is watering before he sets it on my lap and I manage to nod thanks at the same time as gulping the first spoonful.

'Glad to see you've found your appetite. You're all bone and hair.'

I wince. 'Thanks!'

'Nice bones and nice hair. But could do with a bit of covering.' He smiles, opens his mouth to say something. Closes it.

The Hound, at a loss? 'Well?' I put down my spoon and wait.

'Finish your food, Zara. Eat up and I'll tell you.'

Slowly, keeping my eyes on his troubled face, I begin to

eat again.

'I can't get outta my head what you said . . . about what I'd do in your place.' He stares at the ground like an unhappy boy, not a man of thirty. 'You're right. I'd chance it. I'd do everything. Anything. And . . .' His eyes look up at last, holding mine, and I see the struggle eating him – between what his mistress wants and what he thinks is right. I guess that the Hound has never before gone against Floster's wishes.

'I'll help you, Zara.'

Hope lights up inside me like a sudden sunrise.

The Hound's eyes widen in alarm. 'Now hold on. There are conditions. I gotta be sure there's a chance. If the Mistress is right and you got no hope of getting in and out of the palazzo, it's off. But . . .' His eyes narrow as he studies me. 'Something happened to you when you was lost in yourself. I think you went to Elsewhere.'

'You said before. What is it? And why does it matter if I went there or not?'

'I shouldn't tell you this. You're a mage. I'm a thief. Sworn enemies. You're the top of the tree and I'm gutter-life.' His lip curls in derision. 'Elsewhere is how we do it, Zara. Elsewhere is what we use to keep folks from seeing us or hearing us.'

'Not-seen-not-heard!'

'Partly that – partly skill and talent. But Elsewhere is more'n that. It's a place we go in our heads. It keeps you lot out. Before a single middling is allowed out into the city they're experts at Elsewhere. If necessary, we go there and we stay. And not even your daddy can get a thief outta Elsewhere. If we go too deep and too long, we'll die. Like you nearly did coming back

217

last time. Which proves mages can learn to go Elsewhere too.'

'Mind-magic!' Heresy. Beyond heresy. But it makes sense. And as I stare at Marcus, I see that he's figured it out before me. He smiles. A bitter, bleak smile.

'I reckon so.'

'But that means . . .'

'*It don't matter!* Look.' His voice is suddenly menacing. 'Don't tell no one, Zara.' He shakes his head. 'Thieves hate anything to do with magic. Do you think they'd accept, any of 'em, that we're related? That somehow, somewhere, thieves and mages . . . besides . . . we may be able to play with a bit of mind-magic and call it something else, but we've never had none of the other stuff. We can't shift things with our minds. I've . . . um . . . tried.' A shamefaced smile. 'And I don't think we can go into someone else's head either. All we can do is block.'

'Have you tried going into someone's head?'

A sardonic smile is the only answer I get.

'But don't you see, Marcus? If this is true – and I think it is – it changes everything! Mages think they are preordained. Chosen by the gods to rule over the non-magic. If thieves can do magic, even only a bit . . . it destroys all that. It pulls the mage world down by its foundations!'

'And ours.' His eyes are gimlet sharp. 'Not a word, mind. Or I don't help you. And I might just have to stop your mouth for good.'

I think the Hound has just threatened to kill me. And I think he means it. The hair on the back of my neck stands on end. 'I thought . . . you . . . liked me,' I manage at last.

'I do. And more.' A light in his eyes shines wickedly and my stomach turns over. 'But you're a wee bit young. Even for me.'

'The Mistress . . .'

'Hasn't been in my bed for years. She loves me. But she won't. Not since her last kid was killed. Five she had. Three girls and two boys. The mages got every one. Benedict had a hand in two himself. She's sworn off love till your daddy's dead, you see. And she don't mind. Love isn't the same as cuddling, child. You may find that out one day . . . if you live long enough.'

I stare at him, my mouth hanging open, trying to take in everything he's just told me. Including the fact he fancies me. 'I wouldn't let you, you know!' And feel my face burn red when he roars with laughter. '*Not that!* I . . . I mean I wouldn't let you kill me. I'm more than a match for you or any thief! I'm nearly an adept! Do you think I'd just hold my neck out for your knife?' I'm furious now. It's obvious the Hound knows I'm a virgin. He's finding all this far too funny!

'Well. You *might* kill me instead, Zara. Let's hope it don't come to either. A shame between such good friends. Nor the other either. But in five years, if your Maker lad doesn't work out, well . . . consider it an invitation.'

He's teasing. I think. About wanting to share my bed, at least. But would he really try to kill me to keep me from telling the truth about thieves? Looking at him, I don't know. Which isn't a comforting feeling. So I change the subject.

'How are you going to help me, then?'

'Train you up. Teach you not-seen-not-heard and practise going to Elsewhere until you can stop your mind off as well as a thief.'

'Do you mean that I could keep my father . . .'

It hits me at last. I could stop him ever doing that to me again. The only thing that really frightens me. The thing he did when Swift died. If I knew he could never do that to me again . . .

'Gods, child.' A look of repulsion flickers across the Hound's face. 'What did that bastard do to you?'

'No.' I shake my head. 'I don't talk about that. But I'll do anything . . . I promise, Marcus. If you can teach me to protect my mind from other mages I won't rest until the thieves – until all kine – are free. I swear.'

He nods. 'I believe you. We have a deal, Zara. So let's get to work. Time's running out for that Maker boy of yours.'

We work in a distant tunnel far away from the thieves' den. In the flickering light of smoking oil lamps, the Hound teaches me to walk as silently and delicately as a cat. To use shadows to hide in plain sight like a rat. I struggle to do the impossible: be strong and quick while totally relaxed. Balance, fluid body and quick brain. And magic. I'm sure there's magic here, but it's subtle and so different from the magic of the mage that I can't be sure. By the end of the morning, I've made slow progress and although I need to keep working, every muscle in my body is screaming in protest.

'That's enough, Zara. You're making mistakes 'cause you're tired. Give it a rest.'

'There's no time! I'll try again –'

'No.' He catches my arm.

'Let go –!' I yank away, exhaustion and frustration spinning into fury. How dare he touch me?

'Dirty thief?' His smile is humourless. I'm flooded with hot shame. Those were the words on the tip of my tongue.

'Sorry,' I mumble.

'We're both doing our best, Zara. But you need to listen to me and trust me or you haven't got a chance. Now let your body rest while your mind works. Learning to be invisible and silent is the easy part, child. Going Elsewhere . . . that's a bit tricky.'

I stare up at him dismay. I've just worked harder than I ever have before in my life . . . and I'm still rubbish at not-seen-not-heard. I've always found magic easy. Known I was one of the talented ones – destined to be an adept, the elite of mage society. I'm not used to facing the possibility that I might not be good enough.

'There's a place in your head, Zara. A door.'

We sit facing each other on the damp clay floor. The Hound's dark brown eyes stare into mine, willing me to understand. There are shadows in his eyes; the skin under them is bruised, the lines at the corners of his mouth carved deep with stress. Suddenly I sense his worry and fear: he's betraying his mistress. And he's not sure he's right. He's trusting me with everything he holds dear. What would Floster do to him if she found out? I don't even like to think.

I have to succeed; and she must never find out that the Hound helped me.

But the door doesn't open for me.

'Where?' I'm almost crying as I stare up at him. I've failed. Utterly. 'Where is this pestilential door? What do you *mean*?'

'Calm down, Zara! You can't get to Elsewhere if you're

fighting it. You gotta flow . . .' He groans and rubs his face with both hands. 'Try to remember what it felt like after you were in the cat. Where you were before you came back to us. That was Elsewhere. Musta been.' He's trying to convince himself.

But what if Marcus is wrong? What if I was never there? Can't ever go there? If I can't learn to do this, Aidan will die. Worse than die.

He sees the panic in my face. 'Look. I'll do it now. I'll go into Elsewhere. Deep in as I dare. You watch. Maybe it'll help. It's all I can do, Zara.' He sighs. 'Middlings seem to be born knowing about Elsewhere. I don't know how to teach it.'

The Hound settles himself back against the nearest wall. Closes his eyes. I watch intently as the muscles in his face go flaccid, see his eyes turn upwards behind their lids. His breathing deepens and slows. I reach out and touch his hand. It's cold as the clay we sit on.

I crouch on my heels, looking at the Hound, knowing he's far away in a place I can't reach. It's a lonely feeling.

The part of my mind that's listening for Marcus hears something. But it's not the Hound returning from Elsewhere. It's Death.

I am the hawk. I hear the twang of a bowstring; see Aris choking his life away.

I am Zara, sitting with her back exposed to the long empty corridor. I hear the bowstring twang as my murderer releases it and lunge to one side, hardening the air behind me as I do so.

The arrow rebounds from the crystallized air shielding my back and flies on. Death's own fingers guide it. It strikes the Hound and buries itself deep in his chest.

27

'*NO!*'

Two voices scream the word together.

I roll over and jump to my feet, all tiredness driven out of me by shock and fear. Oh gods. *Marcus!*

Somehow I manage to do it all at once. Strengthen the shield of air in front of me. Send out a thread of consciousness to seek for life inside the Hound, and tear the bow from my would-be murderer's hands and splinter it into a million fragments. I sense the iron at her belt and take that too in my rage. Almost. Almost, I could kill her. Except I want to protect her too. She's crying. Stumbling forward to drop to her knees beside the Hound.

'Don't touch him,' I hiss. 'He's still alive. I have to try and get the arrow out. Go and get Quint. NOW!'

I roar the last word. Stupid child! Stupid, hate-filled child. She's probably killed Marcus. And that means Aidan is dead too. I'm shivering with rage. But I can't hate her. She's Twiss.

'Go on. I need to concentrate on repairing the wound. I can't do that if I have to worry about you stabbing me in the back.'

'You . . . you m-melted my knife.'

'Just go! Fetch Mistress Quint. Unless you want Marcus to die.'

Something inside Twiss breaks. I don't know if it will mend again. Or if I even care. She takes one look at the loathing and disgust in my face and turns and runs.

I release the air-shield and kneel beside Marcus. I've found his life force. It's struggling. And now I have to do something no mage attempts. Something the books say is nearly impossible. Dangerous. If I'm clumsy I could kill him. But I won't be clumsy.

I gather all my talent, all my skill, all my determination not to be beaten. I won't let Marcus die. Not like this.

I close my eyes and send my consciousness into the Hound's body. Into the wound in his chest. I feel the shape of the hole. Feel damaged muscle fibres, tendons. Blood vessels sliced and bleeding. The arrow is lodged in his lung, which is filling rapidly with blood. The Hound is drowning in his own blood.

Slowly, carefully, I reverse the arrow's flight path. I pull it, fraction by tiny fraction, out of his body. And I repair as I go. Muscle, blood, tendon. They aren't harder to work than stone or air. Just more delicate. I lose myself in the intricacy of the task. Fascinating! I feel confidence growing. Danger there! Arrogance begets carelessness. Just keep slowly regrowing the blood vessels, reattaching muscle fibre. My body is shaking with effort when I reach the last few layers of flesh.

At last, the arrow eases free, leaving only a small round puncture in the Hound's leather tunic. The shaft drops to the ground with a dull plunk, a blood-stained stick with a narrow point of stone at its tip. What a stupid, frail-looking thing, to take a man's life.

I've stopped the bleeding, but Marcus's left lung is still full of blood. I feel for his life force. It's dwindling. The Hound is dying. I don't know how to get the blood out of his lung.

Think!

My head hurts. I'm cold and shivering. And on the verge of panic. Please, gods! Time's grace, help me. But there's no one to help. I have to do it. Alone.

'I'm so sorry, Marcus,' I say. Tears are streaming down my face into my mouth. 'It was supposed to be me. Not you. It isn't fair.'

He'd laugh. The Hound has never expected life to be fair. But he doesn't let that stop him. It won't me, either. I gather my shredded concentration and force my mind to the job. I find the blood bubbling in his lung and make it change. *Water to air; air to earth; earth to fire.* The cycle of life. Elements. Much of the blood I change to air. The rest becomes earth. A small amount is left as water. And there. It's done. He's breathing easier. But so cold. So far, far away.

Where is he? I need to pull him out of Elsewhere or he'll die. So I follow him there. And find I knew the way all along.

Twiss sits in a corner of Floster's chamber, hunched small, arms and legs wound round each other as though she is trying to keep from flying apart in a hundred small, wretched bits of twelve-year-old child. Her face is tear-stained, her eyes empty of anything except misery. Anyone looking at her would see her crime writ plain. I glance at her when I think Floster isn't watching, and silently urge the little fool to stop looking so guilty. But she has always delighted in making my life difficult.

'Who shot Marcus? I don't want to ask again.' Floster glares at me as though she'd like to dig the information out of my head with her bare fingers.

'And I don't want to have to keep telling you, *I don't know*! I had my back to them. By the time I turned around, they'd gone. And then I was rather busy trying to save Marcus's life. Which, if you've forgotten, I did!'

'What were the two of you doing in that part of the catacombs? Stop lying to me, Zara. Marcus wouldn't have been shot in the first place except for you!'

I wince. My own guilt pounds my head as violently as the headache that has punished me since I dragged Marcus's consciousness out of Elsewhere. 'I know. Do you think I don't feel sorry? All right. I'll tell you the truth. Marcus was teaching me to go to Elsewhere.'

'Only us thieves can do that.' Her eyes narrow. 'He's no fool. He wouldn't waste his time trying to do what can't be done.' She raises an eyebrow. 'Or was it something a bit more basic? He's taken an interest in you.' Her eyes flick up and down my body. 'You're a good-looking girl.'

'No.' To my horror I find myself blushing and my face grows even hotter. 'He wasn't . . . Look. I can prove it. Because I had to go to Elsewhere to bring him back.'

Floster looks at me as though I've grown an extra arm. 'That's impossible!'

I shrug. 'There's only one way to prove who's right.'

She nods. Her face is pale. I settle myself cross-legged on the floor. I won't go far into Elsewhere. If I can find it at all. Suddenly I feel uncertain. I've only managed once. Perhaps I won't be able to find it again. Of their own accord, my eyes search out Twiss. She's aroused from her stupor of self-torment sufficiently to watch me, suspicion battling belief in her face. Why do I care for this girl? She tried to murder me and nearly killed the Hound. And she may have doomed Aidan to horrors beyond even what she can imagine. But I can't give up on her. Or Aidan. Or Swift's memory. So . . .

I close my eyes, and it's so different, this magic. For I know in my soul that it is magic. This is a letting go, not an engagement of will. I give up my will, and there, there is the path. It's a warm place, Elsewhere. Welcoming. Inviting me to stay . . . to melt into a place of warmth and comfort the like of which I've never known . . . to let go . . .

'*Zara!*'

Mistress Floster has followed me. She herds me like a collie dog, nipping at my heels, forcing me back into life.

I open my eyes with a gasp and a sigh. I hadn't meant to go deep. I'd only meant to go a little way. I shiver. Elsewhere is so beautiful. Beautiful and dangerous. I look up at Floster's strained, frowning face. 'Thank you. I . . . I didn't mean to –'

'Don't try that again on your own, Zara. You have a powerful spirit and a strong will. You were deep so quickly I nearly couldn't find you. I will undertake your tuition myself until Marcus is well enough. I don't know . . .' She falters to a stop. 'You're a mage, but also a thief. I don't understand. But I can't deny what I've witnessed myself. Don't speak of this! Nor you, Twiss. I need to think. I don't know what you are now. And I don't know what I am either. Until I can decide what to do about this, speak of it to no one.'

I nod.

'Not even to Philip.' Her voice brooks no disobedience. And I agree. Our world has subtly shifted.

'Very well.' Floster sighs, moves to her chair and sits heavily in it. She props her head on her hands. Then looks up; first at Twiss, who seems more alert, then me.

'Twiss shot Marcus,' she states. It isn't a question. 'She was trying to kill you. To avenge her blacksmith.'

'No.' I look the Mistress in the eyes and lie. I almost believe it myself. 'I know it wasn't Twiss because I mind-called her and told her to fetch Mistress Quint. I knew I could reach Twiss. We know each other quite well. She doesn't believe I betrayed the foundry workers any more. Do you, Twiss?'

The child turns wondering eyes from Floster to me. Tears stand in her eyes and she speaks for the first time. 'No,' she says, her husky voice barely audible. 'You never done it. I know that now.' She shivers and hides her shorn head in her arms.

Floster sighs again. And makes up her mind. 'Very well. You have Zara to thank for your life, child. Get out now. Go on back to the den.'

Twiss hunches to her feet, head turned away from both of us. She slinks to the door and disappears through it without a backward glance, taking her misery with her. I can breathe again without its heaviness polluting the room. My headache begins to fade.

'I know she did it.' Floster's voice breaks the silence left in the child's wake. 'You're protecting her. And . . . I thank you for that. And for what you did for Marcus. They're the only two souls left in this world I care about. It would have hurt to have sent her away. So I thank you, Zara, daughter of Benedict.'

'Daughter of Eleanor.' I meet her eyes, neither denying or admitting.

'Yes,' she says. 'You are. And I thank the gods that you have come to us. Look after the child. And look after yourself.' She stands, heavily, awkwardly, and moves around the table to me. I'm still sitting cross-legged and chilled on the floor. Floster reaches down and takes both my hands and pulls me to standing. Her face is solemn. 'Welcome to my tribe, Zara.' And she kisses me on my forehead. On my mage mark.

It must be the first time in the history of humanity that a thief has kissed a mage.

My chest feels tight enough to burst. Surely. Surely now.

'Aidan,' I stammer. 'The Maker.'

'No.' Floster lets go of my hands and steps back, all warmth gone and her will rock-like. 'It would take too long to train you up so I could be sure of you. And you're too valuable, Zara. You are meant to do great things. I'm sorry. We will stop Benedict. Philip and I are making plans. But we can't save the boy.'

28

Mistress Quint opens the door to the sick chamber almost at once. When she sees me her eyes widen and she rolls backwards as though wheeled on a cart, opening the door and gesturing me inside.

'Quick-quick,' she says, shutting the door behind us. 'No one is allowed to see him. But of course you are different. The heroine of the day! Exceptions will be made. Come in, come in! He's awake.' Nodding and rubbing her hands, black-button eyes gleaming at me sideways on, Quint all but pushes me through the curtain screening off the bed where the Hound is lying.

'Hello,' I manage.

He just smiles. He's lying bare-chested beneath the covers. My eyes immediately go to the scar, a red moth hole in a blanket of dark chest hair. I have been inside his chest with my mind, I think, and suddenly everything feels far too intimate. Impossible.

I turn briskly to Quint. 'Could you leave us alone for a moment, please. I promise not to kill him.'

She looks disappointed, but nods. 'Of course. Kill him . . .

most amusing. Interesting to observe that mages have a sense of humour. I will go, but not for long. I will return soon. Mustn't tire the man.' She reverses out of the room, snapping the door closed behind her.

When she's gone, I still can't think of anything to say. Except the obvious: 'How do you feel?'

'Weak as a day-old pup.' He grimaces. 'But glad to still be here. It were Twiss, weren't it? She came to see me. Sat next to the bed and cried her eyes out. Mad Quint sent her away and to be honest, I was pleased to see the back of her.'

I say nothing. After a moment, he smiles. 'You got it planned, haven't you? Twiss is the most talented middling I've seen in twenty years training 'em up. She'll work with you.'

I can't find a smile to give back to him. 'I'm sorry,' I say. 'You nearly got yourself killed trying to help me and I just wanted to tell you that it wasn't for nothing. I got to Elsewhere.'

'I know. I owe you, Zara the mage. I'll not forget.' He reaches out and clasps my hand in a crushing grip. All laughter fades from his face. Eyes troubled as a stormy night stare into mine. 'Look out for yourself. Come back, girl. Promise.'

I release my hand from his, then bend down, as though to kiss his mouth, which curves invitingly. I feel my face grow warm; I'm blushing. The blood sings in my head and . . . almost . . . I allow myself to taste those passionate lips. But at the last moment, I turn my head and kiss his cheek. A sisterly kiss. I try not to laugh at the disappointment in his eyes as Mistress Quint bustles into the room.

'I promise,' I call to him as she tidies me out the door.

It takes me most of the rest of the day to track down Twiss. She's hiding from me, flitting like a ghost through the living areas of the catacombs. As I stalk through corridor and chamber, I notice a new atmosphere. News of the Hound, and my part in saving his life, has permeated every dark corner of the caverns. Eyes follow me, but most are no longer hostile, merely curious. A small draggle of middlings gathers and follows me like the long shaggy tail of a market dog. Whispers, giggles, the pattering of bare feet trail behind me as I search the catacombs for Twiss.

Finally I corner her outside the very cell I was first placed in. She's been hiding in the prisoner holes. She sees me coming and turns to run. I'm so tired and frustrated I have to fight the temptation to stick her feet to the ground.

'Talk to me, Twiss!' I shout. 'You owe me that.'

'Aay, Twiss!' shrills one of the wolf-pups. 'Ain't scared, are ya?'

She whirls round, fists clenched, and I'm pleased to see that all fight hasn't been knocked out of her. Quickly, before she runs again, I walk forward, but stop a careful two feet away. 'I've got something to ask you,' I say in my most matter-of-fact voice. 'It won't take long.'

She hesitates, watching the middlings edging nearer. 'Piss off, you lot!' Twiss scowls at them, glances quickly up at me then looks away. 'All right. But not here. Not with them listening.'

'Follow me,' I say. And turn and walk away. The wolf cubs scatter at my approach. I don't look back to see if she's coming. I have to trust. If I look, something tells me she'll melt away and any hope will be gone for good. I can't hear footsteps but this is Twiss – she moves without noise. *Time's grace*, I pray, *let the child be there.* She's Aidan's last chance. My last chance.

By the time I reach Philip's chambers my heart is thumping wildly and the urge to glance over my shoulder is almost overwhelming. But I push the door open and walk in. Sit at the table scattered with the Seeker's drawings and vellum scrolls. And only then do I look.

She's there. Standing just inside the room, her back to the open door. Balanced on the balls of her feet, eyes wide and frightened, looking like a feral cat, ready to hiss and scratch and run away.

'I don't think we want to be overheard, Twiss.'

I listen to my own breathing for a long time until her mouth tightens and she turns and closes the door. And comes to the table and sits opposite me. This time, she doesn't look away from my eyes. I imagine it's the hardest thing she's ever done.

'I need your help,' I say without preamble. 'I'm going to Asphodel. To the palazzo. I have to find the Maker and get him out. Bring him here.'

She stares at me. The unhappiness and guilt in her face is replaced with disbelief. 'You're crazy!'

'Possibly. But I still have to get him out.'

'Why?!'

'Because Benedict is going to use him to attack the Makers. A lot of people will die. And if the Archmage's plan works as he intends, the whole Maker world could be destroyed.'

'Don't Floster know?'

'Yes.'

'Then why ain't she helping? She don't want you to do it, do she?' Twiss's eyes widen. 'Marcus was training you up, weren't

233

he? That's what you were doing there.' She flushes, glances down at her hands twisting and twisting on themselves. 'I . . . I'm sorry. I know now you didn't rat on Bruin. I . . .' She trails off miserably.

'That's all over, Twiss. I don't have time. None of us have time to worry about mistakes. We have to defeat Benedict. To stop him. He's the one who killed Bruin. It's his fault. Whoever betrayed the foundry workers may already be dead. If they're not, well, we'll find them sooner or later. But right now I have to get the Maker out of Asphodel. Marcus understood.'

Her shrewd eyes examine me. 'What does Floster say?'

I can't afford to lie to the child. She's too sharp not to guess, and if I want her help I'll have to trust her completely. 'She intends to attack the convoy taking the Maker back to his own. Try to stop Benedict that way. But it's too chancy. A band of thieves against the best warrior adepts in Asphodel?' I shake my head.

'But if we get caught, that's the whole tribe done.'

'No. I can block now, Twiss. I can go to Elsewhere. You saw me.'

'I saw you nearly lose your soul!' Scorn. She sniffs. 'Floster's right. You gotta train up. You ain't near ready.'

'And that's where I need your help.'

'No.'

'Marcus can't do it, Twiss. You stopped him. So you've got to take his place. You owe me.'

Stubbornness all over her face, the hunch of her shoulders. She stares me out. My heart sinks.

'I don't owe you to be an idiot and get yourself killed or

worse,' she says.

I don't have a third plan. Twiss was my last hope. Unless I can learn to control my trips to Elsewhere, I can't risk going to Asphodel.

Aidan will have his mind crushed by my father and his body invaded. And then either he'll be killed in Floster's ambush or, when my father has achieved his aims, he'll discard Aidan's body and what's left of the Maker will die. I don't even try to hold off the pain. It's just. This is my punishment for letting myself love again. I have no hope left.

'Go on, then,' I say. 'Go away, Twiss.' My heart hurts hellishly; all of me hurts. The pain is just beginning and I'm barely holding on. When I have to let go I don't want an audience.

Nothing moves in the room, and at last I leave the tormenting pictures in my mind to look at the thief. She's watching me. 'Go away,' I repeat. 'Please.' I struggle not to shout at her. I need to be alone. To grieve.

'You love him.' Her voice is surprised, shocked. 'You love the Maker lad.'

'Just go away.' My voice, my body is shaking. I whisper: 'Piss off, Twiss.'

She laughs.

My frustration flares into fury and I leap to my feet. 'That's it!' I'm shouting now. 'Get out of here now, or I swear to Time, I'll make you.'

Twiss stands too; her stubbornness is back worse than ever. 'You won't hurt me. You ain't got it in you.'

'I don't have to hurt you to remove you from this room, Twiss. Don't forget what I am.'

'I don't rightly know what you are,' she says. 'But I've changed me mind. I'll help.'

Shock knocks the anger out of me. I sit down. Quickly. And stare at her until I think to shut my mouth. She's grinning, as though she's played a clever trick on me and expects praise and admiration.

'Why?' I manage to ask. 'What changed your mind?'

'You love him,' she explains, shaking her head at the stupidity of the question. 'I loved Bruin. You love the Maker. I done all I could to save Bruin.' The old shadow of grief flickers over her face but she carries on talking. 'You helped me then so I'll help you now. And if we can get him out, then I pay back that bastard Benedict. So yeah. I'll help train you up quick, Zara. But only if I go with you to get the Maker.'

'Two is even more dangerous than one. I go alone.'

'Then I don't help.' She glowers at me, all her sudden cheerfulness vanished.

'But . . . why?'

'I swore.'

Two words, and her mouth shuts like a rat-trap. She doesn't have to tell me what she swore to the ghost of the blacksmith. I understand. I swore to my own ghost when I was younger than this girl.

'All right, Twiss.' I take a deep breath, wondering, even as I promise, if I've just condemned another child to death. 'We go together.'

'Go where?'

We both, the thief and I, jerk our heads around to stare at the door. Philip stands on the threshold to the room, the open door behind him. I curse myself for not sticking it shut with magic. And think up a lie quickly: 'To visit Marcus. Twiss wanted to make sure he's getting better.'

'And apologise, possibly?' Philip's voice is dry. 'Well she won't need you to go with her for that. Off you go, Twiss. I want a word with Zara.' He's watching me, his clear blue eyes seeing far too much. Damn the man!

'Go on, Twiss. I'll find you later.'

She slips from the table and out of the room like a shadow, and Philip shuts the door with his usual precise movements, then goes to the cabinet to pour himself a beaker of mead. As I watch, he adds, one by one, the drops of poppy juice.

'That isn't good for you.'

'It helps free my mind to think. It's a tool, nothing more. Do you want some, Zara? To clear *your* mind?' He turns with a slight smile and knowledge in his eyes. 'You and that child intend to run away and kill yourselves trying to rescue the Maker.' He isn't asking.

I keep my mouth firmly closed. Lying to this man is a fool's occupation. I wait. For there's more . . .

'I should report you to Mistress Floster.'

I hold my breath.

'But . . .' He takes a slow, savouring sip and focuses his eyes and mind on me, as though I am a problem he wants to solve. 'I don't happen to agree with the Mistress. I fear our chance of successfully ambushing the convoy and killing the Maker is . . . small. We haven't the technology yet. Bows and arrows!' He clicks his tongue in disgust. 'I need my crossbow manufactured. But there's no time to refine the design, let alone build it. I have . . . discussed my concerns with Mistress Floster. For reasons of security, we haven't told our plans to the rest of the Council, even though it seems impossible a non-thief could smuggle information out of the catacombs.'

'You think one of them is the traitor!'

'It's possible, Zara. If unpleasant to contemplate.'

'You're wrong! It's Otter.'

He shakes his head. 'Put him out of your mind, Zara. A distraction, no more. The traitor – *if* they are still alive – is a minor problem compared with stopping your father's assault on the Maker world. As I was saying, the Mistress remains convinced her plan will work. I cannot dissuade her. And so, much as it grieves me, I fear I must dissemble and join in your plot.'

'You'll help me?'

'There's little I can do, practically. But I won't tell Floster of your plans. On one condition.'

My heart sinks. This can't be good. 'What condition?'

'Do you remember Mirri? The archer who killed Archmage Aris then took her own life?'

I shudder. 'Yes, of course.'

'The poison she took was an alkaline supplied by our own dear Mistress of Apothecaries. You will take a sufficient supply with you.'

A chill of horror crawls up my spine as I remember the twisted, agonised face of the dead woman.

'For yourself and Twiss, if you are in danger of capture,' Philip continues. 'But more importantly, for the Maker.'

'*What?*' But I don't need to ask. I understand only too well.

'In case rescue is impossible. Then, child, you must kill him.'

29

For two days and nights, Twiss and I have spent every possible moment training. Philip lets us use the smaller of his two chambers. Sometimes he stands in the doorway, watching as Twiss guides me in and out of Elsewhere until I learn to ignore the urge to let go of everything and fall into its soft, warm nothingness.

'It's like when squirrels go to sleep for the winter,' Twiss says, wrinkling her nose in an attempt to explain this place which is both inside and outside my own being. 'Only, if you go all the way you'll never wake up again.'

'A form of hibernation?' Philip asks from the door. 'Fascinating theory but impossible to prove. Do you suppose you could teach me, Twiss? I've been attempting to join in but with no success.'

Twiss frowns at him mistrustfully. She's nervous of Philip. His relentless curiosity when faced with a new idea or problem to solve seems almost to annoy her. 'Only thieves can go to Elsewhere,' she says bluntly.

'But Zara is not a thief. So your statement is obviously false.' Philip waves a hand impatiently. 'You must learn to see what exists, Twiss, not what you wish to see.'

'Zara's a mage. That's different. I can't train you up and I wouldn't even if I could. Elsewhere belongs to us thieves, not to you . . . you *crawler*!'

'Twiss!' I do my best to hide my grin. 'Crawler' is what the thieving clan call other kine – the city-dwelling merchants and guildspeople who, in normal times, are their prey.

Philip merely raises his eyebrows. 'The logical deduction, if you are right, my young friend, is that accessing your "Elsewhere" requires magical ability.'

I jump to my feet. I need to get Twiss out of here before she gives Philip any more hints about Elsewhere. 'You promised to give me another stick-fighting lesson, Twiss. Let's find a quiet tunnel where you can show me how bad I am.'

'And you are!' Twiss retorts with a grin. She's on her feet and out the door before Philip can say another word.

I glance at his face as I follow. His bright blue eyes aren't watching me, or anything in the room. He's off in his own Elsewhere, thinking and puzzling. Time take Twiss for giving the game away! Philip has guessed what I now know: thieves are magic users. Their magic is different from any I've experienced as a mage, but it's definitely magic.

I'll have to confront Philip later and swear him to secrecy. If he starts interrogating thieves, asking them to explain how they get to Elsewhere . . . I groan aloud as I trot into the twisting tunnels of the catacombs after Twiss. Floster is right: most of her tribe would violently reject any notion that they are cousin to their hated enemies, the mages.

Twiss lunges at me out of the dark. The fighting stick in her left hand swings with deadly force, aiming for my head. I jerk backwards. The blow misses but I overbalance and the next second I'm sprawling on my back, my own stick flying from my fingers, spinning across the ground out of reach. Before I can scramble to my feet, Twiss kneels on my chest, her bony knees all but knocking the breath out of me. She pokes her stick under my chin, forcing my head up. She's scowling. Something tells me my teacher isn't happy.

'Ow!' I grunt. 'Get off! That hurts, Twiss.'

'It'll do more'n hurt if a Guardian breaks your head open. Which they will do. You're rubbish!'

She rolls off me and jumps to her feet. There's no pleasure in her voice at my incompetence any more, only frustration at the hopelessness of her student. I groan as I stagger upright. We've been training for over an hour without a break, doing the same attack and defence sequences over and over. And I'm no better than I was yesterday. If anything, I'm worse.

'Look,' I say, rubbing the cluster of bruises on my shoulders. 'Let's take a break. I'm too tired. I'll just carry on messing up.'

She scowls at me. 'We ain't got time for resting. We're outta here tomorrow night.'

'I know.' My heart lurches unpleasantly at the thought, and I slide down onto the damp ground. My mage light illuminates my teacher's unhappy expression. 'If there's any fighting to be done, I'll have to use magic, Twiss. I'm not used to fighting with my hands. I'll probably always be rubbish at it. I don't like the idea of hitting someone anyway.'

'Rather peel the skin off 'em?' she snaps. I roll my eyes but ignore it. She's tired too. And worried.

'You told me they could feel it if you did magic near 'em.

So you need to know how to fight without it!'

'I know,' I say with a sigh. 'But I won't train up in a few hours, Twiss. Sorry. Just forget it. Let's practise not-seen-not-heard instead. At least I can do that.'

'Huh.' She snorts in derision. 'Boney can do it better and he's only five.'

'He's had more practice. You said yourself I was getting better.'

'Hmmm.' She nods reluctantly. Then shrugs. 'Well, maybe you're a little better'n Boney. You can hide all right. It's fighting where you stink. I been thinking. There's someone can help us with that.' She reaches down and tugs me to my feet.

'Where are we going?'

'To talk to a friend. I asked her if she could help.'

'What? You haven't told someone! Twiss, I told you not to tell anyone what we're doing. If Floster finds out –'

'She won't.' Twiss leads me on into darkness, her voice confidently dismissive. 'Tabitha won't tell no one.'

Tabitha. I should have known. Bruin's lover. It's only to be expected that she and Twiss would seek each other out. But how can Tabitha help? She might be an expert in hand-to-hand combat but, remembering the gentle nature and delicate grace of the silversmith, I doubt it.

Tabitha's chamber is dark. One stuttering oil lantern battles the gloom and mostly loses. Is oil being rationed in the catacombs now, as well as food? Philip has dozens of lamps and candles burning all day, but he might have first call on supplies, I suppose, because of his work. A silversmith? For the first time, I wonder how the Knowledge Seekers keep themselves occupied and sane.

Not that Tabitha looks completely sane. Her eyes are dark-shadowed. The skin of her face is tight-drawn over her bones, her cheeks deep hollows.

'Are you ill?' The words burst from my mouth before I can stop them. She looks feverish and half-starved. This room, I think, will kill her. I've been here barely five minutes and feel ill myself. Not because of the damp walls and floor or the stale air – all the catacombs are like that and I barely notice any more – but because of the pain haunting the place like an evil spirit.

'She don't eat enough. I tell her that.' Twiss takes the silversmith's hand with a gentleness I've never seen in her before, drawing the woman to a chair and pushing her into it. The girl fusses around Tabitha, fetching a woollen shawl and draping it over the silversmith's shoulders. 'You sit still and warm yourself up a bit. I'll fetch it, shall I?'

Tabitha looks up at Twiss's solemn face with a gentle smile. 'As you like.'

Twiss darts away into the shadowy part of the room and silversmith turns to face me. Her eyes have a hunted look and I feel a pang when, after the first meeting of our eyes, she blinks and looks away.

Tabitha gazes at her hands, lying like two dead birds in her lap. 'Twiss told me, I hope you don't mind . . . She told me you are going back to the city. And what you hope to accomplish.'

A flare of alarm. Philip, Marcus, Quint, and now Tabitha. Too many people know my plans. I glare after Twiss. 'She shouldn't have told you.'

'No.' The woman's grey eyes, owl-like in her fine-boned face, peer briefly into mine, then turn and stare into emptiness again. 'But she's had no one else she could talk to. About Bruin. It's hard for the child.'

'And for you.' This room holds layers of suffering like the papery skin of an onion. Old, stale pain. Pain so raw it bleeds. It's making me ill. I try to block off the part of my mind that feels emotions. Try, for the first time ever, to slide towards the sanctuary that exists in the outskirts of Elsewhere. Immediately the sense of oppression lifts. I nearly gasp with relief. *Thank Time!* I almost don't hear Tabitha reply:

'. . . are past curing. They must simply be endured. But Death will bring release in the end. Do you believe in the afterlife, Lady?'

'I-I don't know.'

'I believe,' she says softly. 'It must be so. Life is terrible. If there is nothing else, then there are no gods. Or at least, no gods I would wish to pray to.'

I have no answer. I look at her, struggling to find words to comfort this wreck of a woman, and failing. At last Twiss scurries back, holding something before her in outstretched hands. As she enters the circle of light, my spine crawls as though with a hundred ants trailing up and down my back.

'A sword!'

Twiss kneels beside Tabitha and places the scabbard of oiled leather on the silversmith's lap. For a moment, the woman stares at the weapon as though wondering what it is, and why it has been brought to her.

She grips the scabbard with both hands until her knuckles turn white. Her downcast face grows intent. It's as though she's struggling within herself. Finally, her mouth thins and she nods. With deft, slender fingers, which I imagine in their right work – twisting and beating gleaming silver into objects of beauty – she slides the sword from its scabbard. And holds it before her, turning it so that the blade catches the light.

'We made it together,' she says. 'Bruin and I.'

The strength of the man and the grace of the woman. Yes: their making. I see that clearly and, even though the sight of a weapon made with the sole purpose of killing mages fills me with an atavistic fear, I can't help admiring its beauty.

The whole is not three feet long, short enough to be used with ease by someone no larger than Twiss. The hilt is leather-wrapped, the simple cross guard bronze inlaid with silver in a simple, linear design. Tabitha's work, I guess. And the blade . . . I've never seen anything like it. It isn't bronze, nor yet iron. Twisting bands of subtly different colours, silver to dark grey, shimmer over its surface, as though the blade was made of hundreds of thin bands of ore hammered and forged into one. The edge of the blade has a deadly purity of line.

'It is a masterpiece,' I say, knowing it to be true. 'But what is the metal? It isn't iron.'

'But it is!' The silversmith smiles in pride. 'A new sort of iron, hardened with firerock. Bruin worked for years on this idea. He used thin rods of iron twisted together then hardened in the forge, tempered, beaten. Hardened over and over again. He tried a hundred times to make a perfect blade, and a hundred times he failed. Then, a month before he died, he came to me with this blade and asked me to make a hilt as beautiful as the blade.

'He was a great man.' Her voice is quiet, calm. Her grey eyes, gold-rayed like the eyes of a bird, stare into mine. This time they do not fall away. They hold a world of sadness and loss. 'This sword is our child. The only one we will ever have. I give it to you.'

She holds out the sword. 'Take it. Kill the Archmage. Avenge my love.'

30

I move through the twisting intestines of the catacombs, crawling up out of the earth into life again. I'm walking the threaded pathways of Time itself. Forward to a future I cannot predict, a dead man's sword strapped to my side, a mad woman's poison bottle around my neck. Backwards to my old self . . . to the mage, Zara.

Swift's voice, muted during my life underground, whispers once more in my ear. But it's Aidan's face I see.

Philip fed us last night, Twiss and me.

'Funeral meats,' he said, smiling at his own macabre humour as he presented a table spread with a feast. Meat! After weeks living on beans and cabbage. And real bread. I can't imagine where or how he got it. 'Or perhaps,' he added, glancing slyly at me, 'a wedding feast. Let us hope for the latter.'

His words cooled my appetite for a moment, until I saw that Twiss was likely to gobble up every scrap. She piled her wooden trencher full to overflowing and gulped food like a starving cat, barely pausing to chew.

'Slow down, Twiss. Or you'll make yourself ill and I'll be

going alone.' I sat beside her and loaded my own trencher. My shrunken stomach couldn't hold much so I ate my fill and looked longingly at the bread and meat left on the table.

A small satchel slung over my shoulder carries the leftovers. We might be gone a day. Or a week. Or forever. I touch the glass bottle at my neck that carries Death, feeling her presence. 'Worse things,' I whisper. And am rewarded by a hissing reprimand from my tutor. The food has put new life into Twiss. She vibrates with a deadly intent and I remember her vow to Bruin.

Like the shadow of a thought, she flits ahead of me down the tunnels. We travel blind, true thieves, finding our way by touch of earth and smell of air. Soon we reach the stretch of tunnels that lie beneath the palazzo. I can almost feel the cold, heavy weight of it over our heads.

Where is my father? In his library, reading into the night? Asleep in his chamber? Occupying himself with yet another female mage desirous to mate with power? Disappointed in his sole offspring, my father has never lost an opportunity to attempt another. But the gods have not been kind and I know he dislikes me all the more because of his barrenness.

I smile grimly into the darkness and am jerked out of my thoughts by Twiss's hand on my arm. 'Now,' she whispers. 'You do what I taught. Go just far enough into Elsewhere so that the mages can't feel you. And don't do no magic!'

I squeeze her hand to show her I understand, loving her in that moment for her predictable bossiness. Suddenly, I'm terrified. Twiss, I wish you weren't here. Time's grace, keep this girl – this annoying, charmless, passionate being – keep her safe this night!

We wind our way out of the catacombs, into the forgotten corners of the palazzo cellars. Twiss and I retrace our footsteps of that long-ago night. My naked feet walk over Aluid's grave and I barely spare him a thought. I feel older, colder than the stones themselves.

I have been transmuted. Earth, water, fire and air. A mage's playthings. We order the elements and use them to kill, but we are not gods. It's the gods who play with us. I am not the same Zara who fought my old tutor. I am reborn into the world and I don't yet know who I am . . . or what. I only know that tonight I must rescue the boy I love. Or kill him.

We travel the outskirts of Elsewhere and move through the physical world at one and the same time. Twiss walks beside me, a small bright flame. I sense her presence and that of our enemies. Close! I freeze, go deeper. Become invisible. Not-seen-not-heard. Wait with a thief's patience until the guards pass. I feel Twiss's approval – her growing confidence – as I slip through the palazzo's corridors, threading between shadows.

Moonlight scours the courtyard, washing it silver-bright. I take a chance and send out a fine, seeking thread of consciousness. It twines round and round the courtyard. And finds a cat. A rat. Lizards. A solitary amorous toad belching his desire to the night. Nothing human hides in the shadows of marble statues and slender cypress trees. But there are at least two guards stationed at the prison entrance.

I look up. Up and up to the window which is the only way to reach Aidan. So near! Emotion flares through me, threatening to jerk me out of Elsewhere. I push thoughts of him out of my mind and turn to Twiss, who crouches in the shadows beside me. I explained yesterday what would happen now. She didn't like it then and it's clear she still doesn't. Thieves, she told me in no uncertain terms, like to touch the earth.

Thank the gods for semi-starvation. Twiss scowls in protest, but after a moment's hesitation she grabs my shoulders and clambers onto my back like a monkey. She weighs surprisingly little. I take a moment to adjust my balance.

I have to come totally out of Elsewhere to do adept's magic – flying takes all my concentration, even without a twelve-year-old thief clinging to my back. I thicken the air beneath my feet, push upwards. We are airborne! Twiss's arms do their best to strangle me; her legs clench my waist and I hear a small, shuddering whimper. Which I ignore. I'm flying. Freedom! It's been so long. My blood sings with joy. This is what I was born to do.

If there's an adept nearby they might feel the magic and investigate, but there's no other way into the prison – the risk has to be taken. A simple roll of the dice. So many lives wagered.

Swoop, balance, press, step. I dance, and air is my partner. I've never felt closer to the gods. Air, earth, water, fire. Life – miraculous and terrifying. I remember what the Hound said on the hilltop: *Life ought to be enough*.

It's more than enough for Twiss. The moment I reach the prison roof she slips off my back, crouches on hands and knees and is efficiently and quietly sick. Before I can even begin to worry, she scrambles to her feet, wiping her mouth on the back of her hand. She pads to the edge of the roof and lowers herself over the side with an acrobat's grace, swinging from her hands and dropping feet first into the open window. I follow more slowly, manipulating air, remembering the weak floorboards which might support Twiss but certainly won't take my weight.

The room is still whitewashed with bird droppings, luminous in the moonlight; the lock on the door still shattered. I nod to Twiss. She pushes the door open and we step into the empty corridor. And back into Elsewhere. There are adepts near the prison. I feel them. More than one. Have we lost the wager?

Fear slides a chilly finger up and down my spine before the calmness of Elsewhere takes over and I become thief once more. We are flitting shadows, more silent than the cats and rats that chase each other through the city.

The way to Aidan's cell is clear. The atmosphere has calmed; I no longer sense adept magic nearby. But I stay firmly in Elsewhere and, when we reach the door to his room, I let Twiss take out her lock picks and deal with the lock. No more magic. She opens it more quickly than I could have and grins up at me triumphantly. The next moment we are inside with the door closed behind us.

Aidan lies in a beam of moonlight, curled on his side, one hand tucked beneath a cheek shaded with a young man's downy beard. Twiss tiptoes up to him, cocks her head on one side, then turns to wink at me, a thumb held up in approval and a cheeky grin spreading over her face. Even inside Elsewhere, alarm flashes through me: she's having too much fun. It's been easy so far. Too easy? I grasp the sword at my side and the feel of the hilt in my hand gives me comfort.

Benedict is lord here; this is his domain. And I don't think he'll let me walk off with his hostage as easily as all that. Reaching Aidan is one thing; getting a magic-less kine out of this place is going to be much more difficult. Which is why I carry Mistress Quint's poison bottle around my neck. Whatever happens now, at least I will be with Aidan and share his fate. Joy and terror merge into one thudding, breathless heartbeat as I edge past the outskirts of Elsewhere and bend over him. I place a warning hand over his mouth and whisper into his ear: 'It's Zara. I've come for you.'

His eyes flare wide and he twists onto his back, hands clenching to fists. Then he sees me and lies still, breathing heavily, staring up at me with half-focused eyes. His breath is warm; his face inches from mine. I lean deeper and kiss him. The first kiss I have ever given.

Aidan's lips grow soft beneath mine. His hands come up and cup my face, one either side, thumbs softly tracing my mage lines. Gentleness tumbles, swift as a diving hawk, into passion. And I fall from the fringes of Elsewhere into the Maker's arms. They encircle me, pull me tight. Too soon, they push me away and hold me at arm's length. Aidan lurches upright.

'Thank the gods!' The relief in his eyes darkens with pain. 'I thought they'd killed . . . I thought you were dead! Oh, *gods*!'

He's shivering with emotion. I feel joy, fear, anger – all tumbling together.

Aidan shakes his head. His eyes are wet. 'I don't want you to be dead, Zara. I want us to live. To . . .' His hands tighten on my arms. His eyes stare into mine then frown as anger flares.

'Where the *hell* have you been?' He shakes his head. Groans.

'I'm sorry. I didn't mean that. I know you came as soon as you could. It's just that I've been so worried. I've dreamed . . . Are you a dream?' He reaches out a finger and touches my mage mark, my lips.

My heart aches because there isn't time. As Twiss reminds me with a sharp jab between my shoulder blades.

'We gotta go!' she hisses.

'Who's here?' Aidan lurches backwards on the bed, staring round the room, and I remember that he can't see her.

'A friend,' I say quickly. 'We need to leave. Get dressed quickly. There's no time . . .'

'I know there isn't! I couldn't keep putting your father off. I had to mend the clock. He threatened . . .' He shakes his head as though to dismiss a bad memory, rolls out of bed, grabs up his breeches and tugs them on. I'm very aware of Twiss's interested gaze and would like to smack her bottom and turn her to face the wall. But he's dressed in less than a minute and whirls to face me, his eyes alight with excitement.

'Let me have the sword,' he says. He reaches for the scabbard at my hip.

'No!' I step out of reach. 'Not the sword. Here.' I unstrap the knife-belt Twiss supplied me with and hand it over. 'But don't go looking for a fight, Aidan. You won't win.'

'Can you even use that thing?' He frowns stubbornly at the sword.

'The knife or nothing! You're wasting time we don't have.'

He glares, but straps the knife around his waist.

'Let's go.' I take his hand and pull him towards the door.

'Wait!' He pulls away. 'I can't go without the boy.'

'What?' Twiss whispers in my ear. 'What boy? We can't take anyone else!'

'You promised,' Aidan growls. 'I'm not going without him. He's the only . . . he's what's kept me from going mad. Looking after him.' Battle light kindles in his blue eyes.

'I'll keep my promise.'

'We can't take some kid as well!' Twiss hisses. 'Tell him to shut up and do what he's told!'

'Shhhh!' I hiss back, watching Aidan's blank amazement as he looks from me to the shadow where Twiss sits in Elsewhere. 'Where does he sleep?'

'Here in the prison. Two floors down.'

I lead the way to the door. Twiss brings up the rear. 'Don't worry if you suddenly can't see me,' I tell Aidan. 'I'm not leaving you until we're out of here. All of us.' Or we're dead. No need to say it aloud. Aidan knows.

I move sideways in my mind, just to the outskirts of Elsewhere. I hear Aidan gasp but ignore him and place my palm flat on the door, fingers spread, to steady myself as I spin off a cobweb-thin wisp of consciousness and send it through the door to check for enemies. I seem to be able to sit lightly in Elsewhere now and perform basic magic. With practice, I think I will be able to manage the skills of an adept. If the Lord Time allows.

My breath catches in my throat. Maybe, if I hold my breath, I can stop Time. Return to a place of safety. Because it's happening. The nightmare has begun.

There are mages somewhere below us. I sense eight . . . ten . . . far more than normally patrol the prison. I've gambled and lost.

Panic surges and I clench my fist to keep calm. Nearly a dozen mages are gathering in the prison entrance and courtyard, half of them adepts. They're coming for us. And then, with a shock that nearly makes my knees give way, I feel my father's presence. I gasp; whirl around and clutch Aidan's shoulders.

'Do exactly what I say,' I whisper. 'Go to the boy's room. Quickly! Don't make any sound or we're dead. We'll be following, even if you can't see us. Go now!'

He's breathing hard. I feel his fear, but he nods and sets off, darting towards the stairs.

'Lock the door, Twiss, and catch up,' I order. If they think Aidan is still locked in his cell, it might give us a few minutes. *Time's grace, be with us!*

I don't stay for Twiss. I'm tailing Aidan, moving with the silent stealth of a thief. I don't dare put a soundproof shell around him: a burst of magic would draw every adept to us, so I'm relieved to see he's light and quiet on his feet. In a moment, he's down the stairs. Twiss is already at my heels, quick as a cat.

Two flights down and, with every moment, I feel my father's presence grow stronger. I retreat a step further into Elsewhere, seeking calmness, because the taste of my father sours my mind with thoughts of blood. And if I can sense him, he might well sense me. He's no empath, but Benedict is one of the most powerful adepts ever born and I don't know the limits of his skill.

Aidan halts outside one of the wooden doors lining this corridor. He jumps when I touch his shoulder. I grab his hand, holding it tightly, as Twiss unlocks the door and pushes it open. I guide Aidan in after her. The room is smaller than his. Bare, cold even in late summer, with only a narrow straw mattress on the floor and a chamber pot in a corner. The barred window has no shutters to stop the wind.

The small boy curled tightly under a thin blanket shivers in his sleep. I see a mop of white-gold hair as Aidan kneels beside the bed. He places a silencing hand over the child's mouth and whispers into his ear. The boy wakes with a convulsive start, flailing his fists, and the next moment is wrapped in Aidan's arms. The Maker's voice murmurs and the boy calms. Two blond heads press together. When Aidan looks up, I step out of Elsewhere. His eyes widen and he draws breath.

'I'll never get used to that.' He glances down at the boy, who is staring at me, transfixed between terror and fascination.

'Hello again,' I say gently. 'Aidan and I are going to take you somewhere safe. Out of here. But you need to be very good and not make a single sound. Can you do that?'

The boy nods and presses his face hard into Aidan's shoulder. Aidan rises to his feet, holding the child close. As he opens his mouth to speak, I feel the enemy. They are coming for us.

I put my finger to my lips. My heart is beating so loud I think I can hear it. I fear that those coming up from below must hear it too. Aidan's face goes rigid as he hears the sound of footsteps tramping down the corridor towards us. I give him a warning glance, then step sideways with my mind far enough into Elsewhere so any approaching adepts won't be able to sense my presence.

Slowly, carefully, Aidan moves to stand in the shadows beside the door. The boy clings to him with a fierce, silent terror.

I listen and count as they pass: three mages, two adepts . . .

and my father. I don't bother to count the guards who troop after them. Footsteps pass the door and continue down the corridor towards the flight of stairs leading up to Aidan's cell. My father is checking his prize prisoner first of all.

I send a quick thought thread to check the prison roof. As I guessed: more adepts wait there, at least three. Thank the gods we came for the boy. Otherwise we would be on our way to the roof and certain capture.

It's now! I touch the sword at my hip, feel the weight of the poison bottle resting on my breastbone. *Time's grace*, I pray. *Protect us.* But even as I pray, I know Death waits just out of sight. 'There are worse things,' I whisper soundlessly. It may be true, but knowing that truth doesn't seem to make me any less scared.

'Let's go,' I say aloud.

'Wait!' Twiss is at my side, coiled tight as a cat about to pounce. She grabs the scabbard. 'Let me have it, Zara! If it comes to fighting now, you can use your magic. You won't need Bruin's sword.'

Hunger in her eyes – burning in the depths of her soul: the longing to kill. I hesitate. Tabitha entrusted Bruin's sword to me. But Twiss is right: I've no use for it now. Still, part of me rebels at helping this child become a killer once more. *Fool!* We don't live in a world where she has a choice. A gentle soul might prefer to die rather than kill. Twiss is not gentle. Nor am I. I have changed. If I met Aluid tonight, I would kill him without a moment's hesitation. It's not a comfortable thought: life and Time between them are forging me into something new.

I unlatch the buckle of the belt and hand the scabbard to

the thief. She buckles it on in a mere tick. Practised. She's worn this sword before, gripped it in her hand and felt its purity of purpose. Longed to use it. I fear that before this night is over, she will get her chance.

Aidan has been waiting impatiently. The child is terrified but Aidan's fear is tempered with excitement and a desire to be doing. His eyes bore into mine. I nod and Twiss, still firmly in Elsewhere, goes before us and opens the door. Aidan follows, carrying the boy.

I step back into Elsewhere and go last, closing the door. Listening with ears and a thief's senses: no magic now. Too many adepts; too much risk.

Slipping down the stairs, one flight, two, and the ground floor. No mages here; only a single guard at the entrance. Aidan spots her at the same time and slides to a halt. I put my hand on his shoulder to let him know we're here too, then turn around just in time to grab Twiss's arm as she slides Bruin's sword from its sheath. She glares at me and I shake my head. I won't kill a Tribute unless forced.

Twiss rolls her eyes in exasperation. She slides the sword away and pulls out her fighting stick. She holds it up as if to say: 'Will this do?'

I nod. We have to take out the guard quickly but with my father a few yards away I can't risk magic.

Twiss strolls up to the guard as though she's sauntering through the catacombs with her gang of middlings. The girl on guard is my age, or even younger. Twiss raises the stick and brings it down with efficient force on the guard's head. The dull thunk makes me wince: I've been on the receiving end of Twiss's stick. The girl topples forward to lie on her face, unmoving.

Twiss leaps over her like a long-legged kitten, then waits in the entrance while I collect Aidan. He's already moving, stepping over the prone body. I follow.

The courtyard is a game board of knife-edged shadows. Twiss is already across the open space, busy picking the lock of the long window onto the palazzo. Someone must have re-locked it since we passed. The courtyard holds no difficulties for a thief, but Aidan and the boy can't walk unseen in Elsewhere.

I push him to the sheltering darkness of a column. He shrugs off my hand and begins to dodge like a courtball player, flitting from shadow to shadow. He's good: a barely visible flash of movement. But it's as though he cradles a torch in his arms: the boy's hair glows like a white flame when the moonlight strikes it. It will only require one of the enemy to glance down at the wrong moment. I race after them, hardly daring to breathe.

Twiss is still battling with the lock when we arrive, out of breath and panting. She glances up, only a sharpness in her eyes betraying any nerves. I'm stinking of fear, and so is Aidan. I put my hand on his arm to comfort myself as much as him as Twiss tackles the lock with a new pick. And then: it happens. The Lord Time has counted off our allotted minutes and seconds of freedom.

'*Zara!*'

My father's voice sears through the courtyard. He's felt my presence.

He knows that I'm alive, that I'm a heretic and that I have betrayed him.

31

I hear and feel them. I see them with my mind's eye as though I was standing next to them. Mages swoop from the prison rooftop, sweep down the stairwell on a carpet of air. My father comes.

Aidan reaches out a searching hand, finds the unseen Twiss and shoves her aside. She scrambles up with an oath and I grab her arm to keep her from thumping him as he steps back, raises a foot, and kicks the window in.

He leaps past spikes of splintered wood and broken glass, shoulders hunched protectively around the boy in his arms. He whirls around, his eyes automatically searching, grunts with frustration as he remembers he can't see us, and sprints away. Twiss scrambles after him. I jump past the remains of the window, tucking up my feet to avoid the broken glass. As I land, I feel my father's sending racing towards me like a tidal wave. Panic crumples my knees and I huddle on the floor. No one can outrun a sending.

'Zara!'

He is shouting with his mind, not his mouth. Bullying. Demanding. Possessing.

Fear transports me back to the old life, the old ways. I'm shaking with terror. I'm nine again, and my father has split open my mind. Then I remember what Twiss taught me, slow my breathing and escape deeper into Elsewhere.

Benedict's sending rages past. Relief rinses through my body, first cold then hot, until I'm dizzy again. Thank the gods he isn't looking for Aidan . . . yet. But the Maker and his boy are in horrible danger. I rise to my knees, searching, and my stomach knots as I realise I can't see them anywhere. Nor the thief. Aidan and Twiss have disappeared!

I scramble up, a new terror twisting in my head, trying to shove me out of the sanctuary of Elsewhere. I fight to stay calm as I race along the corridor, retracing our earlier path from the catacombs. *Where's Twiss?* I can't sense her in Elsewhere. She gone deeper than I dare follow. Damn the child! She's done it on purpose. Scheming. I'll have to trust her to look after herself. At least she has some chance. But Aidan . . .

There! My heart seems to flop over in my chest as I spot him. I'm too late.

Figures loom out of the darkness, silhouetted in torchlight. Aidan lunges back and forth, holding the boy with one arm while he slashes out with the knife with the other, trying to fend off his attacker. The guard is tall, with massive shoulders and long, burly arms. He swings at Aidan with a fighting stick. Aidan dodges, feints, lunges to stab. But with his burden he's clumsy and slow. The child is holding onto Aidan with all the strength of his skinny arms and legs and wailing a constant, high-pitched scream.

'*Put him down!*' I shout at Aidan as I race towards them.

But the Maker holds onto the boy as desperately as the child clings to him. The guard's arm lifts again but my own stick is out and swinging. It cracks on the man's head and he falls.

'Zara?' Aidan is out of breath, panting. He shoves the knife in its sheath, his eyes searching for me. His head is cut and bleeding. At the sight of Aidan's blood, I want to be sick. I begin to shake. I was nearly too late. I clutch his free arm with both hands. I want to hold him tight in my arms, but the child is in the way. The boy has stopped screaming. He clings, monkey-like, to the Maker, his body wracked with shivers. Aidan reaches out a blind hand, finds my face and lays his palm gently against my cheek.

'I love you.'

Did he say it? Did I? Were the words only in my head? Why did I let this happen again? It hurts too much. Panic tumbles through my blood.

'Come on,' I gasp.

And we're running, hand in hand. His grip is warm, strong. My love for him is beyond pain, beyond pleasure, beyond hope or fear. I will die to save him. Or kill.

He holds the boy against his opposite shoulder and runs step in step with me.

His fear has the same bitter-sour tang as my own. My footsteps mark its rhythm – the soul-beat of fear born the night Swift died. Until then I didn't know that your life could be taken: your soul, your love, your hope. So easily. So coldly. That the gods could look upon such evil and allow it to exist. I know it now. And I will not let my father have this second love.

***

My father's sending rips through the palazzo like a tornado spawned in the autumn storms, whirling up and down the corridors, leaping floor to floor. He's stopped calling for me but I sense his fury. I've thwarted him and now he has let loose a rampage of mages, adepts and guards. They pour through the palazzo like a pack of ravening hounds.

So far, I have kept us just ahead of the search. Changing direction, twisting and dodging. Sensing danger and guiding Aidan away from it. But for how long? We need to get to the cellars, but at least half a dozen adepts are in the way. *Oh gods!* I slide to a halt, still clutching Aidan's hand. There's no place left to run and I don't know what to do. We're trapped. Is this it? Is it time for Mistress Quint's poison?

'What is it, Zara? Which way? *Come on!* Tell me what to do!' He's like a blind man, looking over my shoulder instead of at my face. I see desperation in his eyes, but determination as well. A fighter. Like me. We don't give up yet. I kiss him, once, quickly. And whisper: 'We have to get out into the city. They expect us to go down. We'll go up. Up to the roofs.'

And then? I don't have a plan after that. If I use magic to float Aidan and the boy down from the roofs, my father and his adepts will be on top of us at once. But there's nowhere else to run.

My lungs are burning by the time we've raced up two flights of stairs. No guards; no mages. Just marble floors ringing with the sound of Aidan's boots and the slap of my bare feet; closed doors and unshuttered windows looking onto the innocent night. This part of the palazzo sleeps; torches unlit. I allow hope to slip back into my heart. The gamble seems to be working.

The search has fallen behind. We might just do this.

We pass the door to my father's library and a sudden chill falls across my soul. The very air here tastes foul. Dangerous.

Swift, help us! Is praying to the dead blasphemy? She wouldn't care. I force my heavy legs to move faster. I want us away from this loathsome place. Two more floors before we reach the attics. We swing as one round a corner, step in step, hand in hand, and run straight into a small phalanx of Tribute guards. Their leader raises a sword as he spots us.

Sword? My mind stutters with shock as it takes in the weapon. *No Tribute . . . no kine should have . . .* and then I recognise him: Otter. His eyes flash in triumph as he sees us.

'Take them!' he shouts, lowering the sword. 'Alive!'

The bastard! I was right. Otter is the traitor.

I clutch at Aidan to pull him back but it's too late. Four guards rush at us and tear the Maker from me, pull the whimpering child from his arms. Aidan roars and hits out, but there are too many of them. They twist his arms up behind his back until he's hunched in agony. No! I gather my magic to blast them but Otter lunges forward, grabs my shoulders and shakes me so fiercely my head spins.

And I realise: he was looking right at me when he said 'Take them!' *I'm in Elsewhere but my father's Guardian can see me!*

'You need to learn to follow orders, Zara!' Otter growls. 'Let's just hope you haven't killed us all!'

I hardly notice his anger, hardly notice his hands digging into my arms. He shouldn't be able to see me! I stare into frowning brown eyes that look right back at me. I'm too shocked to think, let alone struggle.

'We're on the same side, Zara,' Otter says. Why is he telling me something so crazy? 'This is my army.' He shakes me again, but gently this time, like he's trying to wake me up. 'We're rebels. I'm a thief. Half-thief. But it's enough. Your father doesn't control me – he never has.'

It must be true. Only now does my shocked brain register what I should have seen at once – Otter is straddling the very edge of Elsewhere, balancing as though on the edge of a blade. It's a rare skill and one of the Hound's favourite tricks, so difficult even Twiss can't manage it, to her disgust.

I go limp with relief and for a few seconds Otter's hands are the only things keeping me standing. My father's trusted Guardian is a thief! Floster's plant? But that would mean . . . I shudder at the implications for the child Otter once was.

Then the wordless crying of Aidan's apprentice reminds me that Death lives neither in the past or future. Death is now; and she's coming.

'It's all right,' I call to Aidan, who's swearing and trying to twist away from the guards bending his arms behind his back. 'They're on our side.'

'Zara?' Aidan stops struggling; stands hunched over, his head twisted sideways as he tries to look up. 'Where are you? What's going on?' He's panting with pain.

'Let go,' I say to Otter. He steps back and I come completely out of Elsewhere. Aidan needs to see me. *Danger!* thrills part of my mind, but I push the thought away. It's only for a moment.

'Let go of him!' I snap at the Tributes.

They glance at Otter for permission, then release Aidan's arms. He lurches forward, swearing, and I grab him to keep him from falling. He holds me tight, then looks up at Otter. 'We can trust him?' He sounds dazed, stunned.

Aidan shudders; gasps in horror. His hands tighten on my upper arms, fingers digging into my flesh, bruising and crushing.

'Aidan! Stop it! You're hurting me!' I'm whimpering in pain but it's Aidan's face that contorts in agony. His lips draw back from his teeth and his eyes twist upwards in his head. I hear Otter swear. But it's too late.

Oh gods! Don't let this be happening!

Aidan's face convulses again, goes blank. And then . . .

My father looks at me through the eyes of the boy I love. 'Zara,' he says in Aidan's voice. 'Welcome home, my child.'

Aidan's blue eyes have gone cold and flat – reptilian. Revulsion sweeps through me. I jerk my knee up, hitting him in the groin as hard as I can. He yells and collapses forward, letting go of me. As I stagger backwards Otter's guards pile in, burying the Maker in a pile of bodies. My father roars in Aidan's voice and an enormous wave of magic blasts through the corridor. Tributes explode off Aidan like stones from a catapult.

I watch as the Maker's shoulders twitch, his head lifts and a ghastly smile of triumph spreads across his face. Benedict searches me out and Aidan's eyes fasten on mine, glazed, wide-spread, the whites shining. A gloating laugh bleats from Aidan's lips: my father's laugh.

I stagger backwards. I'm helpless. And he knows . . . Benedict knows I'm helpless while he's in Aidan's body.

Aidan begins to rise to his feet. He lurches, arms and legs jerky, like a badly controlled marionette. *What do I do? Where do I go?* I remember the poison, grab the bottle. As I move to

266

uncork I see a flash of movement. Otter brings his stick down, hard. Aidan collapses on the floor.

'Get back into Elsewhere, Zara!' Otter roars at me.

I do what I should have done from the first and retreat into Elsewhere, raging at my stupidity. I feel my father's mind roaring among the Tributes, searching for me. Feel his fury when he can't find me. And then he's gone.

I rush to Aidan's motionless body. I hear his apprentice wailing as I crouch down and feel for a pulse. Otter pulls me off. 'He'll live,' he says tersely. He's glaring at me as though he hates the sight of me. 'Get out of here. I'll take care of the Maker and bring him to you. Now, go!'

Too late. I feel an adept approach. I whirl around to see a crimson-cloaked figure racing towards us on a carpet of air. From behind me comes a twang of bowstrings. Three arrows fly. The mage deflects two, but one strikes her in the shoulder and she's falling like a wounded bird. A red, bloody eagle. It's Challen, my father's assistant. Three Tributes are on her before she hits the ground. One screams and falls stone dead. Two pikes stab downwards, lift and plunge again; and Lady Death walks among us.

Otter pushes me away, slings Aidan over his shoulder. Another Tribute carries the child, who's curled in a tight, whimpering ball. Otter glances at the body of the fallen Tribute; the mage sprawled in a pool of blood the same colour as her robes, and then at me. 'Go back to Floster,' he shouts. 'Stay in Elsewhere and get the hell out of here, Zara. I've lost a soldier because of you. I don't want to lose the war. *Go!*'

***

I'm running. Death, guilt and fear chase me. *I stood there, like the weak, useless child I once was and let him take over Aidan.* I remember the scorn in Otter's eyes. *It's my fault! People have died because of me. But Floster would have let Aidan die. Worse than die. And her ambush might have failed and then my father's plot against the Makers would mean death and horrors not seen since the Maker war. I had to come. It isn't my fault the Tribute died. Otter's wrong. He's wrong!* I run and run.

One floor down and I wade through an incoming tide of guards and warrior mages. I stumble into three of them but they blame each other. They only believe their eyes. Even my father. Then I feel him approach and fear sends me cowering against the nearest wall. He strides into view, black robes flapping like the wings of a carrion crow. His shoulders are hunched with hatred and rage. I feel his mind searching for me. Searching for Aidan – who must still be unconscious – searching for Otter. I feel his confusion and it comforts me. The great man can't find his prey and it infuriates him.

I stand with my back pressed against the cold stones of my father's palazzo, wishing I could melt into them. I could, but he would feel my magic. As I watch him approach, I forget to be afraid. Hatred wells up, dark and bitter. Eleanor, the mother I barely remember. Swift. Gerontius. Aidan. Bruin. *I owe you, Father.* Otter told me to run away. But the gods have given me a chance to put an end to this. Now. Here.

As Benedict draws near, I gather my will. An adept can, if skilled enough, kill with a single thought.

A dagger of thought . . . I make a blade of pure air. Condensed and hardened until it's stronger than iron and sharper than broken glass. I've done simple magic from inside Elsewhere, but never an adept's magic. Now I will gamble everything.

My body tenses, my breathing quickens then slows as I focus every particle of conscious thought on the air-dagger. I hone its shining sharpness with my mind; feel the weight, the balance of it.

The Lord Time himself slows to watch my efforts. I focus my gaze on my target: the back of my father's neck. He stalks away, footsteps slowing. Every movement drags; sound itself deepens, lags. My concentration is so intense I'm only partly aware when my father swirls slowly around, arms outstretched, robes rippling outwards as though through thick water. His face is contorted with alarm, ripening to fear.

He cannot sense me but he feels my magic: particles rearranged, the thinning of the air around him as I gather it in to form my knife. Disturbance of the elements. He is Archmage, an adept of unrivalled talent. But your excellent senses will not save you, Father. You are too late. And I fling my dagger at his heart.

32

It speeds through the air, a shimmering spike of hatred. Benedict screams a single shrill note of terror. But my father is quick with his mind and his magic. Stone is too cumbersome. Water wouldn't stop the blade of air. So he blasts it with a fireball. The dagger flames hot, losing its chill sharpness. A fist of air punches my father in the chest, knocking him down. But not, I realise as despair floods through me, killing him.

I've failed. Again.

'My daughter is here! Find her!' Benedict roars at the Tributes and mages milling around him in a noisy tumble of confusion. Two mages lift him to his feet. Tributes brandish their spikes at nothing, looking desperately for an enemy to spear. My father clutches his chest, panting. He flings off the supporting hands. 'Feel for her!' he shouts at the Tributes. 'Form a living wall, link arms and search the corridor. She's invisible but she's here! The blow came from there.' He points to where I was standing a tick before. 'Catch her. Alive!'

I'm already running.

'Shut off the eastern end of the corridor!' roars my father. He's guessed. I could never beat Benedict at chess. He was always one step ahead, expecting my next move before I'd even thought of it.

I dart through the crowd, racing to get ahead of them, but I know I've destroyed myself. I haven't a chance now. My only hope is to find a space of Time wide enough, deep enough, to hide for the seconds it takes to die.

Two mages fly overhead, past the guards sprinting at my heels. They touch down at the end of the corridor. A wall of stone flares out of the floor behind them, stretching up to join with the ceiling. I'm trapped. Please, Time, Lord of all, measurer of lives. Give me a place. Grant me one minute to uncork the bottle and drink the contents.

There's a door ahead. A single door. The door to my father's library. I stumble and almost fall. The gods have an unpredictable sense of humour – Time most of all. It's right, somehow. Fitting that I should die in the same room as Swift.

I sprint towards it. As I reach out for the door handle, I hear the twang of a bowstring. Someone screams. In the corner of my eye, I see one of the mages fall. Their portion of wall tumbles on top of them. *What?* I stagger to a halt and stare in wonder as the belly of the second mage splits open and their entrails tumble out. My nightmares have come to life.

But the stench of blood and bowel is real. And so is my father's scream of rage. Otter's voice rises above the screams and sounds of battle. A general's voice, shouting orders. Both calm and deadly. He's come for me. Hope soars briefly, then dies. He can't win. A handful of Tributes and a half-thief, against my father's adepts? He's doomed himself, but Otter has given me what I need, and I bless him and thank Lord Time.

I yank open the door of my father's library and rush inside. One frantic thought is enough to shut the door behind me and rust the lock solid.

It's a heavy door, made of thick redwood. I lean my back against it, panting, shivering. The sounds of the battle are remote. Another world. If only I could slip out of Time itself. Go far, far away. Well . . . the key to the only other world I shall ever visit lies on my breastbone. I remember Mirri, the archer assassin; her face twisted in agony. And my mouth dries. I'm afraid, but I forgive myself. Anyone would be afraid.

I walk forward on shaking legs. Sit down at my father's desk. My fingers fumble at my neck, find the leather thong. It's warm from resting on my skin. My skin. My warmth. My life. I lift Mistress Quint's poison bottle over my head and set it before me. Such a small, plain-looking bottle of greenish glass. I take hold of it and twist the cork. It comes free with a soft popping noise and an acrid smell rises to sting my nostrils.

I'm numb. That's the fear. My ears are ringing. Buzzing. The desk vibrates with it. And I remember. My eyes swivel, travel in fascination from the bottle of poison along the polished red surface of the desk to where the paperweight sits. The glass disc is glowing. The silver spirals of my father's mage mark carved into its top are illuminated like windows. It is as though a miniature sun is trapped inside the glass. Warm golden light rays upwards. Mage light.

Which is impossible.

I reach out a shaking hand, and touch the paperweight. It should be cool glass, but it feels like skin. As soon as I touch it, emotions flow into me: fear, love, pain, loss. Fear, again. Fear,

I realise, for me.

'*Zara!*' The voice seems to come from inside the glass disc itself. '*Live!*' it calls. '*You must live, Zara!*'

And then a blast of terror that sends me reeling, flinging me back into the chair. My arm knocks over Quint's bottle and it falls to the floor, smashing into poisoned fragments. The library door bursts open and my father stalks inside.

The paperweight goes cold, dead. There's no buzzing. No voice. No love. Only Benedict.

He walks forward. His face is sallow, strained.

I've injured him. He's not used to being hurt; he won't like it. The thought fills me with a bitter pleasure. My only chance of escape is spilt upon the floor but I won't give in. He'll have to kill me. This isn't like last time. Not like when Swift died. He can't invade my mind.

I'll kill him or he will kill me. It's enough. I feel an unholy joy rise in my blood, rinsing away the last of my fear.

The door swings slowly closed behind him, shutting out the sounds of a battle grown more distant.

'My people have the rebels on the run,' Benedict says, his eyes scanning the room endlessly, searching for me. 'They'll be dead soon enough. All but the Maker. Your true love, is it?' He laughs. 'And I believed you to be frigid, like your mother before you. But a kine, Daughter? You tread forbidden paths, lusting after kine. Some would call it bestiality.

'Have you bedded him, Zara? Because if you haven't, it's too late now. I have plans for your Maker. Interesting plans. But you know all that. It was you in the hawk that day at the temple, wasn't it? I underestimated you, Daughter.' His eyes narrow. I sense his determination to dominate, to control. The taint of it makes me want to strike him dead where he stands, but it's not yet the moment. 'I won't make that mistake again.' His voice is dry, severe. It chills me. I must be careful not to strike before I'm ready. I must not let him goad me.

Benedict stands, silent, unmoving, and I feel him stretching all his senses to their limits, searching for any trace of me. Then he makes his next move. 'You belong to me more than you know,' he says, his voice low and caressing. 'I value you all the more for showing me you have passion and talent. Exceptional talent, Zara. We'll soon be a loving family once more. And you can help me destroy the Makers. With you at my side, I shall be invincible.'

He smiles a ghastly smile. I think I have broken one of his ribs. I could mend it, if I wished. It's a strange thought.

'So tell me, Zara . . .' He moves cautiously into the room as he speaks. He's shielded himself on all sides with toughened air. It glistens in the pinkish light from the window. Dawn is coming. Benedict has told me the truth; he fears me now. He knows I could kill him.

'Tell me, Daughter. What magic is this? Why can't I see you? Why can't I feel your mind? Reach into your thoughts? What is the secret? You shield yourself, but I know you're here! You leave a snail-trail of magic, child. You shimmer. I can taste it.'

He lifts his arms out, like a blind man, searching the library step by step. There's a scuttling noise. A rat, perhaps. He whirls around, reaching. His back is to me. I gather my magic but he must feel it, for he turns back as quickly. 'Clever girl, trying to distract me and give you an opening.

274

'We could play blind-man's-bluff, but I grow weary of such games. So I'll tell you a story instead.'

His eyes never stop moving. I feel the heavy tension of his own powers in the air all around me, coiled like a spring, ready to explode with devastating force as soon as he locates me.

Every movement an exaggerated statement of confidence and power, Benedict strolls to his desk and eases into his chair. He lifts the paperweight, rubs a thumb across its surface, a dark smile flitting across his face. 'Such a shame, this speck of blood. You marred perfection, Zara. I find that hard to forgive. This paperweight is a thing of beauty, don't you think? And yet you tried to kill me with it. When I was only enacting just punishment for your own crime.

'But I have a confession. You remember that night? Do you remember the girl? Your Tribute child, Swift? I trust you haven't forgotten her.'

His eyes are brown sludge. Frozen mud. The bastard. He's trying to break me; send me over the edge; make me attack him before I'm ready.

It's working. Blood pounds in my head. Sickness sweeps over me in wave after wave. I squeeze my hands into fists, stab my nails into my palms, fighting for control. I remember Twiss's teaching and edge further back into Elsewhere. Breathe.

Elsewhere brings the calmness to think, to remember: I don't need Quint's poison. That was for Aidan. I have my own path to freedom. I can go so far into Elsewhere that not even my father will ever find me. He might possess my body, but he'll never have my soul.

My father is still speaking. 'Did you never wonder, Zara,

275

why Swift looked so much like you?'

His words catch at my heart. I freeze. I don't want to hear what he's about to say. Benedict is telling me his secret. Something hidden. Something powerful. And somehow I know it's about me, and I won't ever be the same if I hear it. Dread and desire flood over me.

'Don't,' I whisper in my mind.

But he talks on: 'Her hair, if I remember, was the same brown as mine.' He smiles.

Shock hits me. Half-recognition. But my mind is numbed. I can't quite . . .

'You inherit more from me than you know. I too indulged in a low taste for kine. Once. It happens. More than we mages will admit. Your Tribute child's mother was a counter. She was blonde rather than red-haired, but otherwise she looked like Eleanor.'

He groans, shuts his eyes at the memory. Then looks for me again, a self-mocking smile on his face. 'I remember the first time I saw her: the same face, the same body. She could have been your mother's twin sister. And so . . .'

Benedict pauses, his eyes searching, hoping to see that the wound he inflicts is fatal. 'I took her to my bed. Your mother is the only woman I ever loved, Zara. Oh gods, how I loved her. I still do. But she was mad; her mind tainted with blasphemy. A heretic. Even I couldn't save her. So when I saw Swift's mother . . . and then there was a child.'

I can't keep the knowledge out any longer. Pain bends me as I stand. I want to scream.

'Do you understand?' My father's voice drips poison. 'Swift

was your half-sister. I should have killed her at birth of course, as the law demands. She was an abomination. But I am the Archmage of Asphodel and laws are for lesser beings. I am Benedict, the greatest archmage ever to have walked this earth. As history will record when I cleanse the land of every last mage-killing Maker!

'The counter's child had my blood in her. Benedict's blood. And the mother was a superior example of her tribe; but for the fact she had no magic she seemed fully human. I gambled . . . I hoped my blood would prevail. Barrenness is the bane of our race. The gods, curse them, have only granted me one child! And *you* . . . you're tainted with your mother's madness . . .' He breaks off, panting. 'So I let the child live and gave her to you when the time came. It was a mistake. The kine blood polluted mine after all: the child had no magic. Instead, she grew subversive. She would have grown dangerous . . . rebellious. She was seeking out blasphemous texts even then. But it was your fault. You should never have taught her to read. I blame you, Zara.'

I blame you, Zara . . . your half-sister . . . blasphemy . . . She was your sister. I blame you . . . I blame you . . .

The truth that you should have known, when it finally strikes home, hits hard. How could I have been so blind? She knew. I realise that now. *Swift knew!* She actually told me, in her letter, but even then I couldn't see the truth.

I'm crying. Tears are streaming down my face and I'm bent over, hugging myself to try and contain the pain. Something breaks in my head and everything is swallowed in the redness of hate. And the desire, the lust, for revenge.

I step forward, out of Elsewhere, to confront the man who was our father. Child murderer. Eater of his own flesh.

A slow smile of triumph spreads over his face as his eyes find me at last. I feel his will gather, but I strike first. Hatred ignites the blast of fire I send scorching towards him, a white sheet of flame. It cracks across the room, scorching everything in its path, and strikes his air shield, shattering it with the sound of a hammer striking a bronze bell.

He staggers to his knees. But lives. His robes are smoking, his hair singed and melted. But Benedict lives. His eyes fasten on me; his mind swoops to grapple with mine. But I step backwards into Elsewhere.

'Coward!' he shrieks. He staggers to his feet. And I circle him. He sends a blast of flame to scorch the place I was standing. The library smoulders, books catch fire. The room is burning. Benedict's famous library is on fire.

We're both coughing from the smoke. I have to be quick. Air is too slow. Stone even slower. It has to be fire. And he knows that.

I am burning, like the room, burning with hatred. Part of my mind is screaming Swift's name. Elsewhere calms me. I take a breath, step out.

He sees me, and this time he is quickest. A wall of water drenches me, knocking me sideways, sweeping me against a bookcase with a crash that knocks the wind from my lungs. I lie stunned, unable to breathe or move. And listen to my father's laugh as he steps forward. He's put out the fires. The smoke thins, leaving the room stinking of damp soot.

As I struggle to gasp air into my lungs, to gather enough

magic to defend myself, I see her. It wasn't a rat scuttling in the darkened corners of the library.

Twiss appears, sword in hand. She has been so deep in Elsewhere even I couldn't see her. But now she runs forward. And strikes with a cry that burns my soul. Bruin's sword bites deep into my father's back.

Benedict screams. His body arches and his hands claw the air. He drops to his knees, and there is a explosion of magic that scorches my mind with its power. The sword erupts from my father's back, spinning across the floor in a silver-gold whirligig of iron and bronze. But I hardly notice, because Twiss's body is flying through the air like a leaf in a storm. She slams into a smouldering bookcase. And I am nine again. I watch Swift-Twiss slide down the bookcase onto the floor and lie there, crumpled, unmoving.

I find air for my lungs at last. My scream echoes through the room. '*No!*'

My father kneels, groaning in pain. Blood oozes down his black robes onto the white marble of the floor. But he's alive. Before I realise what I intend to do, I've darted forward and grabbed Bruin's sword. I run at Benedict, raising the sword over my head. Hatred gives me strength – the sword is as light as thought. I will finish what Twiss began, what Swift failed to do ten years ago.

But I forgot: I may be invisible but he heard my scream; he can hear me running towards him. My father staggers to his feet and somehow, wounded as he is, he finds the strength for magic.

I'm caught unprepared as a net of crystal-hard air spirals

towards me, glimmering icy blue through the drifts of black smoke. I hurl the sword at him with a blast of magic. But once it leaves my hand, it's visible. Benedict deflects it with contemptuous ease. The net drops over my head and wraps chill fingers around me. My father reels me in hand over hand, like a fisherman. I stagger as I fight the pull, and reach for my magic.

'I don't think so, Zara!' Benedict stops pulling in his net. 'Don't make the mistake of fighting me with magic – you can't win. I've lost a little blood, no more. I won't be dying today. But your colleague has earned a death. I wouldn't like to disappoint them. Or you.' He straightens up. His face is deathly white, but I can feel his strength returning.

I must hit him now! But as I try to gather the shreds of my magic, Benedict ignites a fireball and sends it to hover in the air near Twiss's crumpled body.

'Surrender!' My father's eyes never leaving the net that drapes over me like a cloak. 'Or your companion dies. Let me see you, Zara. Or I promise that whatever creature attacked me will burn hotter than the fires of hell. There won't be anything left but charred bones.'

He will act on his threat. I shift out of Elsewhere and my father's eyes narrow in victory. I'm breathing hard. So much magic is wearing us both down, using our warmth, strength. My legs threaten to give way but I have to hope that he's as near the edge as I. And I have one last weapon.

I look through the ice-cold mesh of crystal air and say: 'You murdered your own child.'

'She should have died at birth.' His eyes are fixed on me as though I'm something so unpleasant and filthy that he can't look

280

away. 'By mage law. All products of miscegenation must die.'

'Your *daughter*,' I repeat. 'Your blood!'

'Kine are not human. You're as sentimental as your mother. I don't know why the gods made me love her.' He snarls, flashing his teeth. 'It's caused me nothing but pain.'

'You don't know what love is! You haven't got a soul!'

He smiles. 'I have yours. You belong to me now. I've won. But before I wipe your memory clean, tell me. What is the magic? How do you hide yourself from my eyes and block me from your mind?'

This is it.

I failed Swift. I couldn't save her. But I might be able to save Twiss. If she's alive. *Please gods!* I glance at the place where she lies curled on the floor. Her fingers are clenched into fists, her head moving slowly from side to side. Not dead. Not dead yet. I look back into Benedict's cold lizard's eyes and suddenly I'm not frightened any more.

I should be frightened. He's stronger than I ever dreamed. Horribly strong, even now. But I have a lifetime of hatred and my sister's death to repay. And there is Twiss. Alive.

'It is magic, isn't it?' I smile as I ready my weapon.

When he sees my smile, doubt flickers in Benedict's eyes. 'But it isn't mage magic, Father. Tell me how it goes. The creed.

'"*The gods made mages and gave them magic so that they might rule the earth.*

'"*And then the gods made kine to be the servants and cattle of the mages, to serve them and worship them all their days.*

'"*Kine have no soul. When they die, they return to dust.*

'"*But the mage, being semi-divine, rejoins the gods at death and lives forever in paradise."*

'Have I got it right?'

'Your mother was a blasphemer, Zara!' He's shaking, staring across the room at me with loathing. 'She died for it. I'll keep you alive, though. I am your father after all. And I have no other child!' he snarls. I watch as he struggles to calm himself. 'You'll just have to be reborn. As with all births, it will be painful.' He smiles too: a ghastly smile.

'You were *her* father too!' I shout. 'You murdered your own daughter! I couldn't stop you then, but I won't let you kill this child. Her name is Twiss. She's a thief. And my friend.'

His face contorts in disgust. 'You can make a pet of a rat – if you have a low mind – but you can't be friends with vermin. I shall be doing my duty as a parent to kill it.' I feel him gather his strength. He begins to turn towards Twiss.

'Wait, Father!' I keep my voice light, contemptuous. It irritates him – as I knew it would. His eyes flick back to me; his hand, half raised to direct the fireball, drops to his side.

'Don't you want to know the answer to your question?' I watch his eyes narrow. He's listening. 'You asked what sort of magic I'm using. I think you'll find the answer interesting: it's thieves' magic.'

'*Thieves?*' His upper lip curls in revulsion. 'Animals! Vermin! Even the kine will not mate with that tribe. And you *dare* use the word "magic" to refer to their tricks?'

His nostrils flare; the whites of his eyes shine as his eyes widen in rage.

I feel a great, fierce joy. I cannot beat my father with magic. But I can destroy his world nonetheless. My heart is racing; I'm shaking as I gather the power of my words.

'And yet it's the thieves you fear, Father. It's thieves we all fear. The knife in the back, the flint arrow flying without warning. For years you've tried to wipe their tribe from existence.

'Remember Aris, dear Father? We both know that arrow was meant for you. Next time it will be *you* lying in the dirt twitching like a dying rabbit as your heart stops beating and your brain chills. How did the sword feel, sliding into your back? You can kill Twiss, but there will be other thieves. They will never stop until you are dead!

'Deny it as much as you wish, but I know the truth: the thieves are magic users. It's how they've survived us all these centuries. They go to a place in their minds where we can't see or hear them, but they can see us. And we can't mind-control them.

'You know now that Otter is a rebel. But let me tell you the best bit: he's a thief. It's his magic that kept him safe from you. Your own pet Guardian. How many times must he have stood behind you, knowing he could kill you with a single blow. Longing to, but waiting. Because killing you isn't enough. He's going to stop it all. 'Benedict – last Archmage of Asphodel. He's made a fool of you!'

He's staring at me white-faced, struggling not to believe.

'I've been living with the thieves, Father. They taught me their magic. I use it to hide in the darkness where you can't find me. Long ago, thieves and mages must have been the same tribe. Mages aren't "the chosen". So, tell me, Father. How does the fact that thieves are magic users square with your litany?'

'*Liar!*'

The horror on his face says everything. His world has just crumbled into dust.

I watch my father go mad. He's forgotten Twiss. Forgotten everything but the need to stop my mouth. I see it in his face, and lunge into Elsewhere just before he bursts into my head.

'You won't ever be able to do that again, Father! Never!'

I've been waiting for this moment. I kindle a knife of fire and slash through the net binding me.

'You're none of mine!' Benedict is raging, spittle foaming from his mouth. 'Your mother must have slept with a demon! *I'll destroy you!*'

A flash of raw power and every book in the room bursts into flame and leaps off the shelves. They bombard the room. Fly down to crash like hundreds of falling stars. One hits me in the back, knocking me down. My back explodes in agony as the fire bites. Screaming, I draw water from the air and shower it over me.

Benedict is waiting. He can't see me but he can feel my magic. He commands the burning books to whirl across the room; flaming missiles. I dodge, bat them away with air. Struggle to suck enough moisture from the air to grow a waterfall wall around me. I'm shaking with exhaustion.

And I'm trapped.

My father gathers all his energy for one last assault.

Through a screen of smoke and flames, I see the door burst open.

Otter races in, followed by half a dozen of his Tributes. From one step to another, he races into Elsewhere as my father whirls to face him. The Guardian raises his sword arm. But before he can slice through my father's neck, Benedict blasts a wall of air towards the door. Otter and the Tributes go flying.

It's my chance. I slash a fireball at my father, cursing as I see him turn towards it and magic an air-shield with astonishing speed. As the fireball strikes, Benedict's shield glows intensely blue-hot and explodes in flames. The flash of light blinds me for a moment. When I can see again, my father is at the window. It bursts open, spraying wood and glass, and my father springs into the air and disappears.

Otter grabs a bow from one of the Tributes, rushes to the window and fires three quick arrows after Benedict. As the Guardian lowers the bow, I can tell from the rigid set of his shoulders that he's missed. My father has escaped.

I've used so much energy I can barely stand. I stagger as I run across to Twiss. The thief is hunched on hands and knees, struggling to get to her feet.

I kneel down and scoop her into my arms, and joy sweeps through me as I feel her life force growing stronger with each second. She lets me hug her close for a moment, then pushes me away.

'I'm all right,' she says. 'Don't fuss. Got the wind knocked out of me, that's all.'

It isn't all. Her nose is bloody and I can feel a lump the size of a hen's egg on the side of her head, but I won't fuss. Twiss will live. But I share her bitter disappointment. She failed. Bruin is not avenged. Benedict lives.

'I didn't kill him either,' I say. 'But there will be another chance. Only next time, don't run off and try to do it by yourself again. That's just selfish.' I pull her to her feet, watching to make sure she's able to stand by herself. She grins at me cheekily and I sigh with relief and turn to Otter. 'Where's Aidan?'

'Safe. Waiting for you. Let's go join him before your father regains his strength and regroups his forces.'

I gather Bruin's sword from where it lies. Its blade is stained with Benedict's blood. I stare at the dull red smears, my mind slow, stumbling. I can't bear to put it into the scabbard uncleansed, to bring a single particle of my father's blood away with me. I'm not sure why, but I don't want to use magic, so I walk to a still smouldering heap of books, kneel on one knee and hold the blade in the dying flames until every trace of Benedict's blood is burnt away. Something unknots in my chest. I turn my head and catch Otter watching me, a strange look in his eyes. Pity? Or contempt?

I'm too tired to care. I stagger slightly as I get to my feet and walk over to Twiss. She holds out the scabbard without comment and I slide the sword into it and strap it once more around my waist.

The library is in ruins. The fires are slowly dying. The shelves of books are blackened skeletons. I take one last look at the place Swift met Death.

The paperweight sits on the desk. I walk over to it. Almost, I pick it up and take it. Almost. But it wears my father's mage mark and the mark of his blood. One undeniably beautiful, the other an ugly stain. Both repulse me. I stare at the elegant, intricate maze of silver piercing the glass. What strange magic does this thing hold? Why did it talk to me? Whose voice was it? If there was, indeed, a voice outside those that live in my imagination.

Nearly ten years ago my sister died. Perhaps her ghost lives here, as well as in my heart. Perhaps it was the voice of her spirit warning me. I can't quite believe it, although it would be a sort of comfort, to think that some fragment of her had remained here, waiting to witness Benedict's defeat. But even if something, some echo of her, was here, it's gone now. The paperweight crouches on my father's desk: quiet, lifeless. I can't bring myself to touch it.

Swift is dead.

I couldn't save you, Sister. I'm sorry.

I turn my back on the room, on my father's paperweight, on my memories of blood spilled and blood denied. I take Twiss by the hand, and leave.

33

We wander through the city at dawn. The mage quarter, with its stone palazzos and marble temples, is far behind us. Columns of smoke rise to the sky. Asphodel is lit by dozens of fires. It is as though the heavens themselves have made war here.

'How many rebel Tributes are there?' I ask Otter as I take in the amount of damage done in these few hours. He smiles grimly and shifts the sleeping form of Twiss from one shoulder to the other. Aidan walks on the Guardian's other side, still carrying his apprentice. The boy cries if anyone else tries to touch him, and even though Aidan's face is streaked with the blood of his head wound, he strides onwards without complaint. But the Maker is changed. My father invaded his mind. I want to tell him that I know what that feels like, but Aidan avoids my eyes.

'My army is small,' Otter answers. 'But well trained. The very best training Benedict could afford.' He smiles at me this time. And I think of all the years we spent in the palazzo . . .

'Why didn't you tell me? You must have known I was working for the Knowledge Seekers.'

'Your mind was as open as this sky, Zara. If your father had ever suspected . . . I wasn't going to take that risk. Sorry.'

Otter's lying. He isn't sorry. Or he's sorry for me, but not sorry for what he's done. I've never met anyone so sure of themselves. It should be irritating, but it isn't. I think that's because it isn't about him. It's about aloneness. I've finally met someone lonelier than me.

I glance past Otter at Aidan and catch his eyes. His gaze is blue ice. He turns his head away and transfers the child onto his near shoulder, so the boy's body lies between us. It's like someone's hit me in the stomach: for a moment I can't breathe. I stumble on. The fight with Benedict ate deep into my store of energy and with each step it's harder to force my legs to keep moving.

It's a relief to have to concentrate on something so simple as putting one foot in front of the other. I glance down and am surprised to see that my feet are cut and bleeding. I suppose if I live long enough with the thieves, the soles of my feet will grow thick and leathery, like those of Twiss and the other middlings. I'm not a mage now. I'm . . . I don't know what. Something new.

It takes a few minutes to gather enough courage to raise my head and look past the white-blond of the boy's head. Aidan stares straight ahead, his jaw clenched. There's a glass wall between us and I can't find a way over or through it.

We trudge into the sector of Asphodel outside the walls. The muddy alleyways run with sewage. The narrow, twisting streets are deserted except for packs of pigs and dogs, scavenging and fighting. Wood and mud shacks lean in ramshackle rows along either side of the alleys. Dozens of dirty black fingers of smoke rise from the nearby hills. The smoke drifts over the shanty town and mixes with the acrid stink of the tanning vats. Skinners, tanners and charcoal burners live here. Untouchables. This place is as far from the broad avenues and elegant palazzos of the mage quarter as it's possible to get and still be in the same city.

'This is our base,' Otter says. 'I can hide several phalanxes here if necessary. Most of my army, of course, stays at the Wall, fighting alongside the other Tributes. Hiding in plain sight.'

Clever of him to use this part of the city as his base. No mage would come here without a compelling reason: it's too filthy, too smelly. We enter an area that contains newer tents and lean-tos. Faces look out at us as we pass. I hear shouts of encouragement, cheers. And a deeper note of sorrow as the litters carrying the bodies of dead Tributes come into sight.

Otter ignores it all. He gives orders to his lieutenants; dispatches his troops. Two Tributes remain with us. Otter gestures for Aidan and me to follow and marches on out of the tent city into the barren brush land bordering the last hovels. The Tributes pull away a brush pile of dead cedar to reveal a hole like the opening of a well, lined with neatly masoned stone.

'Down you go,' Otter says, shaking Twiss awake and setting the yawning girl on her feet. 'You know the way. Lead on.'

Twiss grins at him, mock-salutes and scampers down a rope ladder. Except for the dried blood on her upper lip and a bruised cheek, you wouldn't know that a few hours ago she'd nearly killed the most powerful adept in the land and barely escaped with her life.

Aidan follows, stiffly, still carrying the child. He avoids looking in my direction as he climbs into the earth. I stand, too exhausted to cry, staring after him into the dark hole at my feet. A warm hand takes mine. I flinch and glance up at Otter, relieved to see he hasn't noticed my distress. I couldn't bear sympathy now. Or disapproval. But the Guardian's expression doesn't change.

'Go carefully,' he says. He steadies me as I swing onto the ladder. My arms and legs aren't working properly and I keep slipping as I struggle on the wooden rungs. With each step down, exhaustion rises up my body like the icy water of a well. Soon . . . soon I will make Aidan talk to me. We can go back to where we were.

We love each other. Nothing's changed.

Liar!

My foot slips and I nearly fall. I cling to the ladder, pressing my forehead into a wooden rung until panic fades. It's no good pretending. My father ripped open Aidan's mind and invaded it. No one can ever be the same after that. But I won't give up. I won't let Benedict win. I've done what I set out to do: I saved Aidan's life. I won't let my father steal him from me now.

Twiss is waiting at the bottom. She sees me stagger and grabs my arm. It's like that first night all over again – walking endlessly into the darkness. Only this time, it feels like coming home.

Twiss hurries me along. A smile surprises me as I imagine how she's rehearsing the story she'll tell later tonight to a gaggle of breathless middlings. Adventures beyond their wildest imaginings: Asphodel and the palazzo of the Archmage. Bruin's sword. My smile fades and I fumble for the hilt; hold it tight. We failed this time, Twiss and I. But there will be other chances.

Otter's footsteps crunch behind us, pacing out the darkness. It's comforting having him at my back. Our journey seems outside Time and I don't know if it's hours or only minutes before we reach the outer catacombs.

The thieves in the guardroom must have had advance warning of our coming. They welcome us without surprise, staring at Aidan with a superstitious wonder and speaking to Otter with a deference that surprises me.

They pass us through and Twiss yelps with excitement. She tugs my arm so violently as we trot down the twisting tunnel towards the centre of the thieves' den that I yank my wrist from her grip and let her race ahead. The thief squeezes past Aidan and disappears, bare feet flashing as she pelts towards a faint glow of oil lamps.

I watch her go, surprised by a strange sadness. My feet slow down and stop. I'm almost too tired to move. And I'm aware of Aidan stalking into the half-light a few paces ahead. I don't want to touch him by mistake. I don't think I could bear it if he flinched from me.

Otter rests a hand on my shoulder, pushes me gently on. The next moment I'm squinting into a glare of yellowish light, breathing in the familiar stink of oil lamps, blinking at the raw sound assaulting my ears. Roars, shouts, yells of joy and triumph. I see Twiss bouncing high into the air over and over again, surrounded by cheering middlings. The next moment Mistress Floster sweeps into view, a gingerly moving, bandaged Hound trailing behind. Floster freezes mid-stride as she spots Twiss. The next second she breaks into a run and sweeps the child up in her arms, twirling her round and round. The Mistress of Thieves is weeping and laughing. Then she looks up, over the heads of the throng of chanting middlings, and sees me. Happiness slides from her face and her eyes grow deadly. She deposits Twiss on the ground and stalks towards me.

I'm too tired for this battle, but I'm not going to have a choice. Otter's hand squeezes my shoulder. I glance up to glimpse the tail-end of what might have been a sympathetic smile. The Guardian steps back with a look that says: you disobeyed orders and now you must take your medicine. The cheers and chatter fade. Heads turn, following Floster's progress as she descends on me. When she stops, a foot away from me, her eyes boring into mine, the cavern is totally silent.

'You're very lucky,' she says in a low growl, 'that the child got back here alive.'

'I thought you've given up on loving.' I glance at Marcus, who raises his eyebrows in warning. But his lips twitch.

'That's not the point. You disobeyed my orders.'

'It is the point, I think.' After my father, Floster can't scare me. Not much.

'I'm mistress here,' Floster says. 'I won't stand subordination. You think because you're a mage that –'

'I don't!' Now I'm angry. 'That's not true and you know it. I left here to try to save the life of someone I love.' I feel my face growing hot. I don't dare look towards Aidan. 'And, as it happens, I have stopped Benedict's plot to destroy the Makers. If you'd got your way, Benedict's hostage would be worse than dead and the Maker world facing total destruction.'

'It wasn't your decision!'

My anger splutters out. I stare at her. It's true: I gambled

293

the lives of this entire community. Did I have the right? I don't know.

'Maybe.' I shake my head, lost. 'Perhaps I was wrong. I only know I had to try. Because, much as I wish I weren't, I'm Benedict's daughter. I had to try to stop him because there was a chance I had the power to do it, and none of you did. If I don't fight him I'm no better than he is. If you can't understand that . . . if you want to punish me, well, I don't care very much right now.'

There's a ringing in my head. Floster's face is swinging slowly side to side, like the pendulum of the Great Clock. I look past her, searching for Aidan.

He is watching me. The Maker still holds the boy, who is awake at last, staring around him in wonder. The child spots something and begins to twist and wriggle frantically. Aidan leans over to put him down. When the Maker lifts his head his eyes seek me out once more. They're haunted: desire and horror mingled. My father has damaged something in him, perhaps forever. I've read of heartbreak. This must be what it feels like.

Otter's hand grabs my arm and keeps me from falling. 'This isn't the time, Mistress,' he says.

Floster glares at the Guardian. She is opening her mouth to shout him down when a scream rises above the mutterings of the crowd. A searing wail of joy and pain. Floster's eyes flare wide and she turns towards the sound. Over her shoulder I see the crowd retreating from the centre of the cavern like a waning tide.

Thieves and Knowledge Seekers draw back, edge away. And

294

through the widening gap, I see Tabitha. She's on her knees, embracing Aidan's young apprentice. The child's arms are entwined around her neck and he's clinging to her as though to life itself, shuddering with sobs that shake him from head to foot. Tabitha's face is raised towards the sky we cannot see. Tears stream down her cheeks into her open mouth. Her keening is like the sound of a wounded animal.

I stare at her. At the boy. At Tabitha's golden hair falling onto the silver-gilt head of the child. *Her* child.

And it hits me. Oh gods. What evil has my father done?

Tribute. Hostage. The patterns of Benedict's cruelty repeat; curve back on themselves like the swirls of his mage mark carved in my face.

I wonder how long it will take before the others realise the truth. How long the silversmith has to live. The memory of Bruin's broken body floats before my eyes and I try to hate her. But I look at her face, at the child in her arms, and I can't.

But there is one who will never forgive. Full of dread, I tear my eyes away and search through the crowd for Twiss. I catch sight of her pointed cat-face at the moment that joy fades to confusion. I step forward to go to her, but Otter's hand still holds my arm. He pulls me back.

And then . . . please gods, don't let me long remember the look of horror and pain on Twiss's face as she stares at Tabitha and her son and understanding sinks in.

Mutters of '*Traitor!*' writhe through the room, growing darker and louder. The murmurs rise up, swelling into a howl that circles round and round the cavern walls like the cry of wolves scenting prey. Tabitha's eyes widen in terror and she clutches the child to her, bending over him, cloaking him with her hair. A hail of pebbles and mud, scraped from the floor and walls, begins to rain upon mother and child.

'Stop it!' I shout. I gather my magic, but Otter twists me round to face him.

'No,' he shouts above the howls. His eyes insist I listen. 'I'll do it. You stay here and don't interfere, or they'll go for you too.' And without waiting for my answer, he's gone, pushing through the crowd. Floster gestures, and Marcus darts after him.

Otter reaches Tabitha, ignoring the mud storm spattering him, and lifts her gently to her feet. The howls of rage stutter, then slowly fade as he and Marcus take hold of her arms and lead her and her child away into the darkness, out of the sight and reach of those the silversmith betrayed.

Floster's voice rings through the air, shouting for order. I'm shaking with shock and exhaustion. Twiss wriggles into sight, aiming for me like an arrow. She grabs the hilt of Bruin's sword, trying to wrest it from its scabbard. I push her away. Stumble and nearly fall. I back up as Twiss attacks again.

'The sword is mine, Twiss!' I say, fending her off with a warning hand as she lunges forward. Her face is a mask of hatred. My father would delight in making her the silversmith's murderer. 'Bruin's sword has one job to do. Only one. Leave Tabitha to your mistress.'

Suddenly Aidan is beside me. 'Piss off, brat,' he says to Twiss.

She scowls up at us, her face a snotty mess of frustration, rage and pain, then melts away into the crowd.

I stare at Aidan, aware that there are tear stains streaking though the dirt on my face and that my own nose is running.

I sniff and wipe it with the back of my hand. 'I'm sorry,' I say. 'I'm so sorry.'

He ignores my words. His eyes are cold, his mouth grim. But he's looking at me.

And the next moment, when the world begins to swing round and round and my legs melt beneath me, his arms catch and hold me.

34

'What's happened, Marcus? What has Floster done with Tabitha?'

I was woken half an hour ago in my old bed in Philip's rooms by the Hound. He told me I'd been asleep for a day and a night, gave me five minutes to dress and wash, another five to eat some bread and sour cheese, and said I was needed in the Council Chamber.

'Tell me –'

'You'll find out soon enough. And welcome back, by the way. You got out alive, which is more'n I feared. You didn't do so bad, Twiss says. And that's praise indeed from that little pain in the arse.' He smiles, pushes the chamber door open, and stands aside to let me through.

Six Council members sit at the table. The seventh place is taken by Otter. They glance up as I enter, but it's Tabitha I'm looking for.

She sits on a low bench in the centre of the room, so fragile and elegant that she could have been spun from the finest Tierce glass. Her back is straight, her head erect. Her hands are folded tightly in her lap and she's staring in front of her at nothing. Her eyes move incuriously to meet mine as I stumble to a stop a foot away from her. For the first time since our first meeting, Tabitha looks at me without fear or loathing. It's gone: all her fear, all her pain.

'Zara.' Mistress Floster stands, beckons me to an eighth chair set at the Council table. 'Come. This place is for you. You are a member of the Council now. Ours is a new alliance, and all of us must pass judgement and see that justice is done. We are about to vote to pass sentence of death on the traitor, Tabitha.'

'Death?' My heart sinks like a leaden weight and I gaze around the circle of Council members. 'Has anyone spoken for mercy?' I ask. 'For her child's sake, if not for her own?'

Silence. Floster says nothing. I look from her to Mistress Quint, Philip, Otter. Silence.

At last Tabitha herself speaks. 'My son,' she says. 'Promise me to look after him, Zara. Promise me. You and the Maker. His name is Thaddeus. He's seven.' Tabitha keeps her head upright, eyes looking at nothing. Her voice shakes slightly.

I have to know. 'Is he . . . is he Bruin's child?'

'No. Benedict killed my husband, Titus, and took my son when he was four and a half years old. Three years I've lived knowing that fiend had my child. The Archmage sent a mage called Pyramus to me. He explained . . . what would happen . . . what Benedict would do to Thaddeus if I . . .' Her voice stumbles to a stop, then begins again in a whisper. 'I never betrayed you, Zara. All those years, and I never told them you were a spy. I only told Pyramus what I had to – what he already suspected. But I betrayed Bruin. I loved him but I sent him to his death. They found out about the foundry. They . . . m-made

299

me tell him when Bruin would be there. I had no choice. I'm happy to die now. I don't want live any longer. Only . . . my son.' Her voice chokes.

'Where is he?'

'They've taken him away. I–it's for the best. I knew him at once, of course. But I never dared hope . . . He remembered me!' She takes a deep breath, fighting to regain control. 'He spoke my name. The Maker told me he had lost the power of speech.' She looks at me, pleading in her eyes. 'I beg you, Zara. Don't blame my child for my sins. Promise that you will look after him.'

'No one will hurt him, Tabitha,' I say. My insides feel numb and icy. 'I swear.'

'You must take your seat, Zara,' Floster says. 'And join us in the vote.'

I need time. Time to think, to find a way. But Time has abandoned the silversmith. The woman's death is certain. A useless, stupid death.

Suddenly, I'm furious. 'And who will kill her?'

I wait, but no one answers my question.

'Otter?' I look at the Guardian and he gazes back at me: large, thoughtful, infuriatingly calm. Is there any emotion inside the man? 'You know my father and his pretty ways. You can imagine the choice this woman faced. Are you going to volunteer to cut her throat?'

His face remains impassive. I wish I could tell what he was thinking.

'Or will it be you, Mistress Floster? Will you order Marcus to garrotte her? Will that bring back the dead?'

I point at Tabitha, who sits hunched over, her head in her hands. 'What danger does she represent now? Her child is returned. Benedict no longer has a hold over her. You were a mother. Would you have done differently?'

'Yes.' Floster stares into my eyes, cold as stone. 'I gave my children.'

'And were they five years old when they died?'

Her mouth tightens. She doesn't answer.

'You?' I glare at Philip. 'Are you so eaten up with the desire to learn that you can't feel? Will you test your mechanical bow on Tabitha?'

The Seeker flinches.

'Mistress Quint?' I search out the apothecary with my eyes. She sits with her plump hands twisted into a knot on the table.

'You have the power to give life or death. To heal or kill. Will it be poison for the silversmith?'

Quint blinks. She looks away.

'Knowledge Seekers, you call yourselves.' My burst of passion is fading. I want to believe in these people, but . . . I don't think I can.

'If you kill this woman, it will be in the name of vengeance, not justice. I see no wisdom in this judgement. Know this: if you vote to kill her, I will leave.'

'Where would you go?' Otter asks. He is as calm and unhurried as ever.

The answer comes to me at once: 'Aidan and I will go to the Makers.'

He nods. 'You've spoken your piece, Zara. Now sit down so we may vote. You get an equal vote with the rest of us.'

301

'Those who vote death to the traitor, Tabitha, raise your hands,' Floster says, and raises her hand high. I look at the Hound, and he glances away.

Hammeth the blacksmith raises a burly arm. He leers at Tabitha, who sits white-faced, staring ahead once more.

The counter studies his own two hands, balancing one against the other, as though weighing out iron ore or gold. Slowly, carefully, he raises his hand. And is joined at once by a thin dark woman who I know to be Mistress of the Chandlers' Guild.

Four hands in the air.

'And?' Floster snaps. 'Who else votes for death?'

'I vote she lives,' Otter says in his careful voice. 'I need Zara to fight the mages. This woman isn't a threat now. And there is this: Benedict has made enough orphans in this world. I'm not anxious to help him in that work.'

'Zara's logic is impeccable,' Philip says, after a short pause. 'I vote the silversmith lives.'

'I won't vote to kill Tabitha,' Quint says in a trembling voice. 'I won't! I've tended her. She's nearly killed herself already with grief these past months.'

'Well!' Floster says, her eyes blazing at me. 'Four to four. We need a tie-break vote. Marcus –'

'Will do whatever you tell him,' I interrupt. 'Not Marcus.'

'Very well then,' Floster says drily. But she's given in too easily, and I guess that she's thought of something. 'I suggest we let the person most directly affected by this woman's treachery cast the deciding vote,' the Mistress of Thieves announces. 'Marcus, go fetch Twiss.'

'*No!*' I cry.

'Why not?' Floster asks. 'Does the Council agree? I say Twiss lost the most, so she should cast the deciding vote.'

All around the table, one head nods after the other.

'But Twiss is . . .' I stumble to a stop. Twiss would kill Tabitha herself. The silversmith's fate is sealed. Twiss and I, we know how to hate too well.

'Not Twiss,' I say. 'Surely another Knowledge Seeker – an adult, not a child.'

'Twiss is twelve. She's old enough to fight and die. She's old enough to cast a vote. I say it's fair.' Otter looks at me. There's a shadow of worry in his face now. Floster waves her hand and the Hound strolls from the room like a messenger for Lady Death.

I don't notice how long it takes him to find Twiss and bring her back. I struggle with a new sort of sadness. Sadness for Tabitha, for Bruin, for Twiss, and for myself if I'm honest. I want to fight alongside Otter, Philip and Floster. We defeated Benedict. It was only a battle, but he's never lost before.

Twiss is here, suddenly. She stands beside the Hound, facing us. Marcus must have told her why she's here, for her face is greyish and she looks older suddenly. Almost as old as she is. Twelve. Young to decide if someone lives or dies.

'You get your chance to avenge your blacksmith, Twiss,' Floster says. I open my mouth to protest: she's not even trying to be fair! Otter catches my eye and shakes his head, and I sit back in my chair, defeated. He's right: it will do no good, but at that moment I hate Mistress Floster. I press my lips together grimly and watch Twiss.

'What's your vote, child. Does the traitor live or die?'

Twiss opens her mouth. She's panting slightly and looks totally miserable. And suddenly I feel a flare of hope. Twiss licks her lips and stares around the faces of the Council. Her eyes meet mine last of all. We look at each other for a long time. I can't feel what she thinking. I don't try. Twiss frowns at me. Then, for the first time, she turns her head and looks at Tabitha.

'It were the kid,' she says, in a shaky voice. 'Me own mum died when I were three. I don't 'member her. I wish . . .'

She glares at the silversmith. Tears are running down her face – Twiss, who never cries. 'I hate you! You betrayed Bruin . . . and he loved you. But I know you never woulda done it if that bastard didn't have your kid.' She clenches her fists. 'I'll kill him someday,' she hisses, her eyes black obsidian. 'But I can't kill you. Bruin wouldn't want it.' Twiss raises her head and stares right at me. There's a puzzled frown on her face, and when she speaks, it's as though she asking a question: 'I vote . . . for life.'

35

Summer is dying. The wind has a sharp edge. I shiver and pull the lacing on my woollen jacket tighter. Today the wind is driving the smoke of the charcoal burners away from the shanty town towards the mountains. It cleans the stink of the tanneries, lifts the hair from my neck and whips Philip's robes around his long legs as he oversees the packing of his papers and drawing materials on the back of a mule. The Tribute in charge of the animal rolls her eyes and sighs as she re-ties the ropes for the third time. Philip looks up, catches me watching, and a sudden grin blazes across his face.

'Brilliant!' he shouts over the noise of the wind and the milling Knowledge Seekers. They sling packs on their backs, re-strap footwear, or merely stand blinking at the nearly forgotten sight of the sun. They all turn eventually to stare at the distant city and the stray wisps of black smoke that curl upwards until blown sideways by a sudden gust. Smoke that marks the beginning of a war.

Each face tells a different story: disbelief, fear of the unknown, joy, vengefulness, sorrow. Some, like Philip, cannot wait to be on their way. More have tears in their eyes. The last

Knowledge Seekers of Asphodel are fleeing the city.

I'm going with them. I don't know whether I'm frightened or joyful. I seem to know so little these days. I glimpse Aidan, carrying his apprentice on his shoulders so that the boy's white shock of hair flutters above the crowd like a flag. I avert my eyes and stride over to Philip.

'Does Otter know you've commandeered one of his pack mules and are loading it with useless drawings instead of food and blankets?'

'Useless?' Philip splutters in protest, then sees through my disapproving expression and shakes his head at my teasing. 'You know these plans are our bartering goods for the Makers. They will not take us in out of charity alone.'

A few short months ago, I would have protested that the Makers are our natural allies and will surely welcome us. Now I merely nod and ask the question on everyone's mind: 'Do you think we'll make it to the Wall?'

'I estimate the odds to be fairly even,' Philip says. 'Your father's forces are still in disarray and the border patrols will be less efficient as a result. And we have Otter to guide us. But it's over two weeks' hard walking. Some of these people may not survive.'

I follow his gaze and see Tabitha. The thieves have refused to keep her. Mistress Floster has declared that all non-thieves must leave the catacombs. She is preparing for all-out war. A moat of space encircles the silversmith wherever she goes in the crowd. I know only too well what it's like to live among people who hate and mistrust you. It isn't the wind that sends a chill down my back this time.

Aidan reappears, still holding Thaddeus. He goes to stand beside the silversmith, lifts the boy from his shoulders. The Maker bends down to talk to his former apprentice. I'm pulled forward as if by magic. By the love I hear in Aidan's voice. I wish I were the child and not the mage. I stop a few paces away, not daring to go closer.

'Thank you for bringing him back to me yet again, Aidan. He ran off to look at the mules. I fear he will get lost in the crowd.' Tabitha's voice is a mere whisper. She looks nearly transparent with fatigue.

As she takes her son by the hand, she glances up and sees me. A faint smile flits across her face before the accustomed sadness returns. 'Zara!' she cries. 'I am glad. I've been wanting to talk to you, to thank you – but you are so elusive. I owe you more than I can ever repay. And . . .' She trails off. The haunted look returns.

Aidan turns to look at me. His eyes fog over at once, and he glances away. It takes all my courage, but I move forward until I'm standing close enough to touch him.

'You don't owe me anything, Tabitha.' I keep my eyes on the silversmith, only too aware of the Maker's nearness. 'Except to go on living. It's what Bruin would want. But if you would like to give me something, may I keep Bruin's sword? I still have need of it.'

Her eyes widen. She draws breath. 'Yes. Have the sword with my blessing, Zara of Asphodel. And, if it is truly what you seek, may the gods grant you another chance to use it.' She looks from me to the silent Maker. Aidan's head is still averted. Her face softens in sympathy, and she steps aside and bends to talk to Thaddeus.

I don't say anything. I simply wait for him to look at me. I wait a long time. Finally, he turns his head and looks me in the eyes. I see anger, revulsion, confusion. But also the flickering of love and longing.

Everything I want to say to him is in my face.

'Thank you for saving my life.' He has to pull the words out. I can see and feel what it costs him. 'And for saving Thaddeus. But . . .' His jaw is clenched and I can feel his anger sword-sharp between us. 'You're his daughter. You're one of them. It can't be the same with us. Not yet. Maybe someday.'

It isn't no. A small, dry comfort for my heartache. It will have to serve.

As I turn to go, the high, excited voice of the child stops me. He has pulled away from his mother and now comes to stare up at my face with a searching gaze. 'Are you the same one? Are you the woman in the glass cave?'

Tabitha follows. Her arms encircle her son protectively. His pale face is flushed with excitement.

'A woman in a glass cave?' I shake my head. 'I don't understand.'

'Oh.' His face crumples with disappointment. 'Only you look like her. I thought it was you, when you came to talk to us. You know, when we were fixing the big clock in the b-bad place. I thought maybe you got out too. And I wanted to thank you for looking after me. It was so scary in there.'

'He's not stopped talking about it,' Tabitha says, the note of worry strong in her voice. 'Thaddeus says he was in a sort of glass prison for a long time. And that there was woman who looked after him. Gave him food and told him stories. It must be a dream.'

'It's not, Mother! It's true! It was like the catacombs, with lots of tunnels. And it was sort of dark and light at the same time. You do look like her,' he says again, frowning at me. 'I wish it was you, because she said she was so very lonely before I came. And she's still there. By herself.' He twists around to cling to his mother.

'I want to talk to you about this.' Aidan has taken my arm. It's the first time he's touched me since the night I fainted in the catacombs. My throat goes dry. The Maker propels me in front of him, through the crowd, away from the silversmith.

When we're out of earshot, he releases my arm and steps back. He's frowning. I'm trying, so very hard, not to feel his emotions. I don't want to. It isn't my right. And I'm afraid of what I will find. But I can't block it all. Not the raw anger and self-loathing. Not the tinge of revulsion. I glance away, blinking until the hurt can be borne.

'Do you think he's mad?'

The words are so surprising that I turn back at once to stare at him, and my breath catches in my throat. He's so close. I can see star-shaped yellow lines threading the bright blue of his irises; darker strands of black and copper sprinkled through his straw-coloured hair. The Maker looks older, years older, than when I first met him. There is a faint line between his brows, two more etching a path from either nostril to the corners of his mouth. I long to smooth them away. Instead, I take a deep breath and find my voice. 'Mad? Thaddeus?'

Aidan nods. 'He's been through hell. Enough to make a grown man crazy, let alone a boy.' He takes deep breath.

'He is not the only one who's been to hell and back. What about you?'

Aidan flinches, looks away. Too soon. Why am I so clumsy?

'I don't think Thaddeus is mad,' I say quickly. 'Something very strange seems to have happened to him. A glass prison? I confess it sounds odd, but –'

'I was worried about what it would do to him . . . if his mother . . .' Aidan sighs. 'When she was locked away by the Knowledge Seeker Council he cried for her all the time.' He looks miserable at the memory. Shoots a sideways glance at me. 'Philip told me you saved her life.'

Something in Aidan's voice gives me courage. Our eyes meet, and my heart twists inside me.

'What my father did to you –'

'I don't want to talk about that!' His voice is uncompromising.

I must give him time. Offer Time's grace.

'The boy's words seem odd,' I say. 'But it's true that he seemed almost to recognise me when I first met him. What did he say? That he was inside a glass cave full of tunnels, like a labyrinth? And that there was a woman there with him. Someone who looked like me?'

'A cave-like place with twisting glass tunnels, yes.'

And suddenly, I know. It can't be! But . . . I know. Blood thunders in my head. '*Oh, gods!*' I seize Aidan's hand. Clutch it tight and hardly notice his instinctive recoil. But the Maker lets me keep hold of him. And so I hang on to the possibility of love in the midst of evil as images uncoil in my head and meaning pounces on them.

The paperweight.

'I think . . . Aidan, my sister might be alive after all!'

'Your sister? I didn't know you had a sister.' He thinks me mad now too. Is he right?

'Ita,' I say. 'I told you about her. Only I didn't tell you the whole story. I didn't know it then. I didn't know she was my sister. Benedict told me. He . . . taunted me with it. All those years ago. I thought he had killed her. I thought she was dead.'

'The Tribute child? Your Tribute child?' Shock chases all other emotions from his face. 'You told me someone murdered her. Are you saying . . . *your father*? And she was his –'

'His child by a non-magic woman. Yes. He gave her to me. And I taught her to read. He said her death was my fault. I hate him . . . I . . . but he was right. I can't forgive myself.'

I let go of his hand. I've explained everything now. Everything except the paperweight. He wouldn't believe it. I'm not sure I do.

He's staring at me like I'm a strange, unknowable creature. But then his eyes soften and I see pity. Pity is better than hate.

'I'm so sorry, Zara. But why do you think she's alive? You think she's the one Thaddeus meant?'

'I can't explain yet.' There is too much separating us. 'I might be wrong.'

Slowly, carefully, he reaches out, tucks a strand of hair behind my right ear. His fingers linger, gently touch the side of my face. They leave a trace like silver fire on my skin. His mark. I look into his eyes. And wait.

'I do feel something for you, Zara.' His hand drops away.

Aidan's eyes hold mine for another moment, then the Maker leaves, heading back towards Tabitha. I turn away to find Otter

311

standing beside me.

'Zara? It's time to leave. Are you ready?' His face is as impassive as ever, but he's watching me closely. I realise, for the first time, that the Guardian cares what happens to me. That *is* a surprise. So many surprises.

'I can't go.' I look into Otter's eyes, shaking my head at the impossibility of abandoning Swift for the second time.

'You have to.'

'I'll stay here, with the thieves. Floster will let me.'

'No she won't, and neither will I. You're too valuable to allow you to kill yourself. Benedict knows you're alive. He'll tear the city apart stone by stone to find you. Even the catacombs won't save you now. You're coming to the Maker cities if I have to tie you on a mule.'

'You can't stop me!'

He just looks at me. 'Tell me what's wrong.'

'I can't!' I can't tell anyone. I might be mistaken. I might be mad. Did I imagine it all? I shiver as I think of the skill it would take to make a prison from a glass bauble. Of the magic required to shrink a human being to the size of a speck of sand without killing them. I shudder with horror at both the prison and its architect.

Otter is right. I can't stay. But I can come back. I will travel to the Maker city, and in the coming months I will work harder at my magic than I've ever done in my life, until I am as powerful an adept as my father. I will return to Asphodel, to my father's palazzo. To the place where I thought my sister died. I will hold the paperweight once more in my hands, and find the key to its secret.

'It's all right,' I say to the Guardian. 'I know I can't stay. Where's Twiss?'

Suddenly, I long to have the thief nearby. I need her. If I can ever tell anyone, it will be Twiss. She was there, in the library. She fought my father, as Swift did. I will tell her. Not today, but someday soon.

'She's saying goodbye. To Floster and the middlings. Lording it up, no doubt.' He allows himself a brief smile. But his eyes are still watchful. He doesn't quite trust me.

The Guardian doesn't leave my side until Twiss arrives, wearing a woollen jacket miles too big and strutting in new boots. She carries her belongings on her back, as do we all, and a grin a mile wide on her face. She's practically bouncing with excitement and self-importance.

'I'm a . . . a "emissary", Zara! I'm the first thief ever to go to a Maker City!'

'Yes.'

And, if we survive, I will be the first mage to set foot in a Maker city for generations.

Something makes me look up. There, high above us, I see a dark shape scything the sky – a solitary swift. A crescent of brown wings – the exact colour of her hair. She has come to make the journey with me. To keep the promise she made to herself all those years ago. I watch the swift circling overhead, and am filled with a sudden joy as sharp and clean as the wind that holds her.

Part of me soars high and enters the bird. I look down through the swift's eyes and see myself: a tall, thin girl in leather leggings and a woollen jacket. I carry a pack over my shoulder and Bruin's sword at my hip.

The swift circles.

Otter leads the exodus. A small thief strides beside the mage girl. The Maker walks beside the silversmith, carrying her son on his shoulders.

I walk in the dirt and I fly. I'm Zara and I'm Swift.

I see the shanty town, its stinking smoke trailing sideways in the wind, disappear into the distance. I see the white towers of Asphodel diminish and fade. I see a small army of Tributes and a huddle of Knowledge Seekers plod towards the northern horizon. And there, where the earth curves to meet the sky, I see a wall of stone dividing the land. It marches over hills, through valleys and across rivers – unbroken and unswerving, as though built by the gods themselves. The Wall of the Makers.

GLOSSARY

adept: The most powerful mages (magic users). Mage children are tested from infancy to determine the level of their telekinetic ability (the facility to mentally manipulate the atoms and molecules of the physical world). Those with exceptional talent are chosen to train at the city's Academy, and upon graduating become adepts. Adepts are the political and social elite of mage society.

Asphodel: The most powerful of the mage city-states and geographically closest to the northern plains and the Wall of the Makers.

archmage: The ruler of a mage city-state. Historically chosen through mortal combat, an archmage holds near supreme political power in their city. At any time, a pretender may challenge the incumbent archmage to a magical battle to the death. The winner retains power until defeated in his or her turn.

city-state: The main political unit of both mage and Maker societies. Each city-state is equivalent to an independent country.

counters: The accountants of the mage world, counters are the non-magic guild in charge of counting and measuring restricted materials or resources, such as precious metals, paper, iron ore or coal. Counters report directly to their mage overlords in mage Council. In return, counters are given special privileges and held in suspicion and dislike by other guilds and the general non-magic populace.

Elsewhere: Going to 'Elsewhere' is a mental ability possessed by members of the Thieves' Guild. It makes them 'mentally invisible' and therefore invulnerable to mind-control by mages. Depending on how far into Elsewhere a thief goes, they can enter a form of deep hibernation, used for self-healing. If a thief goes too deeply into Elsewhere they may not come out again and will eventually die.

the first precept: A mage must never mind-control another mage, on pain of death.

Gengst-on-the-Wall: The largest and most powerful Maker city. Its city wall is part of the great Wall of the Makers itself. Gengst is Aidan's home town and the cultural and industrial centre of Maker culture.

guard: A Tribute child chosen at the age of five to be trained to be a mage guard. Guards undergo severe physical training and regular brainwashing to ensure loyalty. They serve as prison and city guards or as officers in the Tribute army.

Guardian: A former guard who has been chosen by one of the seven archmages to be her or his personal servant, bodyguard and assassin. Chosen for their physical and mental abilities, Guardians, like guards, are brainwashed from the age of five and totally loyal to the archmage they serve.

guild: The main unit of social structure in the non-magic society on both sides of the Maker Wall. Girls and boys are apprenticed to guilds around the age of eight. They learn their trade and live with the family of a 'master' of the guild. By the age of sixteen, most young people will have 'graduated' to become a journeyman or woman and continue to work with their master until they attain sufficient knowledge, skills and experience to be declared a master themselves. They may then set up their own business. Guilds in the mage world are strictly overseen and taxed by the mages through the Counters' Guild. Literacy is forbidden in the mage world, so all learning is practical. Technology is strictly controlled and anything which might challenge mage supremacy is forbidden.

kine: The mage word for non-magic people – the approximately eighty per cent of the population without telekinetic powers. The word itself means 'cattle'.

the Kine Rebellion: Several centuries prior to Zara's birth, the non-magic population in the north of the continent rose up in a mass rebellion. The rebellion was bloody and prolonged. Many thousands died but, in the end, the sheer numbers of the non-magic majority overwhelmed their mage masters and every last mage in the north was hunted down and killed.

Knowledge Seekers: A rebel group of guild leaders in Asphodel who are working for the overthrow of the mages in order to end their feudal state of slavery and gain the freedom to learn in a society where literacy is a capital crime.

mage: Approximately twenty per cent of people in Zara's world are born with an ability to perform telekinesis. Because the ability is genetic, strict legal and social taboos exist that outlaw sexual relations between the magic and non-magic (the fourth precept), although mage-on-commoner rape is a frequent occurrence. The crime is neither socially nor legally acknowledged by mage society and therefore never punished.

mage marks: Three abstract designs magically carved in the face of a mage in a ritual naming ceremony performed upon the child's third birthday. The marks are formed by inserting fine strands of silver into the skin of the child's face. The mother's mark goes on the right cheek; the father's on the left, and the child's own personal mark – the soul sign – on the forehead. It is a dangerous and painful ritual performed by up to six adepts working in unison. Rarely, a child will die.

Maker: The people who live on the technologically-oriented non-magic side of the Maker Wall.

middlings: Thief children below the age of puberty.

mind-magic: Although ordinary mages have almost no ability to read or control the minds of others, most adepts have some degree of telepathic abilities. Mind-control of animals is used for intelligence gathering and sport. Mind-control of non-magic commoners is lawful, although even among mages it is considered unsavoury and is seldom used except for the gathering of official intelligence.

not-seen-not-heard: The ability of thieves to become, to all extents and purposes, invisible and soundless. This is achieved through two means: 1) retreating partly into Elsewhere; and 2) great skill in the physical art of smooth, controlled movement.

safe-sworn: The leader of the Thieves' Guild may declare an individual under his or her personal protection. That person is then 'safe-sworn' and any thief who harms them will be cast out of the guild. A pendant (the safe-sworn) belonging to the guild leader is worn around the neck of the protected person.

the second precept: Any child born as a result of sexual union between a mage and commoner is considered a religious abomination by mage society and must be killed at birth. Of course, since rape is so prevalent, half-mage children are sometimes born and escape detection. More often, the commoner mother will expose or kill the child herself, such is the loathing and hatred felt towards mages.

Thieves' Guild: Although the thieving community call themselves a 'guild', they are more accurately described as a tribe. Unlike the other guilds, there is no intermarriage between thieves and other commoners. Thieves prey on the magic and non-magic alike and their community is close-knit and secretive. They are considered the lowest social order in both Maker and mage worlds, and are mistrusted and feared by all. The greatest achievement and honour for a thief is to kill a mage, and their folklore centres on recounting tales of the great mage-killers of the past, both historical and allegorical.

Time: One of the seven gods of Zara's world, and the mages' primary god. Mages both worship and resent

Time. Although they possess near god-like powers, mages are not immortal and Time will kill even the greatest adept in the end.

the third precept: A mage must never physically assault another magic user. All combat must be mental, on pain of dishonour. A mage so assaulted may challenge their assailant to magical combat.

Tribute army: An army of children sent to patrol the Maker Wall and keep the Maker threat under control. The greatest fear of any mage is that the Kine Rebellion will spread to the remaining mage city-states.

Tribute child: Non-magic children given to the mages at the age of five. Tribute children are both slaves and a guarantee against rebellion, as every family must give their firstborn. The children serve as domestic servants when young; at the age of twelve, they are sent to serve in the Tribute army, to fight and die in the war against the Makers.

Tribute tax: A child tax levied by the mages of the seven city-states on their commoner populations.

Wall of the Makers: An enormous wall that spans the continent from ocean to ocean. Built by the Makers in the aftermath of the Kine Rebellion (called the

Great Rebellion in the Maker world), it is patrolled by Maker soldiers and armed with war machines such as catapults and giant crossbows. Much of the Maker economy is given over to arming a defensive force and the creation of machines of war to protect their borders.

wards: A magical alarm system that adepts can use to guard certain rooms or buildings. If disturbed, the alarm will alert the adept who set it. Usually, animal mind-control is the preferred method: a mouse, rat or cat (more rarely, a bee or wasp) will be set to watch for intruders.

Acknowledgements

I would like to thank my agent, Jenny Savill, for the constancy of her support, the intelligence of her advice, and the warmth of her friendship.

My thanks to everyone at Hot Key Books for what has been an engaging creative collaboration; but particularly my two editors: Sara O'Connor, for loving the book and saving me from at least one total rewrite with her unerring guidance; and Jenny Jacoby, for holding my hand so very patiently during the copy editing process.

Thanks to my SCBWI online crit group, for help and support with the first draft; and especially to my writing buddy, Sharon Jones, for always being at the other end of the phone.

Finally, I wish to offer my love and gratitude to my family, William and Kit, for their stoicism during the obsessive and grumpy stages, and for believing in me.

Ellen Renner

Ellen Renner was born in the USA, but came to England in her twenties, married here, and now lives in an old house in Devon with her husband and son. Ellen originally trained as a painter and surrounds herself with sketches of her characters as she writes. She spins wool as well as stories, knitting and weaving when time allows. She plays the violin, fences (badly!) and collects teapots and motorcycles.

Her first book, *Castle of Shadows*, won the Cornerstones Wow Factor Competition, the 2010 North East Book Award and was chosen for both the *Independent* and *The Times* summer reading lists and, along with the sequel *City of Thieves*, was included on *The Times* list of best children's books of 2010.

Follow Ellen at www.ellenrenner.com or on Twitter: @Ellen_Renner